COURAGE BAY SENTINEL

Courthouse sniper leaves one dead, two injured

Gunfire turned the courtyard of the Courage Bay Courthouse into a scene of terror yesterday afternoon.

Only minutes prior to the shootings, attempted murder charges against Dr. George Yube, a well-respected former physician at Courage Bay Hospital, were dropped after it was revealed that police had mishandled evidence. The controversial case created a media frenzy in recent weeks, and as Yube walked into the plaza a free man, he was felled by a hail of gunfire from the courthouse roof.

Courage Bay's SWAT team was on the scene in minutes, but before they could rescue a court reporter injured in the attack, the sniper opened fire once again, wounding a paramedic.

Also in the plaza were Yube's defense attorney, Faith Lawton, and chief of detectives Adam Guthrie.

Highly regarded in their professions, Lawton and Guthrie often find themselves doing battle in the courtroom, and George Yube's case was no exception. But any professional animosity was sidelined yesterday as Detective Guthrie shielded the defense attorney from the rain of bullets before he joined the search for the sniper.

At this point, the shooter has not been found or identified, and suggested motives range from a vengeance killing to a random act of violence. Although Yube was killed, police have not ruled out either Lawton or Guthrie as possible targets.

About the Author

CODE RED

JULIE LETO

With twenty-six novels under her belt, *New York Times* and *USA TODAY* bestselling author Julie Leto has established a reputation for writing ultrasexy, edgy stories. Julie writes primarily for the Harlequin Blaze line and was part of the series launch in 2001, as well as the fifth anniversary in 2006. A 2005 RITA® Award nominee, Julie lives in her hometown of Tampa with her husband, daughter and a very spoiled dachshund. For more information, check out Julie's Web site at www.julieleto.com.

code RED

JULIE LETO

LINE OF FIRE

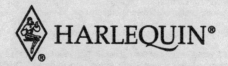

HARLEQUIN®

TORONTO • NEW YORK • LONDON
AMSTERDAM • PARIS • SYDNEY • HAMBURG
STOCKHOLM • ATHENS • TOKYO • MILAN • MADRID
PRAGUE • WARSAW • BUDAPEST • AUCKLAND

Recycling programs
for this product may
not exist in your area.

ISBN-13: 978-0-373-31076-0
ISBN-10:   0-373-31076-5

LINE OF FIRE

Copyright © 2004 by Harlequin Books S.A.

Julie Leto is acknowledged as the author of this work

www.eHarlequin.com

Printed in U.S.A.

Dear Reader,

Exciting times are ahead! I hope you're as thrilled as I've been with visiting Courage Bay, California. Okay, so the place seems ripe for fires, shootings, earthquakes and the like, but the residents, armed with determination and guts, are more than ready to face whatever challenges them—especially when the hazard is something as dangerous as falling in love.

Line of Fire is my first foray into romantic suspense, though I've tried to inject a dose of action and adventure into my Temptation and Blaze novels. Conversely, if you've never read one of my books before, be prepared for a little heat. Well, a lot of heat! Brilliant attorney Faith Lawton and intrepid police detective Adam Guthrie generated quite a bit of steam while they dodged bullets. I'll admit, I stoked them a little. It's what I do. I hope you enjoy the fiery results!

You can drop me an e-mail through my Web site at www.julieleto.com. You can also enter my contest to win free books and learn about my upcoming titles. I have articles for aspiring writers, so if you're a reader or a writer, please stop by and say hi!

Happy reading,

Julie

CHAPTER ONE

PUKA BEADS. Even close up, Adam Guthrie had trouble believing that the necklace the prim defense attorney wore was not pearls, as he had assumed. When she'd approached the bench to question him during the farce of a hearing he'd just left, he'd fallen hook, line and sinker for her ultraprofessional, "never a hair out of place" persona. Same for every other time they'd crossed paths, he as the chief of detectives for the Courage Bay police department and she as the defense attorney from hell. But after her first two questions, he'd been too enraged by her legal wrangling to evaluate her jewelry.

She'd torn him apart.

More specifically, she'd ripped his department's case to shreds and maneuvered the release of a dangerous criminal—George Yube. But out here in the hallway of the Courage Bay County Courthouse, waiting for reporters to disperse so he could speak his mind without having his words quoted in the newspaper, he took the time to notice everything about her.

Trying to ignore Faith Lawton had become a hobby for him, particularly after she'd shown up at the police station a few years ago as attorney of record for a perp he'd personally collared. With honey-blond hair that fell in long, soft wisps to her straight, level shoulders, Faith Lawton had arrested his interest at first glance—and he wasn't wrangling for a reprieve anytime soon. Her steel-gray eyes spoke to him, but usually the message ran along the lines of *don't mess with me or I'll eat you for lunch.*

Luckily for him, Adam brimmed with gristle and bone. She'd have a hard time sinking her teeth through his hide the second time around.

"Ms. Lawton, may I have a word?" He touched her shoulder. Big mistake. Even though her pale yellow suit looked sturdy enough, the delicate rustle of the material against his fingers brought sensual thoughts to mind that Chief of Detectives Adam Guthrie had no business entertaining about intrepid defense attorney Faith Lawton.

She finished her polished answer to a reporter's question, then spared him a glance over her shoulder. "I have no interest in enduring another dressing-down by you outside the courtroom, Detective Guthrie," she answered.

Okay, so he'd lost his temper during her questioning. She'd let him rant for a full minute or so before she'd objected to Judge Craven, who, with a powerless shrug, had sustained the motion. Adam should have known she'd make him look a tad too anxious to do his job—like a vigilante, even. She had a knack for using a person's strengths against them.

"I have no interest in dressing you down, Ms. Lawton. I simply want a word."

With a small grin to the crowd and a whisper to her assistant—who scurried toward the processing area, no doubt to ensure that Yube didn't walk one step into freedom without his legal representative at his side—she motioned toward an unused courtroom on the other side of the hall.

The minute Adam shut the door, she crossed her arms over her chest and leaned cockily against the back of a chair, her weight on one hip. "If you're not going to yell at me for freeing yet another of the alleged criminals your department has arrested, what do you want?"

Her skin gleamed, and not only from anticipation of the pending confrontation, Adam figured. It was obvious that underneath her perfect makeup, the attorney sported a healthy tan. He couldn't resist speculation about her recreational activities. Her sharp mind and devotion to the art of legal defense sent many of his law enforcement colleagues running to cut a deal the minute she took on a case. And worse, when she did go to trial, she won nearly every time.

This particularly didn't sit well with Courage Bay's new chief of detectives. All citizens of the county deserved competent legal defense, but when Faith got someone off, she usually did so by exposing a flaw within the very system Adam had devoted his life to.

Just as she had today. Thanks to Faith Lawton, Dr. George Yube was currently in another part of the building, being processed for release. Never mind that he'd tried to kill Lauren Conway by setting her workplace on fire, tampering with her brakes and, when all else failed, shooting her in the shoulder. Never mind that thirty-two years ago, the former chief of staff at Courage Bay Hospital had drunk too much as a resident moonlighting in the emergency room, botched a difficult delivery that resulted in the death of a baby, then switched several children in their cribs to avoid exposure, not to mention ugly, career-ending lawsuits. The man had spit in the face of his Hippocratic oath, and yet in less than ten minutes, he'd walk out of this courthouse and most likely never face prosecution for his crimes. All thanks to Faith Lawton.

Adam shoved his hands into his pockets. He should be

furious with her. He should give her a rerun delivery of his mantra on the importance of maintaining justice in a civilized society. He should tell her the latest "lawyers are carcass-eating vultures" joke.

But instead, he captured her I-dare-you glare with a steady stare of his own.

"You should be a cop."

"Excuse me?"

"Internal affairs. Maybe you could teach a course at the Academy. You have a knack for spotting weaknesses in the chain of evidence."

She blew out a frustrated breath. "Only because your department mishandles evidence on too many cases. Not to mention search warrants, Miranda rights and—what was it that one time? Oh yeah, a coerced confession."

He nodded, unable to disagree. A police department was only as by-the-book as the people who ran the show. Except for this botched arrest with Yube, all of the other breakdowns in procedure had occurred before Adam had taken over as chief. Not that the timing mattered to the courts. Faith had argued two cases recently where the Courage Bay police department had bungled its job. First, with convicted murderer Felix Moody's appeal three months ago, and now with Yube.

God, they'd been good to go! An ironclad case. Two eye-witnesses. A gun. A receipt for the purchase of gasoline used in the arson attempt. Even photographs of a burn Yube had suffered while cutting the brake line on Lauren Conway's car.

Then Faith had discovered a fatal flaw in the chain of evidence—one that Adam, much to his consternation, hadn't known existed. On the same night George Yube had attacked and shot Lauren Conway, Detective Paul Jerado had lost his son to suicide. The boy's body hadn't been found until after Jerado had gathered all the evidence from the crime scene; he'd been en route to deliver the proof to the department when he received the call about his son.

He'd immediately rerouted, as any father would. The entire department had been shocked and grieved by the boy's death. Josh Jerado had been a fixture at the police station, sometimes doing his homework at his father's desk while Paul worked overtime on a case. After the suicide, there had been a thorough investigation to rule out foul play, a vigil, a memorial, a mass, a funeral. At one point or another, every member of the department had spent time with the Jerado family. And without anyone realizing, the evidence had sat in the back of Jerado's car for two days.

Two days. Forty-eight hours of opportunity for the evidence to be tampered with or otherwise compromised. Under Faith's questioning, Jerado admitted that he had logged the evidence in quietly after his son's funeral, and not until today's hearing had anyone, including Adam, known about the mishandling.

Adam couldn't harbor anger toward Paul Jerado, not after the horrible loss he'd suffered—still suffered from, in Adam's opinion. When Adam returned to the precinct, he'd order an immediate leave of absence and counseling for his friend and colleague. But despite his pleas to Judge Craven to give him and prosecutor Henry Lalane more time to reconstruct the case before he ruled on the motion for dismissal, Adam had realized Yube would walk. Without the evidence, the most they had him on was assault, a far cry from attempted first-degree murder. Faith's discrediting of the physical evidence destroyed Adam's chance to see justice served. A very bad man, a baby-murdering liar, was about to walk free, and Adam didn't much care if the letter of the law had been on Faith's side. The spirit of the law had, with one ruling, flown the coop.

And though Adam hadn't overseen the investigation, the failure chapped his ass like wearing shorts in the summertime for a weekend ride on his brother's hog. First, Moody. Now, Yube. And in both cases, Faith had been right.

"New procedures are in place since I took over, Counselor. Mistakes you've taken advantage of in the past will not be a problem in the future. If I have my way, I'm going to put you out of a job, at least in this county."

She narrowed her eyes, but the slits of silver didn't brim with the anger and resentment he had expected. In fact, the quirk of her generous lips hinted at humor.

"I'll be the first person to buy you a beer if you do."

She uncrossed her arms and dropped her hands to her sides, forcing Adam to note that she wore her skirts pretty damn short. Her fingertips, painted a subdued tone in that popular pink-and-white nail-polish style, barely reached the hem. He might have taken an extra minute to admire the smooth length of her legs, but the sweep of her gaze down his body distracted him.

Wait. She was checking *him* out?

He sucked the side of his cheek into his mouth to keep from grinning like a puffed-up fool. "See something interesting?"

She cleared her throat, then met his stare with that steely coolness that won her the respect of judges, juries and prosecutors alike. Particularly the male ones. "Every time I run into you, Guthrie."

With a laugh he figured she was aiming at herself, she took a step back.

"Look, you're a good cop. And contrary to popular belief, I do appreciate men in blue."

Her gaze swept from his face to his shoulders to his legs. His suit was indeed a dark shade of navy—one of the dozen more expensive outfits he'd been forced to buy after his promotion. He hadn't thought much about how he actually *looked* in the getup, but when Faith released a nearly inaudible sigh, he decided to send the store's tailor a six-pack.

"Lawyers in yellow aren't bad, either."

She sashayed toward him and gave him a friendly punch in the arm as if they'd been friends since childhood. Actually, he'd known of her since high school. They'd never run in the same circles, but Courage Bay, California, was not a metropolis. She'd moved to a neighborhood not far from his in the midsize coastal community just before Adam graduated, and if he remembered correctly, she was nearly the same age as his younger brother, Casey.

"That you can dole out a compliment after I mopped the floor with your investigation in the courtroom says a lot about you, Guthrie."

He chuckled. "I hope it says you're ready for another fight. I'm not done with Yube."

She made a clicking sound with her tongue. "Have at him. If he's guilty, gather the evidence and prove it beyond a shadow of a doubt. But let's be clear—" she leaned in close, so that the delicate scent of her perfume teased his nostrils "—harassment won't be tolerated. So long as Yube is my client, I'll be watching how the police treat him."

Adam inhaled, trying to identify the slight fruity scent that emanated from her skin. "I will see to it personally that all his rights are observed, Counselor. Until I can take his rights away, that is."

"Legally, of course."

"Of course."

She backed up. "So, is that all? Because my client has probably been processed by now, and I need to make sure he gets to his car without being accosted by a mob. People don't like him much."

Adam rolled his eyes. There wasn't much to like about the lying, cheating, murderous creep, even if the soft-spoken old man did remind Adam of his grandfather. Looks could be damn deceiving.

Still, with Faith Lawton playing watchdog, Adam would have to remind his men to act professionally. The prosecutor, District Attorney Henry Lalane, hadn't yet committed to refiling charges against Yube, perhaps for simple assault, but Adam wasn't giving up hope.

"People don't like your client? Imagine that."

She shook her head and gave a frustrated sigh, letting him know that his lame attempt at humor had likely been heard a million times before. Defense attorneys, for the most part, got a bad rap. Some deserved the jokes and loathing, and others, like Faith, took full advantage when cops like him didn't do their jobs right. She was the balance that checked the system of U.S. justice. She wasn't right all the time, but then, neither was he.

The minute he opened the door, he heard the surge of excitement thrill through the crowd. Without hesitation, Faith burrowed into the tide of people rushing toward another door down the hall. Yube was likely on his way out. Adam hung back, turning his head when the burst of camera flashes and the glare of lights blocked his view. Damn circus. Where was security? Probably lost in the shuffle, just like everything else today.

"Win some, lose some" came a voice at his side, but Adam didn't have to turn to identify the speaker.

"You're awfully complacent, Lalane. I thought you didn't like losing."

"I hate it. That's why I usually don't take cases I can't win. You really didn't know about the evidence?"

Stomach acid churned in Adam's gut, sending a hot shot of frustration up his throat. "Of course not."

"How did Faith Lawton find out about Jerado?"

Adam shook his head, confident an internal investigation would expose the source. At the moment, he concentrated on the fact that the skin on the back of his neck prickled. The energy in the crowd intensified. Adam watched a line of additional security guards and uniformed police make their way toward Yube and Faith, but he still crossed his arms over his chest and slipped one hand beneath his lapel, his piece close at hand.

"We could have won this one. We had solid evidence." Adam kept his voice low, though the power of containing his frustration made his teeth hurt. But he stopped his rant before he got started. Again. He'd tried to explain in the courtroom, tried to make the judge understand that Detective Jerado's mishandling of the evidence hadn't changed the results—the evidence was still ironclad, even if it had sat unattended for two days. No one could prove if it had or hadn't been tampered with. In the rational part of his brain, Adam knew the facts didn't matter. The evidence hadn't been handled correctly. But his gut still ached from the injustice.

"Like I said, 'win some, lose some.'" Henry adjusted the belt that secured his pants below a slightly protruding gut. He hand-combed his thinning gray hair and winked a sharp eye that matched his devilish grin. "Buy you a beer?"

Adam snorted. "It's four-thirty in the afternoon."

"Hell, Adam, it's seven-thirty in New York City, Washington D.C., and Miami. Pick a metropolis. We'll pretend we're there and cut loose for an afternoon. We deserve it."

Bit by bit, courthouse security thinned the crowd. Then Adam noted more people pouring in from outside, barely clearing security before they dashed toward Faith and Yube. Through the sea of dark-colored clothing, Adam caught a golden flash of Faith. She had a hand on Yube's arm and was maneuvering him toward a reporter with a feed from CNN.

"Damn, she killed us," Henry said, his voice sounding appropriately miffed for the first time since the judge had dismissed the charges.

Adam shook his head emphatically. "No, the only killer around here is Yube. She just added another section to our manual on processing evidence in an emergency situation."

The crowd swelled again, and when Faith pressed through with Yube on one side and her assistant on the other, Adam had had enough. Heading toward them, he pulled out his cell phone and used the walkie-talkie feature to call for backup, then made his way through the swarm of lookers-on, reporters and various other courtroom clingers, and tugged at Faith's jacket.

He jerked his head and she seemed to understand that their attempt to leave wasn't going as it should. She pulled Yube toward her, but lost her assistant temporarily in the melee.

"The crowd's just as bad behind us!" she shouted. "What's going on? Where's Security?"

"Overwhelmed, more than likely. Word must have traveled fast." To retain a better hold on her, he slipped his hand around her waist. The intimate move made her eyes flash in warning.

"Just give me a second," Adam insisted. "I'll get you out."

In ten minutes, the uniforms had the hallway cleared. The reporters had been ordered off the premises, relegated to the bottom of the limestone steps just below the expansive court-yard and plaza. The neck-craning citizens had been told to get on with their business or move along—and most had dispersed without argument. The hall still wasn't quiet, as county employees milled toward the exits at the end of the workday, but at least they could talk without yelling.

"We can escort you out the back, then send someone for your vehicles later," Adam suggested, noting how the hectic quality of the moment had brought a slight sheen to Faith's skin.

She seemed to consider the suggestion, but Yube, who'd remained judiciously quiet until now, spoke up. "I'd rather go out the front doors, Faith. I've been exonerated." He pointed his gaze directly at Adam and Henry. "I want everyone to see I'm a free man."

Henry slipped his hands into his pockets and turned his head away. Adam could taste the prosecutor's anger as bitterly as he could taste his own, but he swallowed his rancor and focused on the matter at hand.

"Your choice, Mr. Yube."

"Dr. Yube," the man corrected, his eyes staring daggers.

As if he had any right to still call himself a physician! Adam opened his mouth, but Faith silenced him before he had a chance to give the murderous son of a bitch a piece of his mind.

"Just let's get out of here, George," Faith insisted to her client. "Roma?"

Faith's assistant disconnected her ear from her cell phone. Pretty, young and Hispanic, she glowed, apparently feeding off Faith's approval. "I checked your messages. Nothing that can't wait until morning. I also cancelled your five-thirty and rescheduled for tomorrow at nine. Ready to go?"

Roma's wide brown eyes darted among the party, seemingly oblivious in her youthfulness to the tension crackling around her. Adam figured the girl was fresh out of law school, no more than twenty-four, and likely hadn't even taken the bar exam, much less passed it.

"Yes," Faith answered, then nodded toward Henry and Adam. "Mr. Lalane, Detective Guthrie. It's been a pleasure."

She marched toward the doors, her assistant struggling to keep up on her pointy high-heeled shoes, and Yube strutting with an arrogant confidence that made Adam's blood boil.

"So, you in for the brewski or what?" Henry asked.

Adam was severely tempted. When he'd woken up this morning and gone for his run, he'd jogged an extra mile, thanks to the added energy of knowing Yube's hearing would go their way. He'd never imagined that a distraught detective's actions would blow this case to shreds. Faith might have been right to question the chain of evidence, and the law might have supported her contention that the lack of control over the evidence made its veracity suspect, but damn, didn't she realize she'd just helped a baby-killer go free?

"Faith!" he shouted, before he knew why he'd called her by her first name or what he would say to her if she stopped. He jogged toward her.

Yube and Roma continued toward the wide glass doors while Faith paused, turning on her spiked high heel. "Yes, Detective?"

He didn't stop until her face was inches from his. "This is wrong. You know that, right?"

She let out an exasperated breath and turned away, continuing toward her client, who'd stopped to allow an elderly woman to pass through the door in front of him.

"Thought you weren't going to berate me, Detective," she reminded him, her tone curt. She caught up to her client, but declined his gestured invitation for her to exit first. Typical. The woman probably didn't like guys opening car doors for her, either.

"I'm not berating," Adam said, much more insistent than Yube when it was her time to walk outside. He followed her through the glass doors. Okay, he'd lost this case. He might not have the chance to contribute to making Yube really pay for his heinous crimes against this community and the families his lies and schemes had ripped apart, but maybe he could convince Faith to work for him, rather than against him. It wasn't much of a plan, but it wasn't bad. "I'm appealing to your sense of justice."

That stopped her dead. She rounded on him slowly, her eyes squinting against the reflection of the sun on the limestone plaza outside the courthouse. "My sense of—"

The last word of her protest vanished under a loud *crack,* a sound Adam reacted to without thought, reason or logic— just instinct. He grabbed Faith by the arms and shoved her toward the nearest wall, glancing over his shoulder long enough to witness people on the plaza screaming, running haphazardly, standing still as statues in shock, or dropping to the ground for cover.

Someone had fired into the crowd. Adam didn't know who had been the target, but his stomach tightened. If he didn't act fast, someone would end up very, very dead.

CHAPTER TWO

FAITH GRUNTED. Adam's full weight forced her against the brick wall so that the mortar bit through her jacket into her shoulder blades. A bullet sliced the air, then exploded on the limestone just a few feet away. Oh God! If he hadn't pushed her out of the way, her head might have exploded instead of the stone.

Adam had drawn his gun, a large revolver that gleamed black and dangerous despite the muted sunlight from the shade of the U-shaped courthouse. Except for two people lying on the ground, the plaza had quickly cleared—so far as she could see, with Adam's massive body curled protectively over hers.

"What's happening?" she asked.

"Sniper," he answered curtly, turning to scan the windows across and above. "From the top of this side of the building." He stretched his left arm out, as if bracing an invisible shield across her.

Faith's heart dropped into the pit of her stomach. Suddenly, she smelled it—

Blood. Lots of blood.

"Stay back," he ordered.

"I'm not moving. You shouldn't, either. Let the cops on duty handle this. Someone called for backup, right?"

With a slight shake of his head, Adam continued to peer

upward. "Don't know. Don't move, Counselor, do you understand?"

She growled in frustration. What did he think she'd do, run into the courtyard like a big yellow target?

"Do I look like I'm going anywhere?"

He wasn't facing her, so he likely didn't know that she was scared spitless and couldn't move her legs even if she wanted to. She forced dry gulps of air into her lungs, fighting the instinct to grab Adam when he started to inch away. She fisted her hands at her sides, then flattened against the wall as much as her 36-C breasts would allow, and tried to ignore the ringing in her ears. She had to let him do his job. He was the chief of detectives, for Pete's sake. He didn't need her help. Besides, she loved her life and didn't much fancy losing it to a faceless coward with a rifle, a scope and a deadly vendetta.

Adam extracted his cell phone from his pocket and instantly connected with the dispatcher. "Yube is down. So is…looks like Lorraine Nelson. Shots seemed to come from the top of the south annex." He requested an ambulance, then paused before speaking again with calm precision. "No, the area is not secure, but the back entrance is likely clear. Can't tell from here. Have EMT on standby just inside the doors. Evacuate the building. Alert SWAT. Inform Zirinsky that we need an Incident Command System. We're sitting ducks!"

Adam crouched, moving slowly toward the two bodies. When she saw the blood pooling reddish black against the stark white stone, oozing from the back of George Yube's head, Faith's stomach roiled. A gasp lodged in her throat, blocking her airway. She pressed hard against her stomach, forcing her diaphragm to work.

"Is he—?"

"Yes," Adam answered. "Can't tell about Lorraine. I don't see a wound."

Faith covered her mouth with her hand. Lorraine Nelson was a court stenographer who probably should have retired ten years ago except that she was the best recorder in the entire county system. Faith knew her, had worked with her, had relied on her perfect court records to file at least a half dozen appeals.

Adam inched his foot out ahead of him, but the action was met with the *crack* of another gunshot.

Faith screamed, but caught the sound in her hand. Her heart slammed against her chest and her ears rattled with the pounding beat so that she didn't hear what Adam said next.

"What?"

He crab-walked back to her, and once flush to the wall, stood up. "Get back into the building."

"Isn't the sniper *in* the building?" she asked.

The courthouse was in the middle of downtown, shaped like a U, with the main entrance at the inner curve and two annexed wings jutting out from either side. No other buildings in close enough range were taller than the five-story complex, which housed offices for several county services, not all of them related to the court system. The only places from which someone could shoot down into the plaza were the upper floors or roof of one of the two wings, since the main building was topped with a dome. And if the sniper were in the north annex, across from them, they'd be dead by now.

"Probably, but there's Security just inside the doors. If we can make it back to the lobby, you'll be safe. You can evacuate with the others."

"Aren't we safer right here?" she asked, not certain she

wanted to leave Lorraine alone, or abandon Yube's body. She suddenly remembered that Roma, her assistant, had been walking with them, too. Where was she? "Oh God. Where's Roma?"

Adam grabbed her arm and met her stare with clear intent. "Roma must have gotten away. Don't worry about her. Worry about you. But I can't stop the sniper from here," he added through clenched teeth.

Lorraine moaned but didn't move. Had she been shot? What if she woke fully and panicked? If she thrashed or tried to flee, the sniper might shoot again to finish the job.

Faith leaned around Adam. "Lorraine, it's Faith Lawton. Help is on the way. Please, just stay still." Then to Adam she said, "I'm out of range here, right? I'll stay with Lorraine."

Another shot fired, this one cracking limestone at the other end of the plaza. Two people Faith couldn't identify had attempted to make a break for the door. Adam blocked Faith with his body again and shouted for the people to remain where they were.

"Damn it! I want you inside!"

Faith could see the rage building on Adam's face.

"If I can arrange a diversion, you can make a break inside," he told her.

"I'm not going," Faith said.

He met her gaze with wide eyes, apparently shocked that she wanted to stay out in the open. "You can't do anything for Lorraine," Adam argued. "The paramedics and SWAT are on the way."

"I'll stay where I am until they arrive," she answered calmly. She watched Adam's expression change from irritation to single-minded determination.

"Stubborn even outside the courtroom, Counselor?"

She smirked at the humor in his voice. "Absolutely."

A strong vibration pulsed against her hip, right where Adam's leg was pressing against her waist. She nearly cracked a totally inappropriate joke when he dug into his pocket and retrieved his cell phone.

"Guthrie."

Faith took the time to pull deep breaths into her lungs in an attempt to achieve a little balance. One minute she wanted to laugh hysterically, the next she wanted to scream. Good God. George was dead! She'd known he was accused of some horrible things, but to be murdered by a sniper on the court-house plaza? What kind of justice was that?

Vigilante justice. Faith seethed, unable to comprehend the logic of matching evil with more evil. What if, somehow, even the slightest possibility existed that Yube *had* been innocent of the baby switch thirty-two years ago? No one had any physical proof. Or what if his state of mind had precluded him from discerning right from wrong when he'd attacked Lauren Conway? His appointment with the court-recom-mended psychiatrist had been scheduled for next week. Faith hadn't thought too much about that aspect of her defense once she'd discovered the mishandling of the evidence, but she suspected the one-time hospital administrator had recently taken a jump off the deep end.

Faith believed in right and wrong. She'd lived by the tenets of accountability and lawfulness for as long as she could remember. It was hard not to develop a strong set of morals after her father was murdered right in front of her by a man who ended up serving no time for the crime. Unbidden, the coppery smell of death seeped into her nostrils. Willing the memories away, she shook her head and took in deep breaths through her mouth. She'd been so young. Still, her vigilance about living on the straight and narrow had intensified after she'd learned how a drug deal had led to her father's death. Then, two years later, her mother was sent to prison, leaving Faith alone in a world that didn't want her.

She had lived in the midst of crime and poverty for her entire childhood, until the state interceded after her mother's conviction and placed her with the Apalo family, who'd moved to Los Angeles from Hawaii. Shortly after taking Faith in, they'd moved to Courage Bay. The family's luau-style restaurant was only a few blocks away. Her sister, Kalani, knew about Faith's emergency hearing today. Had she heard the news of the shooting? Her foster family was probably worried out of their skulls!

Adam disconnected his call, snapping Faith's thoughts back to the present. Lorraine still hadn't moved, but Faith thought she saw the woman's chest rise and fall. She shouted a few more words of encouragement, yelping when two more shots rent the air. This time, the sniper didn't seem to be aiming at anyone in particular. Again, Adam used his body to shield hers.

The scent of pine trees teased her nostrils. Not the antiseptic odor she associated with household cleaners, but the crisp, green smell of a forest bathed in sunshine and dew. She inhaled, surprised to recognize the hint of sage, the tang of citrus, until she realized she'd rather focus on anything than breathe in the sickly sweet stink of fresh blood.

"He's shooting from the other end of the plaza, probably from the roof of the north annex. He's lost his aim. The cops must have tried to move in."

"Can't they get him from the inside?"

"That was Max Zirinsky on the phone. He's setting up an emergency command center at the back entrance. Apparently, the elevators aren't working. Cut power line. The south annex has been evacuated, but the north annex stairwell from the second to the third floor is blocked."

"Blocked? By what?"

Sirens whined, loud and harsh. Fire trucks. The firehouse was behind the courthouse and just a block down at Jefferson and Fifth. Suddenly, Faith realized the whistling sound she'd heard earlier wasn't just ringing in her ears. It was a fire alarm inside the building.

"There's a fire? And you want to go inside?"

"Max thinks the sniper has a fairly good chance at reaching the front doors if he's so inclined, but I've got to get in. Stay here with Lorraine, but keep out of the line of fire. You could be his target—"

"Me?" she protested, unable to tear her eyes away from Yube's body. "That's absurd."

"Is it?" Adam asked. "The sniper got Yube. I haven't noticed him stop shooting, have you? That means maybe he's not done yet."

Faith bit her lip and crossed her arms, hugging herself tightly. Okay, defense attorneys weren't exactly popular. Maybe some psycho had decided to take out the city's latest high-profile criminal—and his attorney. The thought made her spine freeze with terror. Panic gurgled like acid in her stomach, but she closed her eyes tightly and said a silent prayer. She was strong, smart and resourceful. She had Adam and, soon, the entire Courage Bay emergency response team looking out for her. For the moment, her location flat against the wall kept her out of the sniper's sight. She'd be okay.

When she nodded, Adam smiled, his hand gripping her shoulder as if he meant to inject her with his strength.

"Zirinsky is suiting someone up to retrieve you. But I have to go in. They're having trouble evacuating those above the second floor."

"It's late. Who's still up there?"

"Don't know. A few judges in chambers. The office of Child Services is on four. The day-care center for county employees on three."

She nodded, understanding. Adam didn't have it in him to sit and wait for his colleagues to do all the work, just as she couldn't leave Lorraine alone with no one to comfort her, no one to remind her to keep still.

"I know CPR," she told him. "As soon as it's clear, I can help her."

He glared at her. "Don't be a hero, Faith."

"I could say the same to you, but it'd be too late."

He rolled his eyes humbly, then flattened himself on the wall and moved as quickly as he could toward the glass doors they'd just exited moments before. She held her breath, knowing that when he rolled away from the wall, the sniper might have a clear shot. Beyond the glass, Faith saw two men in black prepare to open the doors. The moment they did, one tossed a canister into the middle of the plaza and shouted for the bystanders to look away. Faith complied, then heard a loud *pop* and caught a bright flash in her peripheral vision. By the time she turned back, Adam had dashed inside.

Surprisingly, the sniper didn't fire, but Faith knew they weren't out of danger yet. She turned her attention to Lorraine.

Tears sprang from her eyes when she heard the older woman moan, this time with anguish.

"Don't move, Lorraine!" Faith shouted. "I'm near you. Just try to stay still a few minutes longer. Help is on the way."

Faith closed her eyes for a moment and repeated that last bit of information to herself, hoping beyond hope that she was telling the truth.

ADAM DASHED INTO THE LOBBY of the courthouse, sparing one last glance at Faith through the glass doors before rushing toward Police Chief Max Zirinsky and his assembled emergency team.

He hadn't expected hysterics from a cool customer like Faith Lawton, and she hadn't disappointed him. The woman could think on her feet, and he had to trust that she'd be safe until they could catch the maniac who'd popped George Yube. Yeah, Adam thought the guy should have paid for his decades of crime, but vigilantes pissed him off nearly as much as criminals. The cops might not be perfect, but nine times out of ten, they did their jobs and they did them well.

The lobby echoed from the sound of combat boots on the terrazzo floor. Adam glanced around, not surprised to see the large space free of civilians. The SWAT team, headed by Flint Mauro, swarmed into the space, dressed in black and wearing intense expressions. Courage Bay had one of the best SWAT teams in California. They were in good hands.

"How's the attorney?" Max asked the minute he spotted Adam coming toward him. Though only five years from turning fifty, Max Zirinsky could bench-press his weight with ease. Dark haired with cool green eyes, he was the kind of cop who belonged at the top. Quick with a joke, but deadly serious when it came to fighting crime, Max had the respect of everyone in law enforcement, with the exception, perhaps, of the many criminals he'd locked away.

"She's cool. Staying put until one of your guys can reach her."

"What about Mrs. Nelson?"

Adam shook his head. "Not good. Faith's trained in CPR, but she can't get near her until we stop the shooter."

He had noticed Lorraine Nelson's chest rising and falling, but otherwise had seen very little movement. She wasn't young. She needed medical attention and she needed it now.

Max clapped Adam on the shoulder. "Ms. Lawton won't have to put herself in danger. I'm suiting up one of the paramedics in SWAT gear and sending her out with Flint. He's pulling out a bulletproof shield from the riot gear. Thinks he can angle it and keep them safe until they can determine Mrs. Nelson's condition."

Adam nodded, not the least bit surprised that in minutes, Zirinsky had the situation as near to under control as possible. He wondered if the chief was going to send him out of the building while the rest of the team worked this operation. Courage Bay had a crack Incident Command System. With the city on the ocean, surrounded by mountains and sitting on a fault line, the Courage Bay community had to be ready for emergencies. As chief of detectives, Adam wasn't usually involved unless the emergency was crime-related. Like this one. But snipers were SWAT's business, not his. At least until the danger passed.

Still, he had a personal interest in not only bringing Faith back inside safely, but also catching the sniper alive and making sure he paid for his crimes. He'd had enough of slippery criminals today. He wanted to make sure this arrest went down by the book—and *that* was a job for a top cop.

Max engaged his walkie-talkie. "Johnson, where are the blueprints?"

"Prints?" Adam asked.

The voice on the other end of the walkie-talkie answered. "We're still looking, Chief. Someone misfiled them."

Max let out a stream of curses from between clenched teeth. "I need the prints, Johnson. There's got to be another way onto the third floor!"

The walkie-talkie crackled again. This time, the voice belonged to Dan Egan, the fire chief.

"Fire's out, Max. Smoke is thick, but the fans are working wonders. Send your men up."

Max grinned, his gaze sharpening at the prospect of catching the shooter. "Two teams are on the way. One for the shooter, the other for evacuation."

At his signal, the teams stormed the stairwell. Adam's adrenaline surged through his veins, and he bounced on the balls of his feet. Damn, the SWAT guys couldn't screw this up. He wanted this sicko caught, not killed, though he'd accept killed if that would keep Lorraine and Faith and anyone else trapped on the ground safe. Still, if Adam were up there, he could try to control the situation.

"Max—" Adam began, but knew the minute he caught the twinkle in his chief's eyes that he wouldn't have to finish his question.

"Grab a Kevlar and take the rear position. You supervise the arrest only, got it, Guthrie? I don't need you down, too."

Adam dashed to the neat pile of supplies by the door and snatched a bulletproof vest. He shrugged out of his jacket and slipped into the protection, checking his weapon and extra clip before saluting the chief on his way to the action.

Once out of sight, he fisted his hands and let out a low-key "Yes!"

He'd wanted to snare a bad guy today. And he might still get his chance.

FAITH NEARLY JUMPED FOR JOY the minute she saw the SWAT team easing toward her. One held a large black shield with a clear slot to see through. The other carried a medical kit. Thank God! Lorraine, who'd just started coming around, was going to be treated.

"They're coming, Lorraine," she said, sounding as encouraging as she felt. "Just hold on. Don't move. The SWAT guy has a shield. He'll block you, keep you safe. Can you hear me, Lorraine?"

A low groan was the only response, but that was good enough for Faith. She folded her hands together and repeated another litany of prayers for Lorraine. She'd never felt half so spiritual as she did today. And though she couldn't do anything for George, if Lorraine lived, she might sleep when night finally fell.

Time seemed to pass in slow motion. Days seemed to elapse before the SWAT team reached Lorraine, months before the paramedic had a diagnosis: heart attack. Lorraine needed immediate medical help, but the paramedic couldn't administer treatment out in the open.

"Base, this is Mauro," the man with the shield said into the radio strapped to his shoulder. "We need a gurney. Now!"

No response. Faith's stomach dropped to her knees.

"Base, this is Mauro!"

His radio wasn't working. He gestured toward the doors, and in a split second, two more SWAT guys burst out—two shields in front of them, a gurney pulled behind. They didn't know the precise angle the shooter was aiming from—for all they knew he could still shoot them in the head. Faith held her breath, willing Lorraine's rescuers to succeed.

As soon as the gurney was secure, the two new SWAT members formed a wall with the shields, two on the ground and one angled to protect from shots from above. The paramedic worked furiously, with the second SWAT guy assisting her in lifting Lorraine onto the cart.

Suddenly, a succession of gunshots rang out from above. Faith screamed and ducked, folding herself into a tiny ball, watching from beneath her arm as bullets slammed into the limestone, random, unfocused, splintering the plaza so that fragments bit at her cheek and hands. The SWAT team scrambled toward the exit, the bulkiest man barking orders in rapid succession. The paramedic seemed completely focused on Lorraine, not realizing that she had stepped out from behind the barricades. A bullet broke through their moving shield and struck the paramedic in the arm. Blood spurted as she yelped in pain, but the leader dragged her over Lorraine's legs and, pushing the wheeled gurney quickly, managed their escape.

Then all went silent. Deadly silent. The kind of silent that creeps beneath the skin and chills to the bone. No sirens. No gunshots. No voices. Nothing but her own ragged gasps for breath. Faith fought the hyperventilation that would occur if she didn't pull herself together. She held her breath, counted to ten, blew the air out slowly and then began again until she achieved a halfway decent calm.

George Yube was dead. Lorraine was critical. Now the paramedic had suffered a gunshot wound to the arm, if not worse. Faith blinked tears out of her eyes, trusting that the same police department she'd crucified in the courtroom would find a way to end this nightmare.

CHAPTER THREE

As soon as the SWAT detail cleared the smoke from the fire that had raged through the stairwell, Adam tore off his oxygen mask. His shoes squeaked as he walked across the hall, the soles sucking up the moisture from the fire sprinklers. Dan Egan had disengaged the automatic waterworks, but the damage was done. As the SWAT team moved stealthily in front of him, he stopped and kicked off his loafers. He wouldn't have much traction, but he'd have the element of surprise—if the shooter was still on the loose.

They'd exited the stairwell on the fourth floor. A second SWAT team had scaled the roof and reported that the sniper was not there, nor was there any evidence he'd ever been this high up. The stairwell from the roof into the building had been blocked by a rusted-out panel from a colossal air-conditioning unit, leaving the teams sent up from the lobby to find the sniper. They split up, the first team proceeding to the fifth floor, the second filtering onto the third, with Adam bringing up the rear of the final group, which exited on the fourth. Max reported civilians here and ordered Adam to see to Judge Craven, whose hysterical court clerk had kept them from evacuating.

Despite Adam's raging need to stick with the team as they moved down the hall to search for the sniper, he obeyed the order to protect Craven. If the shots weren't random, anyone associated with Yube's release could be in danger. That included the judge—and Faith. Adam swore under his breath, trying not to replay the scene again, as he had all the way up the stairwell. He'd hated leaving her. No matter how logical the decision had been at the time, no matter how safe he'd considered her to be, shoved up against the wall and out of the sniper's sights, Adam had still abandoned her in the courtyard with only a dying woman and Yube's bloody body for company.

He'd heard Max's update to the team. SWAT had rescued Lorraine Nelson, but what about Faith? Was she still out there? Was she terrified or was she still clinging to that steely attitude she'd exhibited before he left?

From the other side of Judge Craven's door, he heard sobs, as well as a man's voice attempting to soothe. He knocked, quietly announced who he was, then turned the knob. Locked. Good for Craven.

A second later, the judge opened the door, looking nothing like the cool-headed, wise vanguard of law and justice he appeared to be on the bench. His tie was nearly unknotted and his sleeves and hands were darkened by soot. His usually slicked-back hair now hung across his eyes.

"Detective, we need a paramedic team. She's inconsolable." He gestured toward a young woman sitting on the floor, rocking back and forth. Tears ran in beige rivulets down her cheeks, tinged with black from her eye makeup. In a white sweater and pink dress, she hugged herself tightly, wailing loudly and resembling a miserable child rather than the twenty-something Adam guessed her to be.

He nodded at the judge. "They'll be up as soon as the area is secure. May I?"

The judge nodded. Adam holstered his gun, relocked the door behind them and crouched next to the weeping woman. He saw no signs of physical trauma.

"What happened?" he asked.

Judge Craven smoothed his hair back and seemed, with Adam's presence, to gain control of his normally refined and dignified manner. "Her brother died in the Oklahoma City bombing, and she lost a good friend in the World Trade Center. She's petrified of terrorists. I'd guess post-traumatic stress disorder, though I'm no expert," he said sadly.

When Judge Craven disappeared into his private bathroom, Adam leaned back on his heels for a second, hoping to hear something from the hallway to indicate that it was safe to move them out of the office. He heard nothing. Aside from the communications between the command center and the teams swarming the buildings, there'd been no activity from the sniper since that last random volley of shots, which had occurred only moments after the SWAT teams entered the smoky stairwell.

He touched the young woman's arm. A quick glance up at her desk and the engraved nameplate told him who she was. "Mindy? I'm Detective Adam Guthrie. You'll be okay. You're completely safe in here. The SWAT team is in control. As soon as we secure the area, we'll get you medical attention. Whatever you need."

If she heard him, she gave no indication, just continued to rock and whimper. Adam glanced around the office, noticing a spilled can of diet soda dripping across the clerk's desk. She'd probably dropped the drink when she heard the shots and screams. The sirens and sprinklers outside the office must have added to her terror. Yet her clothes were dry, indicating that she hadn't ventured into the hallway. She must have dropped to the floor, where she'd been ever since.

Again, Adam thought about Faith, still outside, safe from the gunfire but not from the terror. Everyone had a breaking point, even sassy attorneys who looked as smooth and sweet as butter in a soft yellow suit. What would make her go over the edge? Seemed to him that a dead body with Yube's injuries—gunshot between the eyes, the back of his skull likely blown out—might do the trick. Right now, Faith's only view was that horrid violence, and for that most of all, he cursed himself again for leaving her alone. Knowing that Max had just ordered Flint to go back out and provide cover for Faith calmed Adam somewhat. But not much.

He didn't know why he felt so responsible. Maybe his brother, Casey, a fellow cop, was right when he claimed Adam took the whole "protect and serve" thing too seriously. Still, a man was dead. Two women, Lorraine and the paramedic, were injured, and countless others terrorized—all in what amounted to a few moments of deadly fury.

Judge Craven emerged from the bathroom, his shirt changed and his hands clean. He held out a fresh but damp towel to Adam, apparently for Mindy, then crouched beside the woman, a small cup of water cradled in his hands.

"Mindy, have a sip, won't you? We're perfectly safe now, with Detective Guthrie here."

For the first time, Mindy acknowledged their presence. She met Craven's caring gaze, then, with violently shaking hands, reached for the cup. Craven smiled at her kindly and held the glass to her lips.

The usually stoic judge then took the towel from Adam and wiped the woman's face clean, turning the terry cloth so that he never used the same spot twice. When he was done, he held up the towel, now streaked in beige, pink, black and red.

"I hate to tell you, Min, but you'll have to redo the war paint before you go on your big date tonight," Craven joked.

Mindy snuffled, and for the first time since Adam entered the room, spoke. "I'm so sorry, Judge Craven. I don't know what happened. If you hadn't come back when you did…"

Adam narrowed his gaze at the judge. "Where were you, Judge Craven? You weren't out trying to play hero, were you?"

The judge leveled Adam with an indignant look. "I leave the heroics to the professionals such as yourself, Detective Guthrie. I checked the stairwell, but the fire and smoke were impassable. Mindy and I were stuck up here—until you arrived. Can we leave now?"

Adam pulled out his cell and dialed into the command system. He got Max on the line.

"Are we clear?" he asked.

"The attorney is back inside and paramedics are tending to Yube, though there isn't a damn thing they can do except pick up the pieces. Mrs. Nelson is en route to the hospital, as is the paramedic I sent out."

Adam couldn't miss the self-recrimination in Max's voice, but he didn't comment.

"Third floor is empty. SWAT is sweeping the fourth and fifth floor offices. Stay put until all's clear," the chief added.

"No shooter?" Adam asked, disbelieving. If the SWAT teams had so much trouble making their way to the top floors, how could the shooter have escaped so easily? The fact that the sniper hadn't been on the roof concerned Adam greatly. Metal detectors and X-ray machines greeted each and every courthouse visitor. How was the weapon brought in? He thought back to the craziness that had ensued immediately after Craven released Yube. Could someone have slipped through Security in the chaos, undetected?

"If the sniper is still in the building, we can't find him," Max answered. "We're sending up two more teams and we're guarding the stairwell. I have teams on the outside watching all the windows. Unless there's another escape route that we don't know about, we'll get him."

Adam frowned. "Maybe it was an inside job."

Max didn't sound any happier about that prospect than Adam was. "Maybe. We'll check out everyone still in the building. You still with Craven?"

"Yes. The situation is under control."

A knock sounded. Judge Craven moved to answer the door, but Adam shouted ahead. "Who is it?" he called out, holding the phone to his chest.

"Randolph, sir. I'm with SWAT. Checking in."

With Adam's permission, the rookie entered and did a quick sweep of Craven's office—coming up empty, as Adam had expected. Despite the growing suspicion that the incident was over with no perp in custody, Max ordered Adam to remain with Judge Craven and his assistant until the floor was clear. Max shared Adam's instinct that the hit wasn't random. Until they knew more, they had to assume that anyone associated with Yube's release was in danger. For all they knew, Faith had been a target as well. Unfortunately, it wasn't a great stretch to think the vigilante who'd pulled the trigger on Yube and Faith could have it in for the judge who released Yube.

Adam also acknowledged that the whole tragedy might have been haphazard, a fortuitous accident perpetrated by a lunatic with a gun, but no agenda. They had no idea—and wouldn't, until Adam and his team of detectives broke the case.

FOR WHAT SEEMED LIKE the tenth time, Faith shook her head at the paramedic stationed a few feet away from her and declined treatment. While she appreciated the fact that the emergency medical technician simply wanted to help, she preferred to sit here, sip her bottled water, ignore her scraped knee and hope the police would interview her soon. She'd already borrowed a cell phone—hers was in her briefcase on the other side of the yellow tape—and checked on Roma, who'd been evacuated after running back into the building. Next, she'd called her foster parents to assure them that she was okay. Once someone took her statement, she'd go show them in person. Besides, what she wanted most of all in the world right now was a slice of her foster mother's guava chiffon cake. Faith could already taste the silky texture of the baked confection, the sweet lightness of the whipped cream icing, the distinct tropical flavor of the glaze.

Her stomach growled.

Great, now she'd made herself hungry. A wonderful addition to feeling traumatized and exhausted.

To take her mind off her appetite, she glanced through the crowd milling through the lobby of the courthouse building and wondered where Detective Guthrie had disappeared to. She owed him, at the very least, a sincere thank-you. When he'd pinned her to the wall, he'd likely saved her life. Even if she hadn't been the target, she could have been hit.

But before Faith could decide exactly how to word her gratitude, Adam emerged from the stairwell behind Judge Craven, who had his arm wrapped around a distraught young woman in a pink dress. Chief Zirinsky approached the judge and, if Faith remembered correctly, his law clerk, Mindy, and directed them to a bank of chairs near his makeshift command center. Two uniforms hurried to stand watch, not unlike the one who'd been trying to stand discreetly behind her; she could practically feel his breath on the back of her neck.

Adam made a beeline for her.

"You okay?"

Though Adam was likely the hundredth person to ask her that question in the last thirty minutes, this time, the sentiment spawned a lump in her throat. She coughed into her hand, then took another sip of water.

"Thanks to you."

He chuckled. "For God's sake, I left you out there with Yube's body for company. I'm really sorry about that."

"Hey, you had to do your job."

"Just like you had to do yours this afternoon," he commented, but there was no condemnation in his voice. More like resolve, as if he'd forced himself to understand.

"Lot of good it's done now. Someone decided to be judge, jury and executioner without the benefit of the legal system we both love. Was the vigilante caught?"

Adam eased into the chair beside her. "No, but we'll catch him."

She smiled, but the effort cost her. Damn, she was tired. Bone weary. She attempted to sit up straighter, until a sharp pain between her shoulder blades caused her to wince. "I believe you. I don't know why my statement is important. I didn't see anything."

Adam motioned the uniform over, then borrowed a pen and paper. He nodded for the guy to step away, and the cop immediately complied. Once they were alone, he poised the ballpoint over the pad, then hesitated.

"You up for an interview?"

"Do I have a choice?"

Adam quirked an eyebrow. For the first time, she noticed how incredibly warm his eyes were—a rich caramel brown with flecks of gold that would likely catch the light on a sunny day.

His voice was deep, but gentle. Like a wave meant for floating rather than surfing. She wondered if Adam ever caught the waves, if he ever experienced the rush of riding the ocean on a mad dash toward land.

"We could postpone this until later," he said. "You look like you're in pain."

"Nah, just a little sore. That's the price of skipping my workouts for the past three weeks."

"No pain, no gain," he commented.

"So they say," Faith acknowledged, though right at this minute she'd like to slap the idiot who came up with that stupid phrase. "Go ahead with your questions, Detective. The sooner you do your thing, the sooner you can catch the sniper—and do it by the book, okay? I won't be defending this creep, but someone will be."

He frowned, cleared his throat and then proceeded. "Had your client received any specific threats?"

She snorted. "You're kidding, right? About a gazillion of them at last count."

"Any to your office?"

"Half there, half to his home, which he immediately forwarded to me. Roma kept records."

"Any of them specific?"

"What, like 'I'm going to shoot your head off in the court-house plaza if you walk in this case'?"

He met her sarcasm with another frown.

"Sorry," she said, not really meaning it. "I tend to get snippy when I'm tired and hungry."

"Not to mention traumatized."

"Excuse me?"

"That was one nasty crime scene, Faith. It's okay to lose it a little."

"Are you the department shrink, too?"

"Am I crossing the line?"

Faith took a deep breath and exhaled slowly. She had a habit of turning into a real toad when she hadn't had a meal and felt as if she hadn't slept in two weeks. But she had to admit, the prospect of climbing beneath the sheets of her bed, in the dark, didn't appeal to her at the moment. Not when the image of George Yube's dead body seemed imprinted on the inside of her eyelids.

"No, Detective, you're not. I'll deal. I've seen worse."

"Like when?"

"I'm a defense attorney. Crime scene photos cross my desk every day."

"It's a little different when the blood is real and might drip onto the tip of your shoe."

She couldn't help but look down. Her shoes were gone. The SWAT team member who'd facilitated her removal from the plaza had instructed her to leave her heels behind so she could run faster. At the time, they weren't sure the sniper had been neutralized. Apparently, he hadn't, though they'd made it into the building without any more gunfire.

"I'll be okay. I always am."

"Survivor, huh?" he asked.

She realized she'd known Adam Guthrie for years, yet they were practically strangers. He had absolutely no idea how the term *survivor* had practically been invented for people like her. But hers wasn't a physical survival so much as an emotional and spiritual one. Not that she'd escaped the backlash of isolation and mistrust entirely, but every day, she made progress.

"You could say that. So…" She was suddenly anxious to cut to the chase. "I'll have Roma prepare the records she kept of the threats, for whatever good they'll do."

"And if you receive any other information—"

"You'll be the first person I'll call."

He nodded, but the movement was just short of agreement. He stood and waved at Max, who gestured him over.

"Excuse me a second?"

Faith motioned in Zirinsky's direction, too tired to argue about how she wanted to go home—now. "Be my guest."

Adam patted her shoulder before he dashed off toward his superior. His silent acknowledgment of Faith's exhaustion taunted her frazzled emotions. Great, where did she finally meet a guy who was actually in tune with her feelings? At a courthouse after a shooting. And though he'd rescued her and was one hot hunk of man, could she pursue him? Not unless she had an appetite for conflict, not to mention irony. On a daily basis, she represented the criminals he was determined to put in jail. Not exactly the strongest foundation for a long-lasting relationship.

But a fling?

Hmm.

Faith leaned forward, cradling her head in her hands. She must be more tired than she had thought. She did skip lunch preparing for Yube's hearing. Maybe she was delirious or, at least, near to it. To even consider a no-strings-attached affair with a man like Adam Guthrie, she had to be losing her mind. Sure, he was handsome in a rugged, tough sort of way. Mel Gibson-ish, without the accent. And he had a strong code of moral ethics. Even though his department had screwed up on more than one occasion, not once had he tried to cover up the mistakes. He owned up to the flaws, and from what she'd read in the papers, put procedures in place to ensure the cops didn't make the same mistake twice.

Worst of all for her, he had a sweet sense of humor. Sexy, ethical and compassionate. If he told her a good joke—preferably one that didn't rely on skewering a lawyer for the punch line—she'd be a goner. How could she resist him?

She couldn't. Not in her current emotional and physical state. She needed to get out of here before she did something really stupid. Like ask him over to her place.

A commotion from the outer doors drew Faith's attention. Standing with her fists on her ample hips, her foster sister, Kalani, was telling a poor uniformed officer exactly how things were going to be.

"Listen, Officer, I appreciate that you don't want the public at large stomping through your crime scene. But if you don't move aside and let me see my sister, this woman at large is going to stomp all over your butt."

She punctuated her very real threat by clomping her foot on the floor and shimmying her neck and shoulders in that soul-sister way that sent most men running for cover. The young officer glanced around, possibly hoping for backup, but not moving out of the way. Faith chuckled. She figured she'd better lend him a hand or she might find herself spending the rest of the evening defending her own sister on assault charges.

Shoeless and aching, Faith stood and crossed the lobby. "Officer, please let her through. You can check with Detective Guthrie. He just took my statement."

He spared an impotent scowl at Kalani, then marched off in the direction Faith had seen Adam disappear with the chief. Instantly, Kalani ran toward her, her dark hair secured in a swinging ponytail, a lei of lilies peeking out from the oversize Tommy Hilfiger shirt she'd thrown over her sarong. Her shift at the restaurant wasn't over until midnight, so apparently she'd taken off during the dinnertime rush.

Faith half expected to be bowled over, but as usual, her sister managed more control than anyone expected from her and folded Faith into a gentle hug. Kalani nurtured the reputation that she was a tough-talking, street-smart, piss-and-vinegar Hawaiian woman with an attitude. And in truth, she was all those things. Unless she liked you. Then she was a pussycat.

"Faith! God, I couldn't believe when I heard on the news. That's what you get for defending scumbags like Yube, and I don't care if that hurts your feelings."

Faith rested her cheek on her sister's shoulder and inhaled the warm sweet scent of coconut oil. Faith didn't know if the scent came from the kitchens of their parents' Hawaiian restaurant, Sunsets, or if Kalani had eschewed kitchen prep work today in favor of hitting the beach.

"It only hurt my feelings the first time you said it. Yube is dead, Kay."

"I know. Don't expect me to grieve."

Faith shook her head and broke the hug. No one in her family made any secret of the fact that they hated her chosen profession, even if they loved her unconditionally. Her foster father, Maleko, would have preferred she'd specialized in corporate law, so she could take over the business end of the restaurant's operations. Her foster mother, Melelu—called Lu by everyone who knew her—didn't much care what field of law she practiced, so long as she wasn't in danger. Unfortunately, criminal lawyers tended to hang out with an unsafe element.

What they didn't understand was that the risk didn't appeal to her any more than it did to them. She had no love for people who knowingly and willfully broke the law. But thanks to her own experiences with her mother, the woman who'd given birth to her in poverty, who had worked her fingers to the bone to put a roof over Faith's head and food in her belly, Faith knew that the innocent sometimes got caught up in the manipulations of the guilty.

She was nine when her father died, and barely eleven when the police barged into their tiny apartment in Los Angeles, yanking her, kicking and screaming, out of her mother's arms. The rage, confusion and resentment still lingered, closer to the surface than Faith would ever admit. She'd been damn lucky to be placed with the Apalo family just a few days later. Melelu had somehow known how to deal with Faith. She'd told her the truth, with no sugar-coating. Her real mother had been arrested for dealing drugs.

Sylvia Lawton had had no money for bail or a decent lawyer, so very soon after her arrest, she'd gone to prison. And not long afterward, she'd died.

While in college, Faith had finally found the courage to request all the documentation on her mother's case. What she'd read had horrified her, and that was long before she'd entered law school and fully comprehended the incompetence of her mother's defense, who'd urged her to plead guilty. The state's case against her mother had been shaky—based almost entirely on the testimony of jailhouse snitches—but even Faith's untrained eye could see her mother's innocence. Faith had decided that no other child should have to lose a parent, even for one night, because the police or the prosecutor didn't have their ducks in a row. In fact, no one deserved to serve a moment in jail if there was a reasonable doubt that they had committed the crime.

Unlike Faith, Kalani had never gone one night her entire life without her parents to take care of her, even during college, since Kay had chosen to live at home. Mal and Lu Apalo never left Kay or Faith, not for business trips or vacations or even stays in the hospital. Sure, George Yube's children were grown, but his grandchildren worshiped him. For them, Faith had decided to at least take a look at the case against the once-respected doctor.

Now he was dead. Oh God—had someone called his kids?

"Contrary to popular belief, Kay, George Yube will be missed," Faith muttered.

"By you?"

Faith shrugged, then realized that if she didn't change the subject soon, she'd have nightmares for weeks. "I hardly knew the man, but murder is a horrible crime, no matter who the victim is. Look, I had to give a statement to the police and I think they'll let me go now. Please tell me Lu made her guava cake for tonight's luau."

Kalani's tanned face brightened with her wide, toothy smile. "You kidding? If Mama doesn't make her guava cake every night, we lose business. I promised I'd call her as soon as I found you and made sure you were okay." She glanced around and spotted a bank of phones by the security station. "I'll be right over there."

Faith nodded, then looked around for Adam. He wasn't hard to find, when likely he should have been. With the exception of the SWAT team, every other male in the place was wearing a suit or a police uniform. Since more than half of the men in the lobby were cops, the majority of the guys milling around were also tall and well-built. Still, Faith's gaze zeroed in on Adam as if she'd developed handsome-hunk radar in her irises. Or maybe she'd formed a connection to the chief of detectives that she wasn't yet ready to acknowledge.

When she started toward him, he waved, but continued to issue orders to the man standing beside him.

"Tim, check in with Sam Prophet immediately. I want to know about the incendiary device in the stairwell. Anything he's got."

The detective made a note in a PDA. "He promises an initial report by morning. His first guess was that it was a small explosive, remote controlled, specifically placed to start a very smoky fire."

Adam swore mildly, but enough for Faith to catch his intensity. She already knew he took his cases personally, but seeing him in action added a layer of understanding she wasn't sure she wanted to possess.

"There goes the random-shooting theory," Adam said. "I also need the visitor list from courthouse Security before you leave. Call me on the cell when you've got it. And contact Ms. Lawton's assistant. She had a collection of threats Faith and Yube received. They kept records—for a brief time, anyway—and I want them. I'll handle everything else."

Tim glanced over his shoulder at Faith and frowned.

"You sure, boss? I mean, taking the choice assignments for yourself could hurt department morale."

Despite Tim's obviously teasing tone, Adam's jaw twitched, and Faith could almost feel a wave of cold emanating from his frosty response. Apparently, Adam Guthrie had his limits.

Through clenched teeth, he said, "I'll buy pizza for everyone on Friday. Will that do?"

Tim grinned, gave Faith a polite salute and then left.

Adam crossed over to her and, with a soft chuckle, banished any seriousness from his face.

"So, you ready to get out of here?"

Faith sighed. "You're kidding, right? I've been ready for hours. What about my briefcase and purse? They're still outside."

"I have a uniform standing by. As soon as Forensics releases the scene, he'll bring your things directly to your home. I've already ordered someone to check out your car, just in case."

Faith was suddenly very glad Kalani had come to the courthouse. Without her keys and driver's license, she wouldn't have any way home or, even if someone gave her a ride, any way to get into her house. Kalani had an extra set of keys on her key ring.

"Do you need me to come by the precinct tomorrow and sign my statement?" she asked.

"We can decide in the morning."

He gestured toward the glass doors. The sun had set, and television camera lights glared on the other side. She groaned. The last thing she wanted was her sorry-looking image broadcast on the eleven-o'clock news. She patted her hair, looked down helplessly at her grubby hands and filthy suit.

Then his words hit her.

"What do you mean, *we?*"

Adam increased his pace, seemingly ignoring the fact that she'd stopped walking.

"I'm going home with you, Ms. Lawton. And I'm staying the night."

CHAPTER FOUR

FAITH GROANED ALOUD. "Is this the part where I'm supposed to protest madly?"

"Excuse me?"

"You know, where I insist that I can take care of myself, that I don't need protection and I certainly don't need a sexy guy in my house acting the bodyguard. That's how it works in the movies."

If Faith had meant her cinematic scenario to unnerve him, her plan had worked. He was trying to get past the "sexy guy" part when a pretty woman, obviously Hawaiian heritage, joined them.

"So who's this hottie?" she asked.

Faith coughed to cover a giggle. Adam nearly blushed.

"Kalani Apalo, meet Detective Adam Guthrie. Detective, this is my sister, Kay."

Kalani's grin was nothing short of predatory. Adam ignored his sudden need to loosen his tie and instead shook her proffered hand. "Nice to meet you, Ms. Apalo."

"Call me Kay. Unless you want to call me 'sweet thing.' We could work that out, you know?"

From the corner of his eye, Adam watched Faith cover her mouth with her hand. Yeah, this was hilarious. Not that Kalani Apalo wasn't a stunning, voluptuous woman—she was. But suddenly, Adam, who'd never had much of a preference for female "types" before, realized he had more of a hankering for a sharp attorney who wore puka beads with her business suits.

If Kalani was her sister, that at least explained why she preferred tropical jewelry to conservative pearls.

"Your offer is tempting, Ms. Apalo, but I'm afraid my interests this evening are focused on your sister."

Faith turned toward him slowly, her gaze curious, but cautious. He could play this bowl-over-with-brashness game as well as she could—probably better.

Kalani nodded approvingly. "Hot damn, sis. You survive a shooting and catch yourself a man, both at the same time. Didn't know you had it in you."

Faith smirked at her sister. "First of all, the shooter wasn't aiming at me. Second, I doubt Detective Guthrie's interests extend beyond the professional. Third, he's just teasing about coming home with me."

Adam jammed his hands into his pockets. "You're so wrong, Counselor, I don't know where to start."

She crossed her arms. Adam hadn't forgotten the feel of those soft breasts crushed to his chest when they were outside against the brick wall. The moment had been too fraught with danger to acknowledge at the time, but now his flesh fairly tingled with the warm memory.

"Excuse me?"

"First," he said, mimicking her tone, "you don't know that you weren't in danger or that you still aren't. The assassination attempt might not have been aimed only at Yube."

Faith shook her head. "How do you know that Yube was the target at all? I'm not saying that isn't a logical assumption under the circumstances, but face it, Detective, you have no proof. The sniper might have been after random targets and George Yube was in the wrong place at the wrong time."

Adam groaned, wondering how he had ever thought assigning protection to her would be easy, particularly when he intended to pick up the detail himself, at least until tomorrow morning.

"You're entirely right," he conceded. "I have no solid proof, but the circumstantial evidence is too disturbing to ignore. And until I know the nature of the attack, you will receive police protection. Max Zirinsky has approved the detail."

She rolled her eyes. "And you're taking it upon yourself to provide my protection, with your undoubtedly busy schedule?"

He glanced back to where he'd stood when he and Tim had sparred over this very topic. Adam had made the decision on an uncharacteristic whim; he couldn't shake the instinct to make sure she was safe. He'd saved her life once, and if necessary, he wanted to be there to do it again.

"Like Detective Masters said," Adam answered, "it's a choice assignment."

Faith wanted to smile. He could see the corners of her mouth quivering as she fought with her reaction to being flattered. Not that he was any great catch, but he also knew he didn't send women screaming in the opposite direction.

Her sister slapped her on the arm. "He's flirting, Faith. Flirt back."

Faith tilted her head toward Kalani, her expression weary. "My sister, a bastion of subtlety."

"She's right," he added.

"Great. You have interesting timing, Detective. Flirt with the woman who's too tired to stand up, much less flirt back. Superlative plan."

Adam conceded his timing could be a little off, but he wasn't one to pass up an opportunity. He could drive her home and make sure she was safely in her house with an officer posted outside, before he was missed at the crime scene, which so far wasn't yielding one single clue as to the sniper's identity.

"At least you're thinking of flirting back," he said. "That's something, right?"

"Can we talk about this after I've eaten and had a shower?"

"No problem." He gestured toward the door. "Lead the way."

Just then, Detective Masters called out to him. "Guthrie, we've pinpointed the shooter's perch. Empty office on the fifth floor. Forensics needs you."

Of course they do.

"There's your reprieve, Counselor," he said reluctantly. "I'll send an officer to see you safely home."

"I'm not going home," she said quickly. "I'm going to my parents' restaurant, Sunsets."

"The luau place?"

"Best guava cake in town. My parents keep an apartment upstairs, so I can crash there tonight if I need to. Lots of people around. I'll be perfectly safe."

Adam pursed his lips, considering. This was a good situation, under the circumstances. Anyone targeting her wouldn't likely think to go after her in such a public place. Still, he'd send the uniform along just in case, and then he'd stop by later to return her belongings and make sure she was all right.

Maybe resume a little of the flirting.

"You'll stay with her?" he asked Kalani.

She saluted. "Absolutely."

"Good. I'll see you later, then? For our slumber party?"

He turned and stalked off quickly after Masters, giving Faith no time to argue or gauge if he'd been kidding. Which he had been—sort of. He glanced over his shoulder and barely contained a chuckle. She stood there with her mouth open and her finger poised, as if she'd prepared an objection that he'd left her no time to make.

"FEELING REJUVENATED YET?"

Swirling her fork, Faith scooped up every last sweet crumb left on her plate. With a flourish, she slid the fork into her mouth, relishing the exotic flavors gliding over her tongue. No one made guava cake like her foster mother. And no one could look both contented and concerned at the same time like Lu could, either.

"Doctors should prescribe this stuff instead of Prozac," Faith said.

Lu wiggled her ample bottom into the rattan chair across from Faith. "I keep trying to convince the pharmaceutical companies, but they aren't buying."

"You could do takeout," Faith suggested, for what was probably the thousandth time. The food at Sunsets was, thanks to Lu and her homegrown culinary skills, beyond compare. The restaurant was fiscally healthy, with a steady stream of regulars and bonus business from special celebrations such as birthdays, anniversaries and office parties. Faith appreciated that not once since the Apalos had taken her into their home had Faith had to worry about her family's finances, the way she had with her mother. And since she'd gone out on her own, she could always come home for a hot, delicious meal and love-inspired pampering. When her career allowed, which wasn't very often lately.

"If I did takeout, you'd never stay more than ten minutes. You'd go back to that little house of yours and work all night and never eat and, more importantly, never see your family."

Faith winced, conceding that if left to her own devices, she'd be exactly the hermit Lu described. Even after more than twenty years of living with the Apalos, she still had to fight her instincts to remain indoors, buried beneath a blanket with a book, or now a case file. The neighborhood where she'd grown up in L.A. hadn't exactly been conducive to outdoor play. Not unless you wanted to get shot, stabbed or mugged while you played hopscotch on the sidewalk.

"I guess I would've turned into a recluse if not for you guys."

"A malnourished recluse," Lu said, waving Paolo over. The waiter, bare-chested, tanned and wearing a colorful half sarong and lei, dashed over with a tray balanced on his hand. "Bring Faith another slice of cake," Lu ordered.

"No, Lu, really. I have to go upstairs and—"

"What? Do more work? Do you have a court appearance tomorrow?"

Faith knew what was coming. "No, ma'am."

"Briefs that need to be filed before the weekend?"

She shook her head. "I called Roma and cancelled all my appointments."

Lu's face broke into a wide smile. "That's my girl." Then with a scowl, she looked over her shoulder and caught Paolo just standing there, grinning, instead of fetching Faith more cake. He was a cutie, Faith thought. Might be good for taking her mind off what happened today, except that he was barely twenty-two and thought surfing was more religion than sport.

Not that Faith wasn't inclined to agree, when the waves were just right. Good Lord, how long had it been since she'd hit the surf? She wasn't even sure where she'd last stored her board. In the attic here at the restaurant? In storage at her office? She doubted that. She'd never bring the symbol of her secret indulgence anywhere near her law firm. Wouldn't want to give clients the wrong idea.

Lu stood, her hands flat on the table as she leaned in and kissed Faith on the cheek. "You have another piece of cake, you hear? Or pork. Or fruit salad. I don't care. Sample the whole buffet. I know you skipped breakfast, and you probably skipped lunch, too."

Faith glanced away, caught. Paolo instantly disappeared, no doubt off to fetch the second helping of confectionery delight. Ah, well. Faith could go to the gym tomorrow. Maybe hit the pool. Or maybe she'd just lounge around for a day and enjoy three delicious square meals and a little more motherly spoiling.

Minutes later she was about to dig into her newly delivered second slice of cake, daydreaming of chucking all her responsibilities for twenty-four hours and enticing Kalani to run off with her to the beach, when a sultry male voice caressed her from behind.

"You look delicious."

She put down her fork and glanced over her shoulder, not surprised to see Detective Guthrie standing there. He looked the way she'd felt two hours ago—exhausted and close to collapse—and he was carrying an accordion file as if it weighed a ton rather than a few pounds. He needed a strong dose of the treatment she'd received from Lu.

Upon her arrival at the restaurant, her foster mother had promptly thrown her into a hot, papaya-scented bath and ordered her to soak for no less than thirty minutes. Lu had remained in the bathroom long enough to give Faith's hair a good washing, just like she used to when Faith was so much younger and having a particularly rough day. Lu had crooned old Hawaiian tunes for ten minutes, before leaving Faith alone to wash off the ugliness of her day. Now, wrapped in one of the spare sarongs the waitresses wore, and sporting two tiny lavender orchids tucked behind her ear into her naturally wavy, air-dried hair, she could smile with genuine warmth and sincerity.

"If it isn't my Galahad," she crooned, offering him a chair.

"Let's not be melodramatic."

"I'll cease and desist on the melodrama if you take a rain check on the flirting."

Not that she didn't enjoy his attention. But during that bath, she'd convinced herself that messing with a man like Adam Guthrie, even if all in good fun, could hurt her credibility in the courtroom. Before today, she'd inspired a modicum of trepidation and fear in the officers of the court with whom she tangled. She wasn't too proud to admit she enjoyed her cutthroat reputation. Then again, since Adam had saved her life, she was pretty sure his grandiose assumptions about her, if he'd had any in the first place, were not quite so larger-than-life anymore.

"No can do," he said. "Comes too easy."

She couldn't argue, so sipped her coffee instead. A lawyer who couldn't argue? What was the world coming to? Still, as a lawyer, she wasn't one to ignore facts.

Adam Guthrie was a major heartthrob. And she hadn't had an honest-to-goodness heartthrob in her life for too long.

"How's Lorraine?"

"Stable, finally. They think she'll be okay, but she'll have to take that retirement she's been avoiding."

Faith smiled sadly. No one deserved a rest more than Lorraine, but she'd be a great loss to the system.

"Any clues about the shooter?" she asked, waving to Kalani and hoping a change of subject would take the edge off her charged response to him.

He folded himself wearily into the chair. "We found shell casings, so we know the make and model of his weapon. Remington M24."

"Standard military issue," she noted.

He lifted a brow.

She smiled. "I defended a former Army Ranger suffering from post-traumatic stress disorder back in Los Angeles," she explained. Some of the knowledge she'd picked up since passing the bar wasn't the kind she'd want to use more than once, but for the most part, her broadening knowledge base came in handy. Like when trying to impress police detectives.

"You practice in L.A., too?"

Clever devil, turning the conversation to something personal.

"Went there first after law school. I still take cases there all the time. Luckily for you, there's more crime there than in Courage Bay."

"But your main office is here now?"

Faith grinned, despite her attempt to contain her sentimentalism. "I'm a sucker for roasted pork and ukelele music, what can I say?"

Kalani scooted over, two tall turquoise drinks poised on her tray. "See, Detective? I've kept her in my line of sight all evening," she said proudly.

"I should put you on the payroll," he quipped.

Kalani snorted. "For my sister, it's free. So are these." With great flourish, she served the drinks, complete with fresh fruit and a tiny umbrella poised on the rim. "Compliments of the house. Order anything you'd like. Anyone who saves my sister's life has earned a complimentary dinner."

After laying a menu beside Adam's drink, Kalani winked at Faith and moved gracefully away, her shoulders swaying to the twang and rhythmic whine of Maleko's steel guitar. Faith's foster father stood on the tiny stage in the opposite corner of the room, playing a traditional tune to an enraptured crowd. Though it was a Thursday night, the place was packed, but for the most part quiet. Maleko Apalo was a true master of Polynesian music, and the mournful strumming took only moments to seep under Faith's skin.

She closed her eyes. She hadn't slept since returning to the restaurant, but while her exhaustion had dissipated, she was now blissfully tired. Like a cat who'd just lapped a saucer full of cream, she wanted a nap.

Until she experienced the sensation of a man's gaze roaming over her face. She opened her eyes and caught Adam staring at her intently, a tiny smile lingering on his lips. A sigh caught in her throat. Having him look at her with such contained hunger was a definite ego-booster, but she wasn't the type to lead a guy on. She'd better tend to business soon so he could leave. The longer he hung around, the harder it was going to be to keep those melted caramel eyes of his—not to mention other choice parts of his delicious body—out of her dreams.

She sat up straighter and took a sip of the Blue Sunset her sister had delivered. The sugary flavors of pineapple and mango juices blended with the distinctive taste of dark rum and blue curaçao. Man, she missed these. The drink was a rare luxury, since she usually left the restaurant and drove straight home to do a few more hours of work.

Not tonight.

She took another long, indulgent sip.

Adam had flipped open the menu. "What do you recommend?"

"The buffet," she said, nodding toward the sumptuous spread of food that took up the entire west wall of the restaurant. "Have a little bit of everything. You'll like it all, I guarantee it. Except the poi. We serve it because it's expected, but it tastes like paste."

Adam glanced around, obviously impressed by the tropical festiveness of the decor. Colorful streamers, floral garlands and twinkling lights in rainbow hues decorated the ceiling, rustling lightly thanks to the lazily churning palm-frond-style fans. The walls sported a collection of antique ukeleles, most resembling mini-guitars, others more oval or pear-shaped with tropical fruits or hula girls painted on the base. The tables glimmered with votive candles crafted with a kaleidoscopic array of colored bits of glass, so that a rainbow danced on the table when the fans shimmied the flames. The air flowed with the sounds of hushed conversation at the tables, the music, and chatter from the kitchen behind them. Faith always chose a table in the back, where she could watch the action and yet remain relatively undisturbed.

Adam smiled when he turned back to her. "This place is really cool. I can't believe I've driven past it so many times and haven't come in."

Faith lifted her glass. "You've been missing out. The food is authentic, the drinks are strong and the fun is contagious. When you're not falling asleep at the table."

"I look as tired as I feel, huh?"

"Worse," she said, exaggerating. Yeah, he had dark circles beneath those caramel-brown eyes, but even with the weight of the world on his shoulders, she figured, Adam Guthrie could find a second wind if he were so inspired.

When Kalani swept past them with a tray of empty glasses balanced over her head, Faith swiped a straw from her sister's apron. Alcohol worked faster when sucked through a straw, and she needed something to tame her raging interest in the handsome police detective.

"I thought food would perk me up," he said, "but now, I'm not so sure."

Adam flipped the menu closed, not entirely certain he had an appetite. The investigation tonight had been a bitter lesson in frustration. Though Forensics still had a report to construct, the initial clues found at the scene were useless. No fingerprints anywhere, no witnesses that had caught even a glimpse of the shooter. An intense meeting with the head of courthouse Security yielded no indication of how someone could have gotten into the building with an M24. Metal detectors arched over every public entrance, and the two emergency exits in the stairwell were locked and monitored by cameras, twenty-four hours a day.

He'd gained some hope of constructing a viable explanation for the gun getting into the courthouse after learning that certain courthouse regulars were waved through Security without checks as a courtesy, a practice Max Zirinsky ordered immediately suspended. Unfortunately, the list of those eligible to be waved through was extensive, though the number of judges, police officers, city councilmen and county employees who actually took advantage of the perk was very small. He saw name after name of properly searched and scrutinized VIPs on the printout from the security station.

Just as he had been about to give up for the night and head

to the restaurant with Faith's briefcase and shoes, he'd received a phone call from Faith's assistant, Roma Perez. Apparently, the fresh-faced attorney, like her boss, understood the workings of a criminal investigation. Shaken from brushing so close to death, Roma volunteered to deliver the threats Faith had received at the office tonight, rather than wait for morning.

Instead, he'd arranged to pick them up himself, although from his quick glance through the pages while at Faith's office, he'd learned nothing new.

So why had he come here tonight? He had no new information to share with Faith. He'd checked in with the police officer he'd assigned to her, the one standing guard in a corner near the bar, looking rather longingly at the buffet. Nothing had occurred to make Adam think Faith was still in danger, and yet, he couldn't ignore the facts.

Someone could have killed her this afternoon, and it might not have been an accident. On the other hand, she might just have been in the line of fire.

"What else do you have?" she asked, the intensity on her scrubbed-clean face telling him she was talking about the clues in the sniper case.

What he really noticed was that he'd been right earlier. She did have a tan underneath her makeup. The kind that dusted pink half moons on the very top of her cheeks, right where her sunglasses would rest.

"We have the shells," he admitted. "We're checking them for prints."

"That's it?" she asked, as disappointed as she was surprised. Chances were high that the shooter wore gloves.

"Unfortunately." He grabbed the accordion file. "And I

have these threats from your office. Your assistant met me there to turn them over tonight."

Faith frowned. "Roma was pretty freaked out. Find anything useful?"

He flipped open the file and dug into the first collection, the ones he'd looked over in the office. "Nothing out of the—"

A single folded piece of paper slipped from the stack. He hadn't seen it before.

"What's that?"

Clearly, she didn't recognize it, either. Roma had treated each and every threat, received via e-mail or by mail, with meticulous attention. They'd all been unfolded, stamped and catalogued. This one obviously hadn't been touched.

Using the tips of his fingers, he lifted the paper from the corner. The stock was heavy—high quality—so he had to shake it to loosen the folds.

Two words stared up at him in thick block letters.

Your next.

CHAPTER FIVE

"NICE GRAMMAR," Faith quipped after he turned the note toward her.

"Seen this one before?"

She shook her head. "Definitely not. Roma stamped all the threats we received with the date and time of receipt. This one is clean."

Adam turned the paper, looking for any identifying marks. "This isn't copy paper. It's got a texture."

Faith leaned in to look more closely. "You can pick up fancy paper like this at any copy shop. Some of them even leave it out in little bins, easily accessible to anyone."

"True," Adam conceded, dangling the paper carefully over the candle. "But this one has a watermark."

She shrugged and sipped her drink. "Most quality papers do."

Adam manipulated the paper until the light behind him gave him the view he wanted. "Not like this. Look."

He backed up his chair, then scooted around until they were sitting shoulder to shoulder. It took a great deal of his willpower not to tilt his head closer, maybe even press his nose against her neck so he could identify the exotic scent wafting from her skin.

He turned the paper again until the candlelight illuminated the distinctive shadow of the watermark. It was in a bottom corner instead of in the center, as was the usual placement, but the company name, while only partial, was fairly clear: Wilder Accounting Services.

"Anyone you know work for Wilder?" he asked.

She shook her head. "That's a temp service, isn't it? Could be anyone. Besides, the watermark is in the wrong place. I had a letterhead like that once. I sent it back to the printer."

Adam turned, impressed. He'd only been half-serious when he'd offered Faith a job at the police department. Maybe he needed to consider the offer again, this time in earnest.

"So what are you saying—the paper could have been tossed in the trash, again accessible to anyone?"

She glanced at him sideways, her mouth a thin line—but one that could morph into a smile at any moment. The rum in the drink obviously agreed with her.

"There's always a hundred possibilities with circumstantial evidence. That's why only the hard, physical stuff works for me."

Adam cleared his throat, forcing himself to keep the natural response about her liking it hard and physical to himself. Faith Lawton sure did a number on his libido. He couldn't remember the last time he'd entertained thoughts so lecherous and yet so invigorating. Like a firecracker tossed beneath a pile of dry timber, Faith could ignite his heart in a flash.

Still, he'd have to find a way to douse the effect—and fast. He had a case to solve, and the last thing he needed after the string of scandalous mistakes within the police department was a relationship that hinted at impropriety. He was a cop. She was a defense attorney. Other than cats and dogs, he couldn't think of any two species who should keep a wider berth.

He carefully folded the paper and slipped it back into the file. He'd have the lab take a look at it first thing in the morning, before he paid a visit to a judge and received a search warrant for Wilder Accounting. The threat was real, grammar error or not.

"So where did this threat come from, if it wasn't originally in the file?"

"Maybe Roma just missed it," Faith offered, though half-heartedly. "She's damn efficient, though."

"I checked through the file at the office and then again in the car at the stoplight. It wasn't there."

"The car was dark. You could have missed it."

Adam cleared his throat. Officially, he was off duty. Until tomorrow, his protecting Faith was voluntary—and he'd been more than willing to raise his hand for the job. Although he wanted to keep his wits about him, another sip of the froufrou drink Kalani had delivered likely wouldn't affect him. He lifted his eyebrows, surprised at how the fruity concoction wasn't quite so cloying as he had imagined. The bartender used dark, spiced rum, giving the bright blue cocktail just enough bite to satisfy his decidedly male tastes.

"I don't think so. I flipped through this first section pretty thoroughly."

"Did you stop anywhere before you came here?"

"I went back to the courthouse. When I left to meet your assistant, Forensics still hadn't released your briefcase, shoes or phone. I left them with the hostess up front, by the way."

"You left the file in the car?" she asked, incredulous. "Did you learn anything from the hearing today?"

"Yeah, I learned defense attorneys can be a pain in the ass," he muttered.

She didn't seem to take his assessment as an insult. "You already knew that."

"I had a uniform keep an eye on the car. That precaution, Counselor, would impress any judge."

"Unless any decent attorney could prove the uniform could reasonably have been distracted by all the commotion going on around him."

Adam took a deep breath, exhaled slowly. He pulled the cocktail closer but didn't drink, certain he needed a clear head for any interactions with Faith, even when she was bordering on tipsy. *Sharp* only started a description of her, one that also included *sexy* and *seductive.*

"Do you plan to file some sort of motion, Faith, or are you interested in finding out who put this in the folder? I mean, it is a threat on your life."

Her eyebrows shot up so high they disappeared beneath her wavy bangs. "My life? Hello? It was delivered to *your* car."

"In *your* file—a folder bulging with promises to see *your* head mounted on the wall of the—" He dug through the letters he'd dropped on the table to find the one that had caught his eye earlier. "Ah, yes. The Legal Eagle Wall of Shame."

She slapped her hand against the paper, dismissing the validity of the intimidation attempt. "You can't prove the new threat was meant for me."

He shook his head, not quite sure why such an intelligent woman couldn't see the obvious. "You defend bad guys. Can't you see how that could put you on the wrong side of an M24?"

She thrust her hands on her hips. "Yes, you're right. I *defend* bad guys. For the most part, bad guys like me. You, on the other hand, put bad guys in jail, where most of them don't want to be. You were standing right next to me, just to the left of George Yube. For all we know, he wasn't the target at all. You were."

Despite the music and laughter behind them, silence reigned between them. Adam toyed with the paper umbrella on his glass, splashing the slice of pineapple into the blue drink. "That's a stretch of logic," he said, knowing there was some truth to what she said. He was more likely to have enemies that sported M24s than she was. Still, she had a cache of death threats unlike any he'd previously seen. She'd riled a great many people by agreeing to represent George Yube, including Adam himself.

"The note wasn't in the file when Roma gave it to you," she continued, "meaning the threat was not sent directly to me. At some point tonight, someone made sure it came into your possession while you had the file. Which could easily mean that it's meant for you. Our sniper might have you marked as next on his hit list."

"Or maybe I'm just the designated delivery boy."

She removed the garnish from her drink, lifted her glass and took a hearty swig. Either she reacted to rum more slowly than he had assumed or she was simply taking off the kid gloves in case this argument got ugly.

Instead, her tone softened. "Both scenarios are possible. Either of us, or neither of us, could still be in danger. So what do we do?"

The endless possibilities made Adam's stomach growl, and few of them had to do with the case. His appetite returned and a sudden jolt of energy surged through his veins, bringing the situation into sharp focus. No matter who was the target of the threat, until the case was solved, he and Faith couldn't avoid spending time together. A *lot* of time together. Which meant that ignoring his attraction to the smart, sexy attorney was no longer an option.

Since he'd joined the force, he'd tried to date women far removed from his profession. Unfortunately, they never understood his devotion to his job. Twice, he'd broken the rule and gotten involved with fellow officers. First, a partner. Then, a fellow detective. Both times, he'd enjoyed the freedom to discuss his latest case with women who shared his dedication to seeking justice and who had often lent insight to the investigation. But both times, he'd ended up resenting that work had soon become the main topic of conversation in the bedroom and beyond. With Faith, a thousand possible subjects popped into his brain—and few had to do with crime.

"First, we eat, though you look like you have that part covered," he said, tilting her empty cake plate.

"Ha! That was just dessert. I've been ignoring the pork skewers all night, and they're my favorite." She stood up and gestured toward the buffet. "Okay, first, we eat. Then what?"

He scooted his chair back. Standing, he could see completely how the blue tropical sarong hugged her body, showing off sandaled feet, tanned legs, slim hips and, of course, impressive breasts. Her skin shimmered in the candlelight, enhancing the healthy glow she had obtained from the sun. He wondered when she did her sunbathing, and noticing the absence of tan lines on her shoulders or neck, he couldn't help but speculate on exactly how she achieved such perfection.

"I don't know, Faith. But I'm open to suggestions."

FAITH WAS FAIRLY CERTAIN that her initial suggestion had disappointed him. She might have had a hearty dose of her Blue Sunset, but she still retained enough sense not to say what was truly on her mind. She'd nearly propositioned him just to see how he'd react, but she'd held back. She wasn't afraid of rejection. She was more terrified he'd actually call her bluff. So instead, they'd talked about their families.

They chatted while they ate, mostly about his brother, Casey Guthrie, who had shared a geometry class with Faith back in high school. She couldn't help grinning from ear to ear as Adam spoke about his daredevil younger brother with a combination of pride and exasperation. She often experienced the same conflicting emotions about Kalani, and for a brief second, she considered asking Adam to help her fix them up. But Kalani had a serious case of mutual lust going with a surfer who lived in Santa Barbara, yet was currently in Australia challenging the waves that poured over the Great Barrier Reef. Faith wasn't one to step in the way of true passion.

Though she did have a real skill for ignoring it, especially when she was involved.

"I'm stuffed," he said, pushing away his plate, empty except for fruit rinds, wooden skewers and the poi she'd warned him not to sample. "You're right. The food here is awesome."

"I wouldn't steer you wrong, Detective. Tired enough to leave me to my own devices yet?"

A half grin gave his face a boyish quality that sapped her breath. Her glass—she'd switched to sparkling water—was empty. Where was Paolo or Kalani when she needed them?

"No can do, Counselor. Officer Bartlett over there is already working overtime. Until I can set up a regular detail of protection for you, I'm your new bodyguard."

She shook her head, tired of arguing this point. While Faith would not deny that she'd nearly been hit on the plaza today and that she had received death threats at her office, she had trouble believing that someone would target her for assassination when her most objectionable client was now dead. What would be the point? To stop her from defending others?

But she sighed, conceding that she had to take precautions until the facts were sorted from the speculation. And Adam Guthrie had to agree to the same.

"Who's going to protect you?" she asked.

"You could always volunteer," he suggested.

She chuckled. "With what weapon? My high-heel shoes?"

"I've seen women do serious damage with spiky sandals. You look scrappy to me. I wouldn't count you out."

She rolled her eyes. The man was, for all his serious devotion to his job, utterly incorrigible. "What do you say we discuss suspects who actually have a motive?"

"Here? I was hoping to move this discussion somewhere closer to where I'm going to pass out. What kind of couch do you have?"

She leaned forward on her elbows, lowering her eyelashes with that sleepy, sultry look she used to practice in the mirror with Kalani, back when they were twelve and trying desperately to be exotic women of mystery rather than clumsy prepubescent goofballs. Over time, she'd perfected the look— and she'd used it to much success. But not in a very long time, unfortunately.

"A very cozy one. It's where I sleep when I'm too tired to go to my bedroom."

"Is that an invitation?" he countered, mimicking her move—elbows on the table, chest forward, gaze intense.

She couldn't help but lick her lips, pleased when he followed the movement of her tongue with his eyes. "I'm a sucker for hard-knock cases, Detective. If it'll make you feel better staying at my place tonight, I have no objections. We could consider working together to figure out what the hell is going on. Maybe we can keep each other safe," she ventured, unable to tamp down a tiny smile at the thought of waking up early and catching Detective Adam Guthrie snuggled in her spare bed wearing nothing but a sheet.

Safe from the sniper? Yeah. Safe from each other? Not likely.

THEY WERE HALFWAY to the door when Kalani ambushed them. "Where are you off to? No one leaves until the last dance."

Adam groaned, holding tightly to the folder Kalani seemed determined to tear from his hands. "This is evidence. Can't let it out of my sight," he explained, catching a flash of Faith's grin.

He'd already called over to Max, who remained at the courthouse. Though the officer assigned to watch Adam's car earlier had already gone off duty, Max had promised to have him report to Adam first thing on his next shift. Adam didn't hold out much hope for a break in the case. Not with so many dead ends already.

"Officer Cutie over there can hang on to it, right?" Kalani suggested. "The Apalo family is very appreciative of your actions today. The least we can do is give you the full Polynesian treatment."

Thankfully, Faith moved forward to run interference. "We're exhausted, Kay. I promise to bring Detective Guthrie back another night."

Kalani's face morphed into a mask of determination. "You two are perfect for one another, you know that? No sense of fun."

Adam slapped his hand over his chest, pretending to be wounded by Kalani's words, when in truth, she wasn't wrong. Kalani Apalo and Casey, his brother, seemed cut from the same easygoing, *carpe diem* cloth. Adam didn't much like that he'd somehow lost the devil-may-care part of his personality that had once made him and his brother a collective force to be reckoned with. And Faith, though no-nonsense and single-minded on the surface, undoubtedly shared a smidgen of her family's love of all things frivolous. He didn't need to prove anything to Faith in regards to being serious and good at his job. She knew that just as well as he knew the same about her.

But tired as he was, he couldn't pass up a chance to show her he also wasn't averse to having a good time.

Not exactly sure why this challenge overrode his need for sleep, Adam gestured to the officer standing by the bar and ordered him to hold the folder, stand at attention and not move a muscle.

"What the hell." Adam reached out to take her hand. "My sense of fun has been challenged once too often lately. What do you say, Counselor? Want to dance?"

Faith's shocked gape made the change of plans worth the ache in his physically exhausted body. But she didn't protest. Instead a grin stretched from her generous pink lips to her sparkling silver eyes. "You're full of surprises, Detective."

That comment was all he needed. He grabbed her hand and led her onto the dance floor, ready to shake more than just his groove thing. He was about to quake the foundations of what he knew about Faith Lawton—and in turn, what she thought she knew about him.

CHAPTER SIX

FAITH RECOGNIZED two of the half dozen couples already waiting on the dance floor. Bob and Linda Doherty, who visited the restaurant weekly to reminisce about their honeymoon years ago, while he'd been stationed on Oahu, and Lee and Nora Wilson, who lived next door, above their sporting goods store, and came to the restaurant nearly every other night. The third couple, arms entwined, had "newlyweds" written all over them. The other two pairs, obviously part of the same office party, reflected the uneasiness at being front and center that Faith shared. She'd participated in the dance portion of the entertainment quite a few times, but never with a date.

Could she call Adam Guthrie a date? No, not really. Actually, not at all. Though her insides fluttered at the thought of him holding her close as Maleko directed them on the dance floor, teaching them his own personally created combination of the hula and the hustle. Faith reminded herself that only a few hours ago, she and Adam had been nothing more than professional adversaries. When had that changed? When he pushed her out of the way of a madman's bullet? When he put her safety above his own? When he risked his life to rush back into the building to try to catch the killer?

A lot had happened today, but some facts remained irrefutable. She still believed in a defendant's right to vigorous representation. He still believed that criminals should go to prison. When she dug under the surface, she realized the two philosophies weren't exactly mutually exclusive—but they weren't exactly the same, either.

"Okay, everyone!" Maleko's sweet tenor voice crackled over the cordless microphone. Dressed in a bright red floral Hawaiian shirt, loose-fitting linen pants and flip-flops, Maleko Apalo was every inch the Polynesian showman. He mingled with the group on the dance floor, his dark hair peppered with white, his ebony eyes sparkling in the spotlight. Those eyes flashed a conspiratorial twinkle when he strolled next to Faith and Adam.

"Here at Sunsets, we end the night with a special dance. We taught you the hula earlier and now we're going to make it a little more…interesting. A little more—" he winked "—one-on-one."

Faith took a deep, calming breath as Kalani joined her father on stage, smiling wide and eating up the attention the same way Faith had scarfed down the guava chiffon cake. Faith wondered if she shouldn't have volunteered to partner with Maleko. At least she wouldn't be standing here, her skin tingling in anticipation of Adam's touch.

Closing her eyes, she became entirely aware of Adam standing beside her. His body heat reached out to her and he smelled so damn good, even after a long, bloody day. He caught her quick glance at him, but he had the decency not to smile, as if he knew how nervous, tired, excited and intrigued she was right at this moment.

Maybe he *didn't* realize. Men were supposed to be dense about those things, weren't they? Although, in her experience, most men only pretended to be dense when it suited them. And she couldn't imagine Adam Guthrie ever pretending to be anything less than sharp as a tack.

At her second not-so-subtle glance, he winked. Just like Maleko. Full of the devil.

Who would have known?

Faith bit the side of her mouth to keep from grinning.

Maleko and the audience applauded when he and Kalani completed their demonstration. "My beautiful daughter! Isn't she a wonderful dancer? It's a hard act to follow, but we're all friends here. Gentlemen, do as I do."

Despite the rush of desire Adam ignited when he stood behind her, his hands lightly grasping her waist, Faith knew this flirtation could lead nowhere. At least, nowhere permanent. A long-term interaction between her and Adam would be fraught with conflicts of interest. Opposing viewpoints. Rancor and resentment.

But no one would be hurt if they got to know each other a little better. Not so long as they laid down reasonable limits.

Which would include…what? She had no clue.

With the live band playing softly in the background, Maleko and Kay again demonstrated the simple, swaying steps of the dance. Adam leaned close over her shoulder, watching intently. Faith tried desperately to do the same, but since she'd known the dance for years, she couldn't help but stare instead at Adam's incredible profile. The late hour revealed itself in the dark shadow of stubble on his sculpted jaw. His eyes reflected the stage lights, and his scent, so male, so intoxicating, worked harder than the rum and blue curaçao to dizzy her senses. When the music began again, this time louder, the sudden movement around her snapped her from her reverie.

As instructed, Adam snuggled close behind her, his thighs pressing intimately to her backside. Without question, the hard feel of his sex against her back convinced her that she wasn't the only one entertaining wild, lascivious thoughts. He braced one hand on her left hip, while the other gently cradled her right hand, outstretched gracefully to her side. They took small steps, twice to one side, rocked, then repeated the stride in the other direction. With a little dip at the knees, she spun away, then rolled back into his embrace.

He stopped her before she slammed against his chest, a smile teasing his oh-so-kissable lips.

"You're a natural," she said, swaying with Adam in a tight circle, her cheek nearly pressed against his chest.

She almost pouted when he swung her away, twirling her beneath his light touch. "I haven't danced since my parents' anniversary party."

"Oh, really?" she asked, stepping sideways, then around him so they resumed the position of her in front, him behind, his hands on both hips, this time while she gestured a brief passage from a story told a hundred times by various dancers of the *hula 'auana*. "Who was your partner?"

"My cousin, Rhonda, from Florida," he answered, his grin widening when he was able to roll her into his arms again. "She's a professional dancer in Orlando. I've learned that if a guy picks the right partner, he can look like Fred Astaire."

"Didn't your date mind you dancing with a relative just so you'd look good?"

He chuckled, spun her out, then twirled her again beneath his hand. "Very smooth, Counselor. I didn't have a date."

"Don't tell me you couldn't get one."

"Wouldn't know. Didn't try. I was wrapped up in a case, and before I knew it, my mother had a tuxedo delivered to my apartment and threatened to send a car for me, too, if I didn't show up at the hotel in two hours."

"Sounds like a woman who knows what she wants," Faith said, her admiration clear. "I'm surprised she didn't send over a companion for you as well."

"My mother?" he asked, eyes wide. "No way. She breaks the mothers' creed on matchmaking. Figures if we can't pick a good woman ourselves, we deserve to be alone."

Faith laughed. She figured she'd like Adam's mother, though she wondered if Mrs. Guthrie would take a shine to her. Faith was, after all, the enemy to her son's success. If Mrs. Guthrie was anything like Lu Apalo, her career wouldn't sit well. Though, so far, Lu wasn't making any objections to her being there with Adam, was she? Instead, her foster mother sat near the bar, grinning as if she'd just won the lottery.

"What about you?" he asked, introducing an extra sway to his hips as the steps of the dance became more familiar. Faith couldn't stop the leap in her belly at finding a dance partner who was actually good, whether he believed it or not. Not that she danced very often anymore, but the in-sync rhythm she and Adam created appealed to the part of her she didn't pay much attention to—the part of her that didn't require a schedule, a PDA or a personal assistant. The part that didn't respond to the trill of her alarm clock or the incessant beep of her watch. The part that had a time clock and agenda all its own and was deeply and intrinsically female.

"I date," she said. By now, the dance had become second nature to him, as it was to her. She couldn't believe a tough guy like Adam Guthrie didn't have two left feet. Gorgeous, chivalrous *and* he could master a dance floor? How could she possibly resist? Despite her upbringing in the Apalo household, she wasn't usually a big believer in signs, but she couldn't deny how Adam thrilled her in so many ways that she was losing count. Could she fight fate? Should she?

"Who? Other attorneys?" he asked.

"Not if I can help it. Talking business when a couple should be exchanging sweet nothings isn't my idea of romance."

He twirled her again, but even as her head whipped around, she caught his nod of agreement. "Then who? Surely not police officers."

"Surely not," she answered, her shock exaggerated. "I don't know, guys I meet places. At the beach, at the gym, here at the restaurant. Mostly men who come in here with their mothers or dates Lu doesn't approve of. Unlike your mom, Melelu Apalo thinks matchmaking is her God-given right and primary talent."

"And you don't mind?"

They swayed together again, his hand on her hip, as Maleko invited the rest of the crowd onto the floor. Soon, the tiny twenty-by-twenty-foot area filled with laughter and music and people, while she and Adam drifted toward the back, near a collection of potted palms twinkling with a tiny rainbow collection of lights.

"I like to be social and Lu has fairly good taste, actually. She's never picked any major losers for me. I've done that for myself a few times, but never Lu."

The music kept on playing, but the conversation sapped the sway out of Faith's body. As an ache crept along the back of her neck and across her shoulders, she remembered how tired she'd been earlier and how she desperately wanted to go home and sleep. If Adam Guthrie wanted to tag along, better for her. Except for the recent turn of the conversation, she couldn't remember when she'd had a better time at the restaurant. Of course, she couldn't discount that her impression might be tinged by the horrible events of the day. In contrast to watching George Yube die and Lorraine Nelson struggle for life, eating, dancing and chatting with Adam seemed like a week at the spa.

"Then how come you haven't settled down?" he asked.

"Why haven't you?"

"Do you really want to go down that road?"

"No, but you're the one that asked."

Adam shook his head, and Faith couldn't help but succumb to his devastating smile.

"I can't imagine you being attracted to a loser."

"Why? Because I'm attracted to you?"

"That's the Blue Sunset talking," he charged.

"Maybe," she conceded. "But it's still the truth."

Faith couldn't help herself. Partially hidden by the lights and greenery, she stepped fully into Adam's personal space, her hands braced on his chest. Maybe it was her imagination, but she could have sworn his heartbeat quickened beneath her hands.

He countered by sliding his palms around her waist, settling his fingers along the small of her back. Her sarong, tied high around her neck, exposed her skin to his touch, and a liquid thrill shot from the base of her spine to the tips of her breasts. Her mouth watered. She wanted him to kiss her. God, she wanted him to kiss her.

"The attraction is mutual, Faith. But that doesn't change our circumstances, does it."

She glanced around at the romantic cocoon they'd settled in. "I don't know, our circumstances look pretty promising from my viewpoint."

His chuckle, warm as heated honey, took the edge off the

doubtful look in his eyes. "You and I are becoming pretty well known for having opposing viewpoints, Counselor."

"We both know what we want."

"But rarely can we both *get* what we want."

"What do you want?"

"Right this moment or big picture?"

Faith sighed. Therein lay the crux of the problem. The difference between wanting Adam right now and being able to hold on to him beyond the sunrise loomed like a great chasm. Once morning broke, he'd go back to trying to catch a killer and she'd move on to her next case, more than likely another criminal Adam or his department suspected of some crime. She'd already come to the conclusion that the careers they'd both dedicated themselves to would make a long-term relationship impossible. But the possibility of a fling appealed to her more and more as each minute clicked by with his scent teasing her, his touch taunting her, his eyes staring intently into hers.

She spoke before she could consider the potential consequences for heartbreak. "What do you want right now?"

"To kiss you."

"Then do it."

"That could be the Blue Sunset talking, too."

"Could be," she said, moving closer so their bodies were pressed tightly, so that she shared the intimate heat sizzling off his skin, "but you'll never know for sure until you do it, will you?"

The minute Adam's mouth met hers, Faith suspected all the alcohol burned instantly out of her system, like brandy poured and ignited over cherries jubilee. His lips brushed hers once, lightly—the strike of the match. Then he kissed her boldly, hot to taste her, searing her with a need she not only shared but equaled. Want for want. Desire for desire. Their tongues swirled, dipped and learned. He slid his hands up her back, holding her hard against him, his erection arousing her nearly to the point of madness. At that moment, Faith could think of nothing more than burning herself into his skin like a brand.

Then with gentle hands on her forearms, he pushed her away.

He opened his mouth to speak, but she instantly silenced him with a finger across his kiss-moistened mouth.

"Don't apologize, Adam. We're adults. We're not forbidden from enjoying one another."

He kissed the pads of her fingers, then tugged her hands away.

"Depends on who you ask."

"I'm not asking anyone, are you? Do you need permission to want me?"

His irises darkened to the hue of rich, dark chocolate. "Too late for that. But you can't deny that we're in a controversial situation."

"That's true." She eyed the couples still dancing just a few feet away. She scanned the crowd for Kalani and Maleko. If they had witnessed the kiss, they weren't staring now. They'd switched partners with Lee and Nora, seemingly having the time of their lives. "But we can resolve this controversy quite easily."

His brow quirked. "How?"

"Making out on the dance floor of a public establishment is not wise for the chief of detectives and the county's leading defense attorney," she assessed coolly.

"Agreed," he said, blowing out a breath that she guessed indicated relief.

Short-lived relief, she thought with a grin. "However, making out at my place is a whole other story."

WOULD SHE OR WOULDN'T SHE? As Faith led him through the front door of her midsize, two-story cottage in the ritzy Jacaranda Heights neighborhood, Adam wondered what additional surprises the night would bring. The kiss had already thrown him. Before tonight, never in a million years could he have imagined himself actually kissing Faith Lawton, actually pressing her so close that when they separated, her perfume clung to his clothes. Even now, the scent of sweet mangoes and musk taunted him, teased him with what might happen in the next few minutes.

Unless he did the right thing. Right now.

"That's far enough," Adam said when Faith clicked on the lamp in her foyer. "I want to check the place out."

She tossed her house keys from one palm to the other. "Be my guest."

By his nature, he was thorough, but he tried to perform the most cursory of searches, so he wouldn't stumble into learning something about Faith that crossed the line. A ridiculous goal, he knew, since they'd gotten just about as personal as they could have on a public dance floor. Try as he could to justify, explain or rationalize their kiss, he couldn't lie, even to himself. He wanted Faith. Badly. His body ached for her in a way he hadn't experienced in a long, long time. If ever. But just as overwhelming was the realization that he couldn't have her.

Not *shouldn't*. He wasn't fooling himself. If they made love tonight, no one would ever know. No one but the two of them—and therein resided the problem. In the short time they'd been together today, Adam's once physical-only attraction to Faith had morphed into something more. Now she wasn't just a bulldog defense attorney, a worthy adversary in his quest to arrest, prosecute and punish every criminal who had the audacity to break the law in Courage Bay. Now she was a smart, brave, caring woman who came from a loving, supportive family and who had an incredible sense of fun and adventure. Now she was the woman who tasted like a Blue Sunset, whose waist felt slim and warm against his palms, whose lips and tongue gave as good as they got.

How was he supposed to forget all that when he came up against her in court? He didn't testify in every case she defended, but they'd crossed paths before and they would again.

But now, instead of simply lusting after her as any red-blooded American male would, he respected her, too. As a person, not just as a professional. He couldn't help wondering why she'd chosen this area of law and why she was so tenacious. How she found the time to get a tan. Topics that would draw them further into friendship, further into trouble.

Her bedroom on the top floor was bright and airy. He flipped on the light switch, and two lamps on either side of a plush queen-size bed cast a warm glow. Mounds of shams and pillows, large and fluffy in crisp white and yellow pinstripes, covered a thick, matching comforter. Various prints and watercolors of beach scenes and tropical flowers adorned the walls, which were painted in a soft ocean blue. Even the floor, polished hardwood covered with a thick carpet patterned with pale pink and tan seashells, testified to her love of the beach.

He never would have guessed.

Her closets, the bathroom, complete with a large sunken tub surrounded by half-melted coconut-scented candles, the guest room—damn—and the kitchen were free of anything suspicious. All doors and windows, securely locked, showed no signs of tampering. Her den was dark, but when he flipped on the light, he found it too crowded and cramped to hide a potential attacker. One last sweep through the living room, decorated in a palm-tree motif, and Adam decided no one had invaded her home.

No one but him.

"We're all clear," he reported to Faith, who waited in the foyer, a semipatient smile on her face.

"Good to know," she answered. From her tiny, somewhat predatory smile, he figured she hadn't been worried.

He took one last look out her front window, which was safely darkened by sturdy wood blinds. The street was quiet. In this tiny collection of homes on a cul-de-sac, no one parked on the street; they tucked their cars safely in their garages. Small lawns dotted with tall skinny palms didn't provide many places for anyone to hide. Adam could, for the moment, assume they were safe.

"Yeah," he agreed. "In the morning, we'll review the case and try to figure out who might want to hurt you."

"Or you."

Adam had expected Faith to shy away from this discussion, but he should have known better. Neither exhaustion nor desire would keep her from a good argument.

"We can debate that point all night," he said.

"I can think of more interesting things to do all night." Her soft whisper crawled along his collar, teasing the sensitive skin of his neck, making him wonder if she would deepen the effect by applying her tongue to the same area.

"There's no harm in thinking," he said.

"Is there harm in doing?"

"You know there is."

Her smile turned down on one side. "The harm is in the long

run, sometime in the future, near or far, when we have to stare down each other in a courtroom. We've faced each other twice in two years, Detective. Those odds aren't too intimidating."

He agreed, but Adam wasn't the type to simply grasp at straws because they made his life—even his love life—easier. Faith had presented nothing more than a circumstantial argument, which was much like evidence of the same kind. Relying on such flimsy statistics could lead them down a primrose path to destruction.

"Admittedly, the odds are in our favor," he answered. "But that doesn't mean we should act on our first instinct."

"I can't remember the last time I acted on my first instinct."

"Because it's not in your nature."

"Not usually."

"Then why now?"

"Maybe because I almost died today?"

She tossed the keys on the hall table and closed the distance between them. When she slid her arms around his neck, he put his around her waist. Holding her felt so good.

"Come on, Adam. You're a cop. It's a well-documented phenomenon that people who've faced down their mortality often react by doing something outside the norm."

"That's true. But, Faith, I'm used to looking death in the eye. Only takes once or twice in your life before you build up coping mechanisms that don't include jumping into bed with someone you shouldn't."

He knew he'd said too much when he caught the dark reflection in her eyes—a mirror of the danger and death he'd faced in his career, and his life. But if she wanted him to recount any of the shadows from his past, she didn't ask.

"So far, Detective Guthrie, you haven't said anything to dissuade me."

"I don't want to dissuade you," he said.

"Then shut up and kiss me."

CHAPTER SEVEN

ADAM DIDN'T HAVE TO BE asked twice. The taste of her still lingered on his palate and he wanted more. Much more. He grabbed her cheeks and pressed her mouth to his, loving how she thrust her tongue into his mouth as her hands clutched his chest.

He shrugged out of his jacket. If the presence of his gun unnerved her, she showed no fear as she unbuckled his shoulder holster and attempted to remove it. He chuckled as he tried to contort his body so the leather straps would slip free easily, but had to break the kiss to finish the job. When he reached for her again she took his hand, and with a burst of energy, dashed up the stairs.

She didn't turn on the lamps, but instead went to a corner of her bedroom and flipped the switch on a novelty light perched on top of a highboy in the corner. The shade, lit with a bright blue bulb, began to spin, throwing undulating images of waves around the room.

The effect was at once cheesy…and erotic.

"Like it?" she asked.

"It's different."

"Kalani bought it for me. She knows how I love the ocean."

With a second flip, a sound machine came on. The rush and flow of waves beating against a sandy shore flowed around the room. Faith had kicked off her sandals downstairs, and on her bare feet, she swayed like a palm in the ocean breeze.

Adam carefully lowered his gun and holster onto a chair beside the bed. He took off his shoes and socks, watching her dance with the natural rhythm of the sea and sand. "Before tonight, I couldn't imagine you outside your office, outside the courtroom or out of your crisp, tailored suits. Now I really want to see you in a bikini."

"Maybe this will do."

She lifted her arms and untied the knot behind her neck. She let the material drop, revealing her sweet, round breasts, as tanned and smooth as her midriff.

Adam's mouth watered. He couldn't move, his feet rooted to the spot while she twisted to untie the knot at her waist. Pulsating blue light danced along her body, and Adam's erection pressed tight against his pants. He rubbed his face, filled with wonder and keen anticipation. What exactly had he done to deserve this piece of heaven?

Her skirt fluttered to the floor. Her panties rode high over her thighs, a tan color that blended into her flesh. She crossed the room with no fear, no modesty, nothing but needful desire in her eyes.

And he couldn't have been more turned on.

"You're overdressed," she quipped, flicking a fingernail against the top button of his shirt.

"You're beautiful."

She smiled softly. "Like what you see, do you?"

"You're kidding, right?"

Shaking her head, she undid the first two buttons on his shirt. "I don't kid about lovemaking, Detective. I don't do it very often, so when I do, I want to enjoy it."

He grabbed the shirt from her and ripped the rest of the buttons free. They laughed together as the plastic discs clattered onto the floor, but he silenced her quickly by pulling her into his arms and covering her mouth with his. She wasn't petite, but she was slim, and his palms seemed to span the entire width of her back. She hooked her arms around his neck and pulled herself higher, grazing his chest with her taut nipples, igniting a fire Adam knew he couldn't rush to put out. But when she curved one leg up his thigh, he thought he'd go insane.

Instead, he maneuvered her toward the bed.

Unwilling to release her from the kiss, he struggled with his belt and pants. She attempted to help, and eventually four fumbling hands managed to do the job. In just his boxers, he kicked his clothes away, lifted her into his arms and placed her gently across the fluffy mountain of pillows and down.

Then a thought occurred to him—a completely unwelcome realization.

He didn't have a condom.

"Faith, I don't have protection with me."

Her grin rivaled the smile on the infamous Cheshire cat.

"Didn't you search the guest room thoroughly?" She clicked her tongue in mock admonishment. "Kay and her boyfriend crash there all the time. I'll bet there's a stash in the nightstand table."

He whipped into the guest room, and beneath a pile of old travel magazines and a tin of sex wax that stopped him dead— until he realized it was for creating traction on surfboards— he found an unopened box of prophylactics. Not his usual brand of choice, but the sheer texture caught his eye. Hell, he didn't care if they were purple with green glowing polka dots, he wanted to make love to Faith Lawton, and despite the lust raging though his blood, he wouldn't proceed without protecting them both.

When he returned to Faith's bedroom, she'd tossed a few pillows on the floor and had pulled down the comforter. Her sun-kissed skin shimmered against the white sheets. She still wore her panties, but with one leg drawn up, he could see the outline of blond curls at the triangle between her thighs.

"Find what you needed?" she asked, her voice as sultry and smooth as her skin.

With a swoosh, he disposed of his boxers and crawled onto the bed. He pressed a soft kiss to the arch of her foot, then proceeded to blaze a trail up her calves, her knees, her thighs. He commanded all of his willpower to skip higher, where he dipped his tongue into her navel and mimicked the swirling action he intended to apply all over her.

She forked her fingers into his hair, massaging his scalp and cooing softly, beckoning him higher with gentle tugs. He complied, and as he had imagined, her breasts were smooth and soft, her nipples hard and responsive. His blood surged, pounded in his ears, as her cries grew louder with each nip, taste and lick. Oh, yeah… He continued, alternating his mouth with his thumbs, plucking and priming her like a fine musical instrument. She called his name, the sound strangled by need. His erection strained. He'd meet her needs—and his—soon. Very soon.

Maybe before he planned. When she wrapped her hand around his sex, he nearly leaped out of his skin. Her strokes were bold, rhythmic and measured, maximizing the pleasure zinging through his body like a sizzling electric current. He groaned, the sound vibrating against the nipple he still held between his teeth. He couldn't help but shift his body, allowing her better access. She rewarded him with a deep and passionate kiss, never once stopping, never once relenting, until he thought he'd burst.

But he didn't. As if she knew how close he was to the edge, she gently released him. She kissed his face, neck, shoulders, all the while retrieving the box of condoms. Together, they tore at the packaging, ripped open a foil packet, and with very little fumbling, rolled the thin barrier over his sex.

When she removed her panties and swung a leg over his waist, Adam thought he must have been shot earlier. Yes, he was dead. This was heaven. Had to be.

"Faith," he said, surprised but clearly pleased.

"I know what I want, Adam."

He grasped her hips, squeezing tight. He found her so intriguing and irresistible. But how could he say that without sounding like an idiot?

"You're amazing."

She smiled and licked her lips. "You're fairly remarkable yourself." She braced her hands on his chest, flicking his nipples with her thumbs. "So muscled and strong. Everywhere." She lowered her hand, grasped him and poised the tip of his sex at her hot, wet lips. "Show me how strong, Adam. Show me."

With one tiny shift of his body, he slid inside her. God, she was wet. Tight. Hot. He knew he wasn't far from the precipice. She moved with sinful slowness, milking him with her body, adoring him with her mouth on his. Unable to adjust the pace, he reached for her breasts, knowing from her moans that after one tiny squeeze, she was just as close to the edge as he.

She sat up straight. He grabbed her hand in one of his, then slid the other between them. She cried out in pleasured surprise. Her eyes flashed open, but he could tell she saw nothing beyond the spectrum of indigo pulsating on her walls.

"Yes, Faith," he urged when she began to move quicker. "That's it."

He continued to stroke her, fire her, and she did nothing less in return. His muscles tensed and his climax surged. She cried out with equal pleasure, his name on her lips, before she collapsed on his chest.

Immediately, he wrapped her in his arms. He kissed her hair, and felt his lust ebb at the same time as his heart soared. He knew this was too soon. He had no right to think, even for a second, about how truly special this woman was. Bold, brazen, unafraid. The exact type of woman he'd want in his personal life—if he had one.

Which he didn't. And more than likely, he never would.

How THEY GOT BEYOND the awkward silence of disentangling and cleaning up after such amazing sex, Faith didn't know. Adam cracked a few jokes, caressed her bare bottom, kissed her on the tip of the nose—generally did all the expected and unexpected things a lover did once the climaxes were spent and the night descended into morning. He wrapped her lovingly in her sheets, then disappeared into the shower. She'd intended to lie there until he emerged, sorting out what had just happened, beyond the obvious, but her brain had other ideas. She fell asleep and didn't awake until several hours later, when the savory scent of freshly brewed coffee teased her nostrils.

She sat bolt upright, certain for a moment that Kalani had used her spare key to come in and make breakfast, a habit she'd formed since Faith had moved out. Kalani still lived at home, though technically, she had her own place next door to her parents. Faith turned to alert Adam to the intrusion, but his side of the bed was cool and empty. Except for his buttonless shirt, his clothes were missing from the floor.

She smiled and ran her hands through her hair. She probably looked like a train wreck, but she felt like a million bucks. No regrets. Nothing but utter bliss. Adam Guthrie was a wonderful lover and she'd had the time of her life.

Only, after last night, she didn't have her excuse to sleep with him anymore, did she? Today, he'd assign another cop to protect her. She could no longer claim that the attempt on her life had pushed her to cross a line she'd never imagined she'd cross with a man she barely knew.

But man, she knew him now, didn't she?

She showered quickly, combed her hair into a ponytail and dusted a bit of powder over her skin. After brushing her teeth, dabbing on a quick swipe of lip gloss and throwing on her favorite plush robe and slippers, she ambled downstairs, pleasantly achy in all the right places.

The minute she crossed the threshold into her kitchen, the aches intensified and pulsed as blood rushed to the intimate parts of her body that Adam had so skillfully aroused last night. If she knew how, she would have whistled.

Adam had his back to her, managing something on the stove that sounded and smelled like sizzling bacon. He wore the same pants from last night, but with no shirt. And she was thankful. Adam was a big guy, well over six foot three, and his back was broad and smooth and incredibly muscled. Her gaze focused on a spot just between his shoulder blades that would be a perfect place to deliver a sexy good-morning kiss. Stepping closer, she noticed a thin scar, barely pink, as if the cut was suffered a long time ago, slashing from his neck down to the small of his back.

Without thinking, she winced.

"It doesn't hurt," he said, without turning.

She took that as permission to come closer. As she'd wanted to, she delivered a kiss right at the spot she'd guessed would be the most sensitive. He groaned in appreciation. She smiled. Then, with a light touch, she traced her hand down the scar.

"I bet it did back then."

After taking a few strips of bacon out of the frying pan and placing them on a paper towel to drain, he turned around, ensnaring her in his warm arms. "I was thirteen. I hardly remember."

"What happened?"

"I almost escaped a slashing by a coked-out kid with a knife."

"Where were you?" she asked, shocked. Cocaine addiction existed everywhere, but she knew Adam's background. He hailed from a relatively safe and traditional neighborhood in Courage Bay, not the mean streets of Los Angeles like she had.

"School."

"School?"

With clear reluctance in his eyes, he turned around and tended to the bacon. After draining some of the grease off into an empty glass jar, he put down the frying pan and retrieved a bowl of eggs.

"How do you like yours?" he asked.

"Over medium. What happened at school?"

Adam turned to the still-hot frying pan, preparing to cook the eggs in the remnants of the bacon grease. He cracked the shells with one hand, dropping the delicate egg into the pan without breaking the yolk. Great. Honorable, brave, dances, amazing in bed, *and* he can cook. Was she ever in trouble.

He sprinkled salt and pepper over the eggs while he spoke.

"We had a kid in my grade who had a lot of problems. Got arrested and dragged to juvie every other week, but he was always released with a slap on the wrist and no discernible interventions. I think he was nine when he was first arrested for stealing a car. His dad was a career crook who never spent more than one or two nights in jail because his crimes were considered petty—not that his victims thought so. Anyway, the punk's name was Todd Lathem. One day, he brings a switchblade to school. Says it's for protection. He held our algebra class hostage for an hour while the cops tried to talk him down. Finally, he decided to let us all go. But on the way out, I guess he didn't like the way I looked or something. I don't know. He sliced my back."

Faith winced again, this time for the emotional crack in his voice as much as for the imagined physical pain. "What happened to him?"

Though Adam rolled his shoulders as if he didn't care, he flipped the eggs in the pan with slightly more force than necessary. "Heard he jacked a car, got caught, then drew a weapon on the arresting officer. Turned out the gun wasn't even loaded."

Faith shook her head as she snagged a piece of bacon. The flavor burst onto her hungry tongue, crisp and savory.

"Suicide by police?" she asked, knowing the phenomenon well since she'd represented a woman who'd been prosecuted in Los Angeles because her husband had goaded a police officer into shooting him. The officer had been so traumatized, the district attorney had made a grab at retribution by slapping manslaughter charges on the wife, who'd actually been her husband's hostage. Faith had managed to have the charges dropped, but the tragedy remained with her to this day.

"Could be," Adam answered. "Don't know."

"Is that why you became a cop? To stop serial criminals from making it through the revolving doors of justice?"

He made quite a fuss over arranging the bacon just right beside the finished eggs. She grabbed two mugs from the cabinet, filled them with coffee and set them on the table. They slid into their chairs and picked up their forks, and for the first time in a while, Faith noticed how bright and cozy her kitchen was. And warm. Very, very warm.

"That's one reason," Adam admitted, sipping his coffee. "Another is, I'm simply the curious sort. Always liked trying to get into people's heads, figure out why they did things. How they did things. Took a lot of science courses in high school, but in college, criminal justice appealed to me most. When you're good at something you love, why do anything else?"

She smiled. She understood the sentiment, even relied on it when her chosen profession brought her more grief than she thought she could handle.

Poking the yolk, she grinned when the yellowy goo didn't seep out too quickly, just the way she liked it. She took a bite, impressed by his culinary skills. "You're one heck of a short-order cook," she said.

"Don't let me fool you. The only meal I can do justice to is breakfast. I've been known to serve omelettes and pancakes at all times of the day."

She could think of worse things than sharing breakfast with Adam at any time of the day, particularly if the meal followed some serious lovemaking. "I love breakfast. Don't eat it much with my schedule, though."

"Me, neither. In fact," he said, glancing at her kitchen clock, "I'll need to clear out of here in about an hour. I'd like you to come with me."

She pulled the sugar bowl toward her and added a dusting of sweetness to her coffee. "So you can protect me?"

His grin was halfhearted. "Partially. We need to figure out who killed Yube and sent that threatening note. I'm not letting you out of my sight until I'm certain the shooter won't go after you again."

"Or you," she insisted.

He exhaled, apparently still fighting her theory that he could have been the target. "Either way, the investigation is already under way without me. I need to get on the case."

They finished breakfast in relative silence, then, after refills of coffee, retired to her living room. Adam insisted on going out himself to retrieve her newspaper, which had front-page coverage of the courthouse shooting.

"Says here the police have no suspects," she pointed out.

"Our department spokesperson knows what to say. We have a lot of suspects, actually. Starting with two that, while I find them very unlikely, will be my first interviews of the morning."

Faith nodded, understanding. If she were a police officer, the first people she'd interview in a case like this would be George Yube's most recent victims—Lauren Conway and Dana Ivie. "His alleged victims."

ADAM FROWNED, not looking forward to the interrogation of either woman. He didn't personally know Lauren Conway, but he'd known her newly discovered twin sister, Dana Ivie, for years. Dana had been present when Yube attacked Lauren, and she had her own reasons for resenting the "good" doctor. Both women had had their lives turned upside down by Yube's actions thirty-something years ago, when a drunken night in the ER resulted in a botched delivery and the death of a child.

In Yube's attempt to cover up his mistake, he'd played a sick shell game, switching the dead baby and two healthy ones and separating Dana and Lauren—until they'd accidentally found each other a few months ago. Still, they'd both lost a lifetime of sisterhood, memories and truth about their parentage because of George Yube. And for his crimes, he'd been about to walk away, unpunished. Was that enough motive to kill?

"Tell me what you know about Lauren Conway," Adam said, genuinely interested in Faith's take. Not that he considered her a great judge of character—look at the scum she represented—but on the other hand, she did like him. And she was an intuitive woman with a great deal at stake in this investigation, even if she didn't realize it yet.

"She's the alleged victim of George's attack," she answered simply. "That's about all I know. She's new to town, right?"

He nodded. "You met her in deposition?"

"Yes."

"How did she strike you?"

"Angry. She believed my client tried to murder her."

"Think she was angry enough to want revenge?"

"Outside the court system?" Faith sipped her coffee, considering her response. "No. She presented herself very well. She was nervous, but articulate, well spoken. Gentle, in the way artists are. I don't think she murdered my client—not that my opinion should matter."

Adam placed his mug on the coffee table. "Until we figure out what went on today, everyone's opinion matters. What about her new husband?"

Faith hesitated, her lips pursed with concern. Yeah, that's what he thought, too. Though Adam had known Alex Shields for quite some time and considered him a great guy, Adam could imagine the firefighter taking his frustration out on someone who tried to hurt his woman. He was a man's man. An instinctual protector.

However, Adam didn't think him capable of murder—especially not the kind of murder exacted by a cold, calculated sniper. Unfortunately, Adam's job wasn't to judge people by their reputation or their character—just by the facts.

"Alex Shields was a bit more over the top," Faith answered honestly. "But again, that's understandable." She put down her coffee and beat her chest mockingly.

He smirked. He got the picture. "So you're saying it's a guy thing."

"What? Murder?" She clicked her tongue.

"If you want me to outline some cases of women committing murder, I can—"

The teasing light in Faith's eyes deadened with lightning speed. "I know women commit murder, Detective."

"Will you stop calling me that?" he asked, exaggerating his frustration in an attempt to bring back her smile.

It worked.

"Stop calling you what?" she asked, clearly aware of what he objected to. "Detective? It's what you are," she answered, shaking her head as if he somehow couldn't see the obvious.

"Yes, but it is not who I am. At least, not every minute of every day." He reached across the couch and laid his hand over hers. Her gray eyes flashed with sudden shyness, testifying that their night together remained clearly in her thoughts. He'd bet his next paycheck that even she, as hot for him as he'd been for her, had never expected they'd go so far. Making love had been glorious, even if it had been too brief. He'd nearly woken her up this morning for another round, but she'd been sleeping soundly, dead to the world. Almost getting killed tended to do that to you.

"No, you're not always a cop. That surprises me," she admitted.

"Why? Are you always an attorney?"

She shrugged. "Lately, seems that I am."

"You weren't last night."

Her gentle smile tugged at Adam's heart. Could he have imagined yesterday that this piranha of an attorney could turn so deliciously into a sensual, giving woman? Her sense of fun and inherent sexiness, albeit not qualities she trotted out often, grabbed him, teased him, tortured him. He knew their time together had to be discreet—and brief. People in power would not be happy about an affair between the chief of detectives and the county's leading defense attorney. There was no rule against such a relationship, but the slightest hint of irregularities in his department could destroy the credibility he'd managed to rebuild since taking over. Max Zirinsky would have his head on a platter if he found out about Adam and Faith. And the mayor? The city council? Adam didn't want to think about the consequences to his career.

And for now, the consequences were a moot point. What Adam and Faith had shared last night was between the two of them, and he felt fairly certain that she didn't want word getting out any more than he did.

"Last night was amazing," he said, tugging her into his arms. She came willingly, and he couldn't help but inhale the scent of her hair and wish they had more time today to explore their attraction leisurely and thoroughly.

She obviously had the same idea, kissing his bare chest with soft, fluttering lips. Adam's entire body reacted. His heartbeat quickened. His skin heated. His muscles tensed and hardened. He wanted her again, and if he wasn't mistaken, she wanted him, too. He glanced surreptitiously at the clock in the hall. They had time. If they hurried.

But he didn't want to hurry. Last night had gone by too fast, in his opinion. When they made love again, he wanted to do it all night long—though he'd settle for another quickie now, in anticipation of carving out more time later.

"Last night was unforgettable," she said, pulling back and grabbing her mug.

"I'm guessing that maybe you were attempting to erect some sort of wall between us by calling me Detective, but I'm also guessing we've already become too familiar for games like that."

She looked up and raised a brow. "How familiar are we?"

Had her voice turned husky, or was his own barely checked lust causing his imagination to work overtime?

He leaned back and took a long, desirous look at Faith. Her hair caught the glints of sunlight breaking in through the slats in the blinds. Her lips were glossy, moist and alluring. "Familiar enough to make love again, right here on the couch, in the daylight?" he speculated, hopeful.

She eased to her feet, her bottom lip caught in her teeth.

"You sure do know how to make a girl an offer she can't refuse."

CHAPTER EIGHT

BUT REFUSE SHE DID, though not by choice. Only moments after Faith's foot hit the stairs on her quest to retrieve the condoms from the bedroom so she could take Adam up on his offer, the phone rang. Adam's cell phone, to be exact.

A few minutes later, he met her in the foyer, where she'd stopped on the stairs to await the bad news. His expression was nothing short of contrite. And incredibly cute.

"Lauren Conway and Alex Shields are in my office, waiting for me."

That was quick. Damn honeymooners. Probably wanted to put this all to rest quickly so they could get back to being newlyweds.

"Did you call them?" she asked.

"No," he answered, his lips curled in a grimace. "They heard the news about Yube late last night and figured they'd better come in, seeing as they expect to be the primary suspects."

"Smart couple. Do they have an alibi?"

Adam grunted, and she wasn't sure if he was happy about the situation or not. "Ironclad. They were stuck on the tarmac at LAX, on their way home from their vacation in Hawaii. I've got as many witnesses to their presence at the time of the shooting as a 757 can hold, as well as airline records, if I choose to subpoena them."

No doubt Adam had crossed Lauren and Alex permanently off the list of potential killers, not that Faith thought either one of them capable of murder anyway. In her opinion, whoever had managed to sneak a gun into the courthouse and shoot with such cool precision possessed an experienced criminal mind. The bad grammar on the note, however, made her less than confident that the person was formally educated, though she knew Harvard graduates who couldn't tell the difference between *your* and *you're*. Yet even if she had no real experience profiling killers, Faith had a strong instinct that neither Lauren nor Alex was mixed up in this mess.

"What about Dana Ivie?" she asked, just as doubtful about the involvement of the decorated firefighter as she had been about Dana's long-lost sister, Lauren.

"I crossed her off the list last night," Adam answered. "Dan Egan verified that Dana was on duty, tending to a fire on the other side of town."

Faith thought about the small fire that had been started in the stairwell, a clear diversion for the shooter. A firefighter would have the knowledge of the incendiary device and the fire safety systems to pull off such a ruse.

"No chance she sneaked away, used the fire as her cover?"

But Adam shook his head. "No way. According to Dan, she was on the radio with him from the location of the fire when the call came in from the courthouse about the shooting. She couldn't have been in two places at once."

She bought the argument. Unfortunately, that left them a bit empty-handed in the potential shooters department. "So now we have no suspects again."

"Back to square one. Welcome to police work."

She relaxed her arms, which she noticed she'd crossed

tightly against her chest. Disappointment rushed through her. When she'd first awakened, she hadn't really thought about making love with Adam again after last night, but when he'd made the offer, the possibility of refusing hadn't entered her mind even for a second. She had no idea where they would end up emotionally, but physically, she expected nothing less than extreme pleasure and bone-melting satisfaction. Not a bad payoff, in her estimation.

Now Adam had no choice but to throw himself into the case. She, on the other hand, guessed that her office would be overrun by reporters and worried clients. Despite the fact that she'd given Roma the day off, she guessed her assistant had clocked in at around seven o'clock, typical for a Friday morning.

"So what's your next move?" she asked.

"I go home, change clothes then head into the office and do a formal interview of Alex and Lauren. I'll take their statements, verify their alibi with the airline and officially cross them off the list. Same for Dana. Then I meet with Tim and go over the visitors list at the courthouse one more time and check out the statements of some witnesses."

"Sounds like you don't need me," she said, not quite as happy about that as she'd assumed she would be. She turned to dash up the stairs, but he snagged her by the arm and pulled her flush against his chest.

"You're very wrong, Faith. I need you more than you know."

She glanced down, keenly aware of his hard erection pressing against her stomach. If he wanted her half as much as she wanted him, they were both looking at a serious delay in arriving at their respective offices.

"Do you need me for what I hope you need me for, or are you back in detective mode, talking about this case?"

He looked askance before focusing on her once more with dark, dilated pupils. "Both."

She sighed. The sun was full and bright outside. In a little less than an hour, her phone would likely start ringing off the hook. Adam had a killer to catch, and if for no other reason than to prove she didn't need a twenty-four-hour guard, she had every intention of helping him. No matter how much the circumstantial evidence pointed to her being the target of the sniper, she couldn't discount the possibility that the threat had been aimed at him. And since Adam wouldn't likely put his own life before hers, someone had to watch his back.

"Does that mean you won't let me out of your sight?" she asked.

He grinned. "Is that so awful?"

She licked her lips. "No, it's rather wonderful. But you know we can't let on that we're involved. Beyond this case, that is."

He nodded. "I think I can pull off discreet. Can you?"

"With the right incentive."

His kiss was warm, and despite the urgency of the investigation, wonderfully slow and thorough. He massaged her shoulders, then drew his hands down her back, bracing her when she thought the dizziness of desire might send her tumbling down the stairs. Instinctually, she pressed her body flush against his, loving how her breasts ignited through her robe, imagining that with only one skillful tug, he could have her naked.

Instead, he gently pushed her away.

"If we don't stop now, we'll never make it to the precinct."

"Promises, promises," she teased, running her finger over his moist lips. "Okay, business now. But you have to promise that you won't hand me off to some baby-sitting uniform. If you're going to drag me around with you, I want to help."

His grin twinkled all the way into his devastating honey-colored eyes. He dropped his palms to her backside, squeezing her possessively. "I'm not handing you off to anyone, Faith Lawton. Not until absolutely necessary."

THE INTERVIEW WITH Lauren and Alex Shields went exactly as Adam had expected. In less than an hour, he'd thanked them for their statement and sent them on their way with no warnings to stay in town. Not only did they have an airtight alibi, but Adam sensed that sometime after the depositions, they'd made the decision to move forward with their lives rather than dwell on the past. He'd gotten the same impression from Dana Ivie, who'd stopped by to see him on orders from Dan Egan. With the exception of Detective Jerado, who'd mishandled the Yube evidence and whom Adam considered the unlikeliest of suspects, even if he did plan to interview his fellow detective that afternoon, Adam didn't have a single suspect associated with Yube's past crimes to look at.

Unless Yube hadn't been the target at all...

Adam filled his stained mug with coffee that he knew would taste like something between tar and sludge and decided he had to abandon that angle of the investigation for a while. He needed to look at Faith, particularly. Her past. Her clients. Her enemies. Moments after he'd shown her to his office, she'd commandeered his phone and started running through some of his files on the Yube shooting. He walked in now, shutting the half-frosted glass door behind him.

She sat behind his desk, one hand gripping a clipboard filled with what he guessed was the visitors log from the courthouse, the other hand toying with a strand of her golden-blond hair. She twirled the cornsilk tress around her finger absently, which made the move even more seductive. Had he taken the time to run his fingers through her hair last night? The lovemaking had happened so fast. Next go-around, he intended to take his time. If they had a next go-around.

Try as he might, Adam simply couldn't redirect his mind away from what he really wanted to be doing this afternoon—making love to Faith Lawton. Couldn't he catch the killer tomorrow?

Besides, he hadn't forgotten that once he accomplished that goal, he'd have no other reason to keep Faith close by. The other detectives and police officers in the precinct had already greeted them with wide-eyed stares when they'd come into the building. The fact that he'd directed her to wait for him in his office only intensified the whispers. Even Max Zirinsky, usually the height of professionalism, had made a crack when Adam stopped in his office to check on the progress of the forensic evidence.

Well, ordinarily Adam didn't give a damn who gossiped about him. He considered his private life private. But with all the rumblings about irregularities in the department lately, flaunting a relationship with Faith—a well-known enemy of the department—was nearly the same as tendering his resignation.

So for the moment, they'd just continue as they'd agreed, keeping their hands to themselves in public. No easy task— at least, not for him.

"Find anything?" he asked.

With a tired sigh, she placed the papers back onto the desk. "I hope you don't mind that I started without you," she said.

He crossed the room and sat in the chair across from his desk, not really caring that she had expropriated the space he hadn't quite gotten used to yet. It was hard enough not seeing Leo Garapedian, the former chief of detectives, in that chair every morning since his retirement. While Adam thought Leo was a great guy, Faith was a definite improvement, aesthetically speaking.

"Not at all. A fresh set of eyes might do some good. Did Tim come in?"

"Just long enough to say he was following up on another case and he'd be back in a while."

Adam gestured toward the clipboard. "Notice anyone's name on there that we should be looking into?"

She shook her head. "No one associated in any way with the case against Yube, except, of course, for the people who were at the hearing. Otherwise, I see no one of interest. To Yube."

"You keep saying that," Adam noted, wondering why she continued to qualify her assessment. Unless, of course, she was following the same assumption he was—that Yube hadn't been the target. "Is there someone on the list *not* associated with Yube who caught your eye?"

She frowned, flipped back a couple of pages, then slid the log across the desk, her pink-and-white fingernail poised beside an entry made in the early morning.

Adam blinked. Why hadn't he known this man of all men would be in court that day? He cursed. "Felix Moody."

Faith sucked in one side of her cheek. "My former client."

"But you got him off. He probably worships you."

She rolled her eyes. "Felix Moody doesn't worship anyone but himself."

He swallowed a chuckle. "But you represented him. You had to have seen something redeeming about him."

This time, she laughed. Loudly. "I don't look for redeeming qualities in a client, Adam. Especially with guys like Felix Moody. I look exclusively at the facts."

With a frown, he displayed his doubt. "No one can be that objective, Faith. Not even the cops or officers of the court. Maybe judges, but even they're human."

She lifted her hand off the page, rubbing a spot beside her temple. "His mother came to see me. She brought Felix's children with her, who, frankly, couldn't have looked more worse for wear. Normally, I never would have taken such a high-profile case, not for a guy with Felix's rap sheet. His mother even admitted to me that he'd run afoul of the law, and that in most cases, he was guilty. But she honestly didn't believe he'd killed that other drug dealer. So I looked into the case."

Adam hadn't been chief during the initial Moody arrest, but he'd been on the case and had testified two years ago in the trial that had led to Moody's convictions on murder and gambling charges. Felix Moody had already amassed a long rap sheet for pandering, drug charges and various other offenses. Moody was, in the minds of every clear-thinking, rational person who met him, a two-bit hood and a menace to society.

Adam had celebrated when Moody went to jail, and figured his work on the case had, in part, led to his first promotion on his way to chief. For two years, the streets of Courage Bay had been Moody-free. But for his appeal, Moody had somehow managed to hire Faith Lawton, and she'd worked her magic like the seasoned professional she was. She'd discovered that a rookie working the case had slipped into an adjoining, but separate, apartment to retrieve the murder weapon—the most damning piece of evidence used at the trial. Faith had motioned fotthe judge to immediately vacate the conviction, arguing that since the apartment complex collected separate rent payments for the second set of rooms, the police should have obtained a second search warrant as well.

The judge had had no choice but to agree.

Moody had walked.

"How did you find the problem with the warrants?"

She blew out a breath. "Sheer luck. At about four o'clock in the morning, after two pots of coffee and a bowl of Hershey's Kisses—" weariness crept into her voice "—I was checking through Felix's bank account when I noticed he'd written two checks in one month to his landlord. Several months in a row, actually. Always two separate checks for the same amount, usually one check right after the other. Consecutive numbers. When I asked him about it, he told me that Jasmine, his girlfriend, had rented the apartment next to his, but they'd knocked down part of the separating wall when the superintendent had gone out of town for the weekend. He wanted 'easy access,' if you know what I mean." She blanched. "Anyway, Felix apparently learned construction during another of his…unfortunate incarcerations.'"

Adam chuckled. His mother watched reruns of *Designing Women* every weeknight. Did Faith? Was that why she chose those particular words, like the ex-con on the sitcom?

So many things he didn't know about her, details he wanted to gather… Would they have time to share and explore each other's lives before they had to say goodbye?

"The checks led you to realize that there were two separate apartments, meaning we would have needed a second warrant to search the girlfriend's side. One we didn't obtain."

She nodded. "Just as I explained in court."

"Why was Felix in the courthouse yesterday?"

"I don't know. I'm not his attorney anymore. I just worked that one appeal. I've refused all other calls from him."

That caught Adam's attention. "Really? Why?"

She leveled him with a stare that said, Why do you think?

"So he had reason to resent you?" Adam asked.

"Me? No. He was never threatening or angry. Just persistent. Annoying. Like a gnat."

Adam chuckled. Yeah, that pretty much summed up Felix Moody in his mind. He was a tall guy, so he wasn't likely called a gnat by anyone who knew him, since he was one mean son of a bitch. No one but the cops would dare call him bug-like to his face.

"Still, gnats can bite."

Her frown turned even further downward. "Felix just figured that with me as his attorney, he could run his scams with impunity. That's not the kind of attorney I am, so I referred him elsewhere. I think he got the message. But I can't discount one fact—one little detail he imparted while we were finishing his appeal. Felix hated *you*, Adam. He blamed you personally for his conviction. I chalked up his attitude at the time to testosterone—but what if, after his release, he decided to make good on his threat?"

Adam couldn't deny the rancor between him and Moody. They went way back, and Adam had thrown the guy in lockup more times than he could count. After the release from prison Faith had secured, Adam had made it his business to arrange a private chat with the con, had let him know that Adam and the entire department would be watching him, waiting for him to screw up.

And except for not knowing why Moody had gone to the courthouse yesterday, they'd done a fairly good job of keeping the ex-con in their sights.

Adam looked up, not too surprised to see Faith studying him with narrowed but concerned eyes.

"There's more to the hate between you and Felix, isn't there."

He sat up straight. "Nothing more than you'd expect."

She pressed her lips together. Tightly. She wasn't buying his explanation. He half expected her to stand and march around him like she often did in the courtroom when interrogating a hostile witness.

Lucky for him, she remained in her place. "Have you spoken to Felix lately?"

Adam shook his head. "I haven't laid eyes on the guy since his appeal went through. So far as I know, he's been keeping his nose clean."

"An unusual situation, don't you think?" She leaned forward, steepling her fingers. "Why is Felix Moody suddenly ignoring his criminal instincts?"

Adam shook his head, then stopped. He had no real reason to lie to Faith. Okay, so putting extra heat on Moody might not have been exactly ethical or practical, but it wasn't illegal, either.

"I've had someone tailing Moody."

"What?" she said, clearly shocked. "For how long?"

He groaned. This was just the type of operation that got defense attorneys all riled up. "Since his release. Look, I'm just looking out for the community. Thanks to you, Moody got away with murder. We put a killer back on the streets because of a legal technicality. I'm not arguing that the warrants shouldn't have been properly executed, but the bottom line is that Felix Moody killed a rival drug dealer and he should have paid for that crime. He didn't, so I'm just making sure he doesn't so much as jaywalk or I'll throw him in lockup."

She slammed her hands on the desk. "Have you heard of police harassment?"

He stood. "Have you heard of 'serve and protect'?"

An icy silence filled the air, and Adam anticipated that arguing with Faith wouldn't progress as he had expected. She didn't rant and rave, didn't lose her temper or become unreasonable. In fact, he could practically see the gears of her brain working overtime behind her sharp, gray eyes.

"Where was Felix when the shooting occurred?" she asked.

Adam grinned. She'd likely remembered that she wasn't Moody's attorney anymore, that what the department did to keep Felix Moody on the straight and narrow was really none of her concern. Catching the man or woman who'd shot Yube was another matter entirely.

"Possibly in the courthouse. No word yet on why. He wasn't on any court documentation as plaintiff, defendant or witness."

"Could he have smuggled a gun inside?"

"Highly unlikely. Doesn't mean he didn't have help."

She leaned back in the chair, locking her fingers in front of her. "What time did he leave the courthouse?"

"Visitors sign in, but they don't sign out."

"What about your tail?"

He spoke through clenched teeth. "Moody shook him."

"Are you going to bring him in?"

"On what? Suspicion of being a jerk? We have nothing but his name on a sign-in sheet."

"That's never stopped you before."

He ignored the snap in her words. She was right—but Adam couldn't afford to be sloppy or risky in this investigation. He had his eye on Moody, but the ex-con had no reason to off Yube. No motive. Unless, of course, Yube hadn't been the target at all.

"I want to check out a few other leads first."

"What leads?"

Adam stood and held out his hand to her. "Come with me and you'll find out."

FAITH LOOKED AT ADAM quizzically as they pulled up in front of her house. Roma sat on the porch, cross-legged, in slim khaki slacks and a dark red blouse, thumbing through a pile of paperwork. Here Faith thought he was taking her with him to interview a witness or review forensic evidence. Instead, he was taking her home.

When Adam drove into the driveway, Roma jumped to her feet and gave them a wave. Faith got out of the car before Adam had the engine off and greeted her assistant with a hug. "You doing all right?"

"Yeah, I'm fine," Roma enthused, her wide brown eyes bright and excited. "I can't say I wasn't scared out of my skin yesterday, but I'm okay now. Give me a job to do and I can take my mind off anything." She punctuated her claim with a decisive horizontal slice of her hand.

Faith turned, fixing Adam with another questioning look.

"I called Roma after I finished interviewing Lauren and Alex. I asked her to put together a group of cases that you turned down or lost in the last two years. Cases where the people involved left your office less than satisfied. I want to go over them for potential suspects."

Faith rolled her eyes. "What about Felix?" she asked. "You remember, the guy at the courthouse yesterday? The one who'd likely love to kill you? The one who has a history of violent crimes?"

Roma winced. "Actually, you've got a couple of real winners in here, too."

"Perhaps," Faith conceded, "but how many people associated with me were at the scene of the crime, at least in the morning?"

Roma shook her head. "Seems to me that if I was showing up at a courthouse to shoot people, I wouldn't sign in with my real name. Even Felix Moody wouldn't be that stupid, would he?"

She handed Adam the stack of files, gathered her bag and retreated down the walk toward her car.

Faith didn't know whether to fume or rejoice. She'd chosen Roma as her assistant from an impressive collection of candidates. And other than being the most organized woman on the face of the planet, Roma Perez had a very crafty mind. And she had a point. If Moody preplanned the attack, which he would have had to do to have a gun on the premises, why would he sign his name in the log? He was a known enemy of many police officers, including Adam Guthrie.

Faith unlocked the door and gestured Adam inside, then followed into the foyer just as they had the night before. He completed a quick walk-through. When he delivered the all-clear, she threw her purse down on the bottom step of her staircase. She'd hoped that the next time she and Adam showed up here, they'd head immediately upstairs for a little slow-motion replay of last night's events. She didn't have much desire to go through old cases, even if sniffing through her files was good common sense.

And to top off her ire, Adam looked as if he'd just won the department football pool.

"Why are you smiling like that?" she asked, annoyed.

He closed the door behind them and secured the lock. "I have you all to myself again. Aren't I clever?"

Seeing the wiggle of his eyebrows, Faith dissolved into a grin. She knew he was only half-serious, but she appreciated the method behind his madness. "What do you say we order pizza for lunch and go through these files?"

He snatched her into his arms, the file folders squashed between them. "That would be the practical thing to do."

She tugged the files free and tossed them on the floor. A few papers slipped out, but she'd scoop them back in later. Business first? Pleasure first? What a choice!

But despite her squirming, he didn't release her. "If you're trying to insult me, Adam, it worked."

"Me?" he asked, eyebrows stretching high over his wide caramel-brown eyes. "How?"

"You implied I'm practical," she said with a pout.

"That's bad?"

"Well, it's certainly not as alluring as exotic, mysterious or sexy."

"Duly noted. But if we can hang on just a little while longer, I'll be able to file a report with Zirinsky that will hold him off for a few hours. A few *uninterrupted* hours. If not, he'll be calling every twenty minutes, believe me. And for the record, you're the most exotic, mysterious and sexy woman I've met in what seems like forever."

The cell phone didn't ring right then, but five minutes later, while Faith was ordering the pizza for delivery on her kitchen phone, she heard Adam's cell. She grabbed a pitcher of iced tea from her refrigerator, listening while Adam ran down his plan for the afternoon to the police chief. She grinned when he disconnected the call, not surprised that he didn't share his plans for a little afternoon delight. But whether it was on the official schedule or not, she knew neither one of them could hold out much longer. The quicker they got through her files, the sooner they could dash to the bedroom and take yet another taste of delicious, forbidden fruit.

CHAPTER NINE

ADAM HAD THE FILES arranged on the coffee table in Faith's living room when she came in with two glasses of tea, each rimmed with a fresh slice of lemon. She'd grown up in the restaurant industry; she knew the power of a pretty garnish. Still, her tummy fluttered when he glanced up at her. She was certain the smoky look in his eyes had nothing to do with how she'd decorated the glass.

He accepted the drink with a wide grin. "You're an expert hostess."

She tugged her pants and sat beside him, close, but not too close. They did, of course, have work to do. "You're not a bad houseguest. Find anything?"

Adam lifted the first two files off the stack. "These are two cases you lost, where Roma found notations of particularly violent behavior on the part of your clients. One is Nick Lansing."

Faith bristled. "He was transferred to a federal prison in Texas last year, shortly before he was convicted of murder in that state. He's on death row and not going anywhere."

Adam put the file in a separate pile. "To be safe, I'll make sure there haven't been any prison breaks. How did he kill his victim?"

"Knife," Faith answered with a shiver. She would always

regret taking on that case, even if the man had been railroaded into a conviction. Lansing had turned out to be very scary.

Adam slapped the second file on his lap. "Helen Cass, convicted of murdering her husband. Currently serving a life sentence at the Central California Women's Facility in Chow-chilla. You handled her first appeal?"

That case had broken Faith's heart. Helen Cass was fifty-four at the time of her arrest, the dutiful mother of two spoiled brat sons with long rap sheets. Faith suspected one of the sons had set Helen up, and that during her initial interviews the devoted mother had been too scared to implicate her sons. Instead, they'd implicated her—all the way to a conviction for second-degree murder. Faith had found a witness who claimed the younger son's alibi was bogus, but try as she might, Faith couldn't convince a judge to agree to a new trial. She considered the case one of her greatest failures.

"I lost her first appeal, if that's what you mean. I referred her to a more qualified attorney. And Helen was never violent toward me."

"She wrote some threatening letters," Adam said, pulling a few sheets of paper from the file folder.

Faith took one, imagining she could see tearstains on the crinkled white sheet. "Not threatening," she insisted. "Just… intense. I let her down. So did the system. Not to mention her sons. I even worked with her new attorney. She'd dealt with a very similar case two years ago and seemed to think things would work out. She managed to get a judge to consider new evidence, so there's a chance Helen could still be released."

"When's the new trial?"

Faith concentrated, but couldn't remember receiving any

follow-up information. "I don't know. I haven't heard anything one way or another."

Adam placed that folder in a second pile. "Let's have Roma check that one out, okay? See where the case is. Maybe the sons aren't too happy that mommy's about to be sprung."

"Okay, but wouldn't they then be targeting the new attorney and not me?"

After a moment's thought, he nodded and took the file off the table altogether. She took a long sip of her drink, glad the tea was icy cold, because staring at Adam when he was in full work mode injected an additional steaminess into their interactions. He was reasonable and complete in his thought processes. He didn't discount what she said because of his own preconceived notions. He listened. She added *open-minded* to the list of his positive qualities. So what was standing in the way of her falling helplessly in love with him?

Only the little thing about him hating what she did for a living—and the fact that he'd likely get demoted back to walking a beat if their affair became public knowledge.

And then, of course, there were her own private issues. After making love with Adam last night, she was forced to think about how long it had been since she'd dated, since she'd allowed herself close enough to a man to feel his heartbeat racing against hers. Over a year? At least. Even Lu had given up trying to arrange dates, since Faith usually cancelled. She hadn't been trying to be unsociable, but socializing with men was so much work! The initial chitchat and small talk were exhausting, and she usually had too much on her professional plate to bother with flirtation and seduction. Since she had such a full social life with her family, she tended to ward off loneliness with nights at the luau or road trips with Kalani.

Until Adam had rushed into her life, she'd forgotten how intoxicating a man could be—how invigorating and dizzying.
Of course, all men weren't Adam Guthrie.

A problem in itself.

"Here's a case you turned down not too long ago," he announced, snapping a file closed. "Mia Peters is the contact,
the client is Roland McGee."

Faith grabbed the file, her stomach dropping. How could
she have forgotten about Mia? Mad Mia, as she and Roma had
referred to her when no one else was around. "Yikes. I put her
out of my mind months ago. Scary woman."

Adam scooted forward. "Scary how?"

"Worked at a gun range, for one thing," Faith said, her
blood chilling even as her heart pumped the stuff faster
through her veins. "I wouldn't take her lover's case. Roland
was a powerful stockbroker in Los Angeles. Married, no
children—but not married to Mia. They'd been having an
affair for years. His wife turned up dead and he was arrested
for killing her within forty-eight hours."

"How'd she die?"

Faith opened the file. She could remember the people, but
not the details. She scanned the text, nodding when she found
the notation she was looking for.

"Drowned."

"Suspicious?"

"Medical Examiner found bruise marks on her shoulders,
indicating that someone held her under the water. Her husband
didn't report finding the body in the pool for a day or two.
Claimed he never went into the backyard and that his wife had
said she was going to leave him, so he assumed she had."

"No alibi?" he asked.

She handed him back the file so he could skim the police reports. He frowned as he read.

"Oh, he had an alibi. Mia. Claimed they were together the night of the wife's death. At her place."

"Then why didn't you take the case?"

"I was busy," Faith answered, truthful, but not entirely so. "Roma had been involved with an organization in law school that sought out appeals for people convicted before DNA evidence came into fashion. When she came to work for me, we took on a few of their cases *pro bono*. At the time Mia came in asking me to represent her lover, we had about three freebie cases in the hopper and five or six law students taking up space in my small office. Roland McGee was a wealthy man from a wealthier family. I figured he could find someone else."

"Didn't help that you thought he might be guilty, huh?"

She grimaced. How could this man see through her so easily? "Didn't help."

"And Mia wasn't happy with your refusal."

Faith flattened her palms against her cheeks, remembering the scene vividly. "I had to call the security guard for my office building to have her removed. She was a piece of work. I think I learned new curse words from her that day, and remember, I've had the distinct experience of hanging around incarcerated prisoners who aren't known for sophisticated language."

"So she threatened you."

"In many imaginative ways."

"Was Roland convicted?"

Faith nodded. "Life, with no possibility of parole."

He blew out an ominous whistle. "So if lover-girl isn't getting her conjugal visits, she could still be mighty angry."

"Not to mention that she doesn't have the millions Roland

promised her," Faith added. "She wasn't too happy about losing her meal ticket."

"And she's a weapons instructor, which means she likely would have the skill to shoot accurately from that office building. Yube's case has been high profile. Maybe seeing you on the news every night reignited her anger."

Faith bit her bottom lip. "But she had nothing against George Yube. Why kill him? A few more seconds and she could have had a clear shot at me."

"She might have miscalculated, missed," he guessed. "Even pros take bad shots sometimes."

"Is her name on the courthouse log?"

"More than likely, no," Adam answered. "But you and I both know that doesn't mean anything. Fake identification is easy to come by, especially since she's from out of town and not easily recognizable."

Faith nodded, the pit of her stomach suddenly feeling a mile wide and two miles deep. And it wasn't from hunger. She could most definitely and with great ease conjure the image of Mia Peters taking a shot at her, missing, then trying again. Though the woman had attempted to dress herself up and act civilized when she'd first come into the office, Faith's polite refusal and offer of a referral had been met with a vitriolic spew unlike anything she'd ever heard before. If her office hadn't been filled with people at the time, she might have been genuinely frightened.

But she hadn't heard from Mia since that horrible day. Not a single word, though admittedly any of the anonymous threats sent to her office could have been from her.

Could Adam have been right all along? Had the bullet lodged in George Yube's head been meant for her?

She folded her arms across her chest. "So what do we do?"

Adam closed the file and placed it in a pile all its own. "First, we find out if Mia Peters is still working at On Target Gun Range. Then find out how old Roland McGee likes prison. Then, after we're armed with information, we pay Ms. Peters a visit. You up to that?"

The doorbell rang, and seconds after Adam answered it, the garlicky scent of pizza wafted through the air. As unappetizing as food had seemed a few moments ago, the minute Adam carried the delivery box into the living room, Faith's stomach growled. When he opened the top and the glistening discs of pepperoni gave off their peppery scent, she knew she'd eat no matter what.

They enjoyed their lunch, reviewing the last few files Roma had provided. None of them produced anything interesting, so they decided to focus, for now, on Mia Peters. But as Faith threw down the crust of her third slice of pepperoni pizza, she decided the time had come to look in another direction—just to make sure they didn't ignore one potential victim in favor of another.

"Okay, we've dissected my past enough to find a potential threat to my well-being," Faith announced. "Now let's look at you."

"I've got too many enemies to count," he said.

"Okay, then let's narrow the parameters. Any perps recently released from prison?"

Adam fished another slice out of the pizza box, his gaze not meeting hers. "Felix Moody."

"Any with sniper skills?" she asked, knowing the answer. Her former client's mother had enrolled her son in ROTC in high school, attempting to cure Felix of his criminal ways.

He'd done two years in the Marines before a dishonorable discharge for passing illegal drugs to his unit.

Adam groaned. "Felix Moody."

She raised her eyebrows. "Don't you think it's time to pay Felix a visit, as well?"

He munched lazily, as if her suggestion was not worth his consideration—or he was one step ahead of her.

"Moody is making himself a little scarce lately," Adam reminded her.

Faith grabbed a napkin and wiped the grease from her fingers. "And he had no business at the courthouse."

"No official *court* business. He could have been there for any number of other reasons. Pulling a building permit. Applying for a license for his boat."

She pursed her lips. She supposed Felix could have had any number of legitimate excuses to be in a public building. And though she really didn't think even he would be dumb enough to sign in on the visitors log if he intended to shoot someone from inside the building, she wasn't ready to discount him as a suspect until they found him and interviewed him. While representing Felix in his appeal, she'd heard him pop off about how he hated cops, Adam Guthrie in particular. He'd bragged about how he'd make them all pay for railroading him, for putting him in prison for a crime he didn't commit. For all Faith knew, Felix had been innocent of the murder that had landed him in lockup. That didn't mean she thought him incapable of killing, just that police and prosecutors had used incorrectly collected evidence to prove that he'd been the one who'd pulled the trigger in the drug-dealer crossfire case.

"Have you spoken to his mother?" Faith asked. "She usually knows where he is."

Adam shook his head. "Can't find her, either. She moved and we haven't managed to find a forwarding address yet. Do you have it?"

Faith pawed through the files Roma had brought, then realized her assistant wouldn't have included Felix's file under Adam's prescribed criteria. She'd won Felix's case, and while her personal opinion of the man was less than stellar, he'd never threatened her. "I'll call Roma."

"I'll clean up," he said, jumping up from the couch, collecting their napkins and the pizza box and then disappearing into the kitchen.

Faith grabbed her cell phone and dialed the office. Roma answered, pert and professional as always.

"Roma, do you have Delia Moody's new address? I remember her sending us a card when she moved."

"Hold on a sec."

Adam returned to the living room, retrieved the glasses and trotted back to the kitchen. When she heard the water running, she figured he was washing dishes, such as they were, again. He'd already insisted on cleaning up after breakfast, even though he'd cooked. Here she was, letting him complete all the domestic duties again. In her house! Lu would kill her if she knew.

As she waited for Roma to find the information, she went into the kitchen and shooed Adam out with her free hand before he could open her dishwasher and clear out the clean dishes to make room for the dirty ones. He'd made the task somewhat difficult by trapping Faith's waist with his arms while he nuzzled her neck, but she'd just managed to put away the saucers when Roma came back on the line.

"I don't have it, Faith. I have a notation that you took the file home to do your post-case evaluations."

Faith remembered. She'd wanted to write down some of the facts she'd learned about Felix Moody after she'd won his case, details she hadn't been happy about at the time and that she didn't want to forget.

"Right, it's in my study. Thanks, Roma. You know, you can go home early today. It is Friday and I won't be in at all."

Roma promised to try to take off before four o'clock, but Faith rolled her eyes, disbelieving. She disconnected the call and turned back to sorting the forks, knives and spoons in her flatware drawer.

"I have the file in my study," she told Adam. "Let me finish this, then I'll get it."

Adam leaned against the refrigerator, eyeing her like she was a choice slab of prime rib and he was the world's hungriest carnivore. She turned her back on him, grinning, relishing the fact he made no secret of wanting her in a really bad way. Some men could be so blasé about desire, expecting her to assume that simply because they showed up for their date at the prearranged time, they wanted her physically.

She'd long ago lost the inclination to inform those yahoos that simply showing up wasn't enough. If a man wanted to make a woman feel beautiful and sexy and unique, he should take a lesson from Detective Adam Guthrie. He could convey a lion's share of passion, arousal and hunger all in one ravenous stare.

"Why don't I get the file?" he suggested. "Then I'll have Tim check out the address, and by the time I'm done, you'll be finished with the dishes."

She liked the way he thought, especially because she could hear the unspoken agenda in his voice. If they coordinated a bit, they'd waste no time in retiring upstairs for the intimate interrogation she'd been waiting for all afternoon. A twinge of hot fire surged to her most intimate places, causing her to bite her bottom lip in barely banked anticipation.

"The file's in my study. Should be right on top of my desk, under the coconut paperweight."

As PROMISED, Adam found the file under the coconut, a polished shell with a trio of hula dancers hand-painted on the oblong nut. One dancer had blond hair, which made Adam look twice before he laughed. No mistaking the likeness—the paperweight featured a caricature of Faith, flanked by her foster sister and foster mother. At the bottom, her father's signature identified the cheeky artist.

Before yesterday, he never would have guessed that tenacious, steely Faith Lawton could have been raised by such fun-loving people. Of course, until yesterday, he'd never imagined Faith had so many facets to her personality. He'd bought into the image she projected of a tough, cold female attorney, down to the last vestige of the stereotype, and he should have known better. Women were never simple to figure out.

He sifted through the papers on her desk, past phone messages, newspaper clippings, legal journals and letters. He didn't see any file folders, and scratched his head impatiently. The longer it took them to find the file, the longer the delay before going upstairs with Faith. Once he relayed the info on Delia Moody to Tim Masters, he planned to call in to the precinct and take himself off the clock for a few hours. He'd never been so distracted by a woman, especially a woman whose safety was in his hands.

For the time being, her house was a haven with him inside and a patrol car running through her neighborhood every twenty minutes or so. Still, he knew he should be focused on the sniper case and only the sniper case—not on rushing through this information so he could rendezvous with her in bed. But how could he ignore the sparks arcing between him and Faith like fireworks on a national holiday?

He couldn't. Despite his string of failed relationships, Adam wasn't one to live in the past. He enjoyed his lovers while things worked out, and when they invariably fell apart, he did his best to cultivate friendships, or at least a comfort zone. One of his former lovers worked with him in the department. Things tended to be a little tense from time to time since they were still both single, but they managed to work together quite well. Could he and Faith do the same?

They'd have to. They'd have no choice. He had worked hard for the level of success he'd reached as chief of detectives, and he couldn't imagine Faith changing her career in any way when she was so good at her job. He hadn't been entirely kidding when he'd offered her a position in the department, working with him rather than against him, but for some personal reason, Faith seemed determined to remain a defense attorney. As he fingered through the tabs of a collection of file folders, he thought about the *pro bono* cases she'd told him about. While some in law enforcement resented attorneys opening old cases and renewing interest in crimes long since solved, Adam didn't subscribe to that way of thinking. When he made an arrest, he wanted the right guy. If DNA proved he'd arrested an innocent man or woman, he wanted that person released as soon as possible. He didn't pursue law enforcement for power, but for justice.

He was speculating about why Faith was so devoted to her job, when a thick file folder brimming with paperwork caught his eye. The name on the tab? *Sylvia Lawton.* One file led to another…and another. He turned around, shocked by the presence of several cardboard boxes against the wall, all marked with the same name. Two of the three were stamped with the seal of the Los Angeles County Prosecutors Office.

Unable to stem his curiosity, he turned back to the first file and was about to flip it open when Faith entered the study.

"Did you find—"

Her smile disappeared from her face, which went pale, then white. She glanced at the boxes, as if she'd forgotten they were there, and clamped her lips together.

Taking a deep breath, she walked toward him. "Did you find Mrs. Moody's address?"

Adam dropped his hands to his sides. Did he dare ask? Who was Sylvia Lawton?

"No luck."

She scooted by him, her shoulder brushing his arm. The room suddenly felt very small, cramped even, as she leaned over and grabbed a file from underneath a second paperweight, this one a statue of a surfer relaxing on his board. "Here it is. Sorry, wrong paperweight."

She turned to leave the room and Adam knew she'd made herself clear without saying a word. She didn't want to tell him about Sylvia Lawton. So why couldn't he keep himself from asking?

"Who is she?"

She stopped before she'd passed through the threshold, but she didn't turn around. "My mother."

He glanced at one of the files, white with bright orange lettering, that read "California Institution for Women." The prison in Corona?

"Your mother is in prison?"

She sighed, her shoulders drooping with a beaten slope that stabbed Adam in the heart. Why couldn't he keep his big mouth shut? As a detective, he was ignoring the obvious clues she'd left him—clear indications that she didn't want to reveal this aspect of her past to him.

Yet when she faced him, her chin was high and her eyes were fiery with rebellion. "She was. She's dead. And the justice system killed her."

CHAPTER TEN

FAITH PRESSED HER FIST against her stomach, suddenly wishing she hadn't eaten so much pizza so fast. Before she'd sent Adam into her study, she'd known the files and boxes about her mother and her mother's case remained in full view. She'd already given Adam free rein to explore her house. Why then was she so surprised when he discovered her secret?

"You don't want to talk about this," he guessed, flipping open Felix Moody's file and pretending to skim through for the notation about the new address.

His empathy, shown by the simple gesture of ignoring the obvious, touched her deeply. He had every right to know if she had a big skeleton in her emotional closet. They had, after all, been intimate. Even if they'd subtly agreed to a no-strings-attached affair, they would forever be connected by what happened in the plaza, and by what happened last night in the bedroom. But was that enough to compel her to tell him about the most painful memory of her entire life?

The Apalos knew, of course. Roma knew, but only recently, when Faith realized she couldn't accomplish her goal of expunging her mother's conviction from the records of the State of California without her assistant's help. A few more months of work and she'd be ready to petition the governor for a posthumous pardon.

She wasn't fooling herself. Her mother was a nobody, a poor widow convicted of committing a relatively petty crime and who died in prison from misdiagnosed cancer. There would be no media coverage, no public outrage, petitions or support—just a daughter trying to clear her mother's name, for the sake of justice and truth.

Adam smiled when he yanked a piece of paper from the file. "Here's the address." His deep voice was pitched with enthusiasm. A little too much. As if he was trying really hard to tell her she didn't have to say another word. "I'll call Tim and have him check this out, and while he's at it, he can double-check on Mia Peters and verify her employment. Then we'll do the interviews. Maybe we can find one of them by later this afternoon."

He marched toward the archway to the living room, but she stopped him by laying her hand gently on his arm. She inhaled deeply, then allowed the words chomping at her tongue to tumble out. "She died over twenty years ago."

Without the briefest hesitation, Adam placed his hand over hers and led her into the tiny alcove she might have used as a dining room if she'd ever bought the right furniture. Instead, she had a fluffy old love seat with tiny pink flowers on a field of Dresden blue, a leftover from her college days. She'd taken incredible care of the compact sofa, and it had always taken great care of her, cradling her tired body at the end of a long workday, providing a quiet space for her to curl into to read a good book.

Never case files. Never work. She'd done enough studying on that love seat, the first purchase she'd made when she moved out on her own. Since moving it to her new house, she only relaxed here, a silly unspoken rule that nearly made her laugh under the circumstances. This was the perfect place to unload the secret of her past.

"You don't have to tell me more, Faith. You don't owe me an explanation."

She nodded. "I know, but I don't want you to get the wrong impression. Not so much about me, but about my mother. I loved her very much, Adam. She was all I had, even when my father was alive. Over the years, her memory has become more and more important to me. Funny how when you're a kid, you think you'll never forget. Never occurs to you that someday, the memories you hold so close to your heart will start to fade, get cloudy, maybe even disappear altogether."

"I don't think you could ever forget her," he ventured, his hand still entwined with hers.

"No, but the State of California did. Her lawyers did. Her family did, except for me. I was an orphan, a child, but I still had family, did you know that? When my mother was arrested, I could have gone to live with an aunt and uncle in Minnesota or a set of cousins in Baton Rouge. They didn't want me." Faith took a deep breath. How could she still harbor resentment after all these years? Especially after her life had turned out so well.

Still, the rejection had happened when she was eleven years old. Emotional scars on a child were as long lasting and cut into the flesh as deeply as the one Adam wore on his back. She couldn't deny the abandonment she'd felt then.

"What happened to your dad?" he asked, reminding Faith that he knew nothing about her past, despite the many years they'd been nodding polite hellos when they passed in hallways.

"He died when I was nine. Murdered in a drug deal gone bad." She chuckled humorlessly, hating how dramatic her younger years sounded in the recounting. "I didn't have a typical childhood. When he was laid off and money was tight, my father sold drugs, ran errands for pimps, did whatever he had to. And my mother…well, she just tried to make the best of things."

"She was clean?" he asked, squeezing her hand as the confident tone of his voice urged her to tell him everything.

She tightened her hand right back. "Yeah, she was. No drugs, no drinking. We were poor, we sometimes had no food except for peanut butter sandwiches on day-old bread, but she did her best. She wasn't educated. She had no real job skills beyond taking care of me. When she was arrested, the police thought she'd finally succumbed to pressure from my father's old cronies and started dealing for him to make ends meet."

"But you don't think so?"

Faith attempted to relax so that her mouth didn't freeze in a thin line. "I know that wasn't the case. If it was, where was the money? Where were the extra toys or a nicer apartment? Took me years to figure it all out, but when I hit high school, I got curious. Started digging. By college, I had the files, and by law school, I knew what to do with them."

As more of the story spilled from her lips, her tone strengthened with confidence and focus. Adam released her hand, but liking the contact, she simply exchanged his hand over hers for the reverse, holding his palm close against her thigh.

He grinned.

"Then about two years ago," she continued, "I got wind of evidence—unsealed testimony before a grand jury in an unrelated case that actually exonerated my mother because it implicated someone else. I was furious! Turns out, I was right from the beginning. My mother had been a disposable body to fill a prison cell, a name a snitch could give up to save his own skin." With each word she spoke, her volume rose, intensified. "And the police, looking for an easy collar, ran with it. They railroaded my mother on false testimony and circumstantial evidence. They dragged her out of our apartment in the middle of the night, transported me to a cold, gray Children's Services office where no one gave a damn about what I'd just gone through. They just wanted to find me someplace to sleep so they could go back home to their families."

Adam sat up straighter, his brow furrowed. "I had no idea what you'd gone through."

She shrugged. "I don't exactly share this sob story with everyone."

"It's not a sob story, it's the truth. How did you find the Apalos?"

At the mention of the name, the bitterness hardening in Faith's veins softened. Without the Apalo family, she might have turned out so differently. Her primary emotions might have ended up being anger and resentment at the law and the world. Instead, she loved the law, enjoyed her world and sought to make it a better place. As much as she'd loved her mother, the only contribution Sylvia Lawton had made to the world at large had been the birth of her daughter. But the least Faith could do in her mother's memory was make a difference—and clear her name.

"Dumb luck brought me to the Apalos, as far as I'm concerned. They'd just qualified to become a foster family. Lu couldn't have any more children after Kay, and they didn't have enough money at the time to adopt. Two days after they were certified by the state, I was sent to stay with them. Because of the restaurant business, they decided they only wanted one foster child. They could have adopted me eventually, especially after my mother died, but we moved to Courage Bay and got wrapped up in life, so we never made it official. But they are my family as much as my mother and father were—sometimes maybe more so. It's sad, but true."

Adam's head bobbed slightly as he obviously digested all she'd told him. He had a deep, thoughtful expression on his face, one that reflected all the empathy and intelligence she knew he had in spades. She couldn't imagine that just a day ago, she'd considered him among the same group—albeit not as corrupt—as the men who'd orchestrated her mother's arrest and conviction. Though she'd respected his integrity and desire to change the operations of his department to ensure injustice happened in only rare cases, she'd still attacked him on the witness stand. She'd made him look like a rogue cop, willing to do anything to convict George Yube, including ignoring the man's right to the use of untainted evidence in his trial.

How wrong she'd been. Despite his not-so-by-the-book tailing of Felix Moody, she knew he only wanted what she wanted.

Justice. For everyone.

How they could share the same idealism while staunchly opposing one another was a catch-22 she couldn't understand. It was so much easier when she pared down their compatibility to the most basic, physical attraction. But like it or not, there was more between them. Or at least, more that could be between them—if they were willing to break some unwritten rules and take some unwise chances.

Was she? Was he?

A LONG SILENCE ALLOWED Adam time to process what he'd heard. Never in a million years would he have pegged Faith

Lawton as a girl who'd sprung from a hard-luck childhood. Drugs, murder, abandonment. The grim portrait as a background for such a keenly intelligent, vivacious woman was almost too incongruous to comprehend.

Her strength and capacity to love her foster family stole his ability to speak. He'd never, ever met a woman like her. Courage like hers was a commodity to value, cherish. Now that he knew the whole story, how could he not want to explore their attraction beyond sex, beyond a fun affair? And yet, they still had only this sniper case holding them together. Once they found the killer and knew they were both safe, the pressure of their jobs would likely tear them apart. Could he bear it? Yeah, he could take the heat. But could he ask her to?

"Thank you," he said, unable to resist the urge to take her other hand in his.

"For what?"

"For telling me about your mother. Can't be easy to relive all that."

Surprisingly, she smiled. The grin was tiny, but it reached her glossy silver eyes. "It wasn't so hard telling you. Isn't that weird? We're so different, you and I."

Adam chuckled. In no way, shape or form could his one run-in with a cracked-out punk compare to her childhood. He'd been raised in a fairly affluent family, by parents who were both college-educated—as were their parents before them. His father worked long hours, but he brought home enough money so that their mother could concentrate on raising her two boys, and on weeknights and weekends his father had organized games of catch or dragged the whole lot of them to dinner and a movie. Adam and his brother, Casey, might have gotten into their share of scrapes and snafus over the years, but they'd never had to face what Faith had.

And yet, a strong compulsion to look at their similarities rather than their differences rushed through Adam. Life was so much more stable on common ground.

"Once you went to live with the Apalos, our lives were fairly similar. I love my family, even when they're driving me crazy. My parents are on a European vacation right now, but normally, I'd be over there once or twice a week to bum a roast beef sandwich off my mom or challenge my dad to a game of darts while we throw down a few brews. Casey and I play intramural softball on the same team every spring. We're probably as close as you and Kalani."

Her smile blossomed, and the warmth her happiness inspired seeped right into Adam's skin. Right into his soul. Making her smile and laugh seemed of dire importance to him, more than it had been with any other woman before her. Man, he was in trouble.

Real, real trouble.

"My turn to say thank you," she said, leaning her shoulder toward his so she could bop him gently. "You're a good listener."

"And you're beautiful," he responded, glancing at the clock in the adjacent room. He wouldn't consider the time they'd spent learning about each other wasted, but they had had other plans for the afternoon—and from the sultry glance she threw his way in reaction to his compliment, he figured she hadn't forgotten, either.

"You make me feel that way," she said.

"Really?" He released her hands and snaked his palms around her slim waist. "Why is that?"

She hooked half of her bottom lip between her teeth. "Because you look at me with such unbridled lust."

He tugged her closer, glancing down at where her blouse gaped, revealing a curve of skin that inspired a rush of heat through his bloodstream. "Do I?"

She shifted so the neckline widened even farther. "Mmm-hmm." With her arms hooked around his neck, she scooted closer, then swiped her tongue along the ridge of his ear. "How much time do we have until Tim calls back with his information?"

Adam's eyes drifted closed as her scent, so sweet and warm and intoxicating, permeated his senses. "I haven't called him yet." He ran his hands up and down her back, loving the silken feel of her blouse beneath his hands, knowing the flesh underneath was even softer, silkier, smoother.

Her lips descended to his neck, where she nibbled a delicious path along his collar. "Don't you think you should do that? Maybe arrange a few hours of personal time? A few long, slow hours?"

He growled at the thought of a leisurely exploration, of taking his sweet time learning every erotic nook and sensitive cranny on Faith's body.

"Slow works just fine for me, actually."

Faith stood, pulling him up with her. She ran her hands down his chest, her gaze following her fingers. When she reached his waist, she spread her hands wide, dipping her thumbs ever-so-slightly into his waistband. Then with a quick yank, she tugged his cell phone off his belt and handed it to him.

He made the calls in record time. As far as the Courage Bay police department was concerned, Adam was off the clock until further notice. Faith retrieved the phone and tossed it on the couch beside her.

"First one to the bedroom gets to be on top," she challenged.

She'd said the wrong words. Adam was a fierce competitor, especially with something so important at stake.

THOUGH HE HADN'T PUSHED HER out of the way, Adam's dash to the stairs stopped her just as effectively. As if she'd ingested helium, her body lightened. He wanted her that badly? How could a woman resist a man like him? She couldn't, so a split second later, she raced after him.

She found him in her bedroom, pulling down the blinds. She hadn't made her bed this morning and the sheets and comforter and pillows were in complete disarray. She sighed at the mess, but from the dark look in Adam's eyes, she knew he didn't care if they made love on the floor, if that was their only option. In fact, by the way he grabbed her around the waist and pulled her into a wet, barely contained kiss, she figured he'd be pleased doing it against a wall.

So would she.

In seconds, their clothes were scattered across the floor. In nothing but a bra and panties, she struggled to remain standing while he bathed her neck and shoulders in hot, arousing kisses. He explored her with his hands, cupping her buttocks possessively and lifting her fully against him. He was hard. Heat radiated off his skin, chased by the inebriating male scents of musk and sandalwood. She had to taste him, all of him. The sooner the better.

Only after he lifted her in his arms to carry her to the bed did she remember that they'd planned to go slowly this time, making love at a leisurely pace. Had the plan changed? Did she care?

"How do you do it?" he asked, nibbling a spot on her shoulder.

"Do what?"

"Get a tan. With your schedule, I'd think you and the sun would be complete strangers. If not for playing ball with my brother every other weekend, I'd be pale as a ghost."

She laughed, not the least bit afraid to share yet another secret with him, but more than willing to tease out the moment. "I can't tell you."

"Another mystery?"

"No," she answered, dotting his chin with tender kisses. "I'd just rather show you."

Gently, he put her down. She took his hand and led him toward the door.

"Wait," he said, pulling her back into his arms, much like he had last night when they'd danced. "I didn't mean my question to stop what we were doing."

She snaked her hand up his thigh, cupping him, stroking his hard sex, before patting him on the belly. "Who said we were? Grab the condoms. And your sunglasses."

When she reached the bottom of the stairs, she fished her Wayfarers out of her purse and slid them on. She crooked her finger toward Adam, who followed her through the kitchen to the back of the house. When her hand closed around the doorknob, he protested again.

"Afraid of a little exhibitionism?" she teased.

He thrust his hands on his hips, looking particularly adorable in boxer shorts, sunglasses and nothing else. She supposed she looked just as ridiculous, though she had no proof he found her anything less than seductive.

"You forget there's a sniper after one of us."

She smirked. "We haven't exactly been out of sight since last night."

As if he couldn't refrain from touching her, even for a moment, he slid forward and pulled her back against him. She could barely hold on to her train of thought as she realized how constant his desire for her seemed. She'd never had a man, even during the lusty first dates, want her so thoroughly. Could it last? Did she care?

"We haven't been flaunting ourselves, either."

"Well, not to anyone other than each other."

His laugh rumbled, thick and delicious. "Point taken."

"Trust me, Adam. Where we're going, no one will be able to see us. It's sort of the point."

He hesitated, then, with a grin, released her. She grabbed a bag she kept on a hook, unlocked the dead bolt on the back door, and dashed toward a tall hedge in her backyard. Her squeal of laughter must have spurred him on, because when she spun around, he was right behind her, panting with excitement.

"You're insane!" he claimed.

"No," she said, reaching around to unhook her bra. "I'm a sun-worshiper. Have been for years."

Part of the reason she'd purchased the little cottage was the way her backyard was situated. Though the house was two-story, none of the windows on the second floor faced the tiny scrap of lawn and hedge where she retreated whenever she had the chance. Previously owned by sunbathers who preferred no tan lines, the garden had been created for both access to the sun and privacy. Tall, trim hedges planted in a square blocked any linear view, and the houses surrounding hers were all one-story. During the right time of day, the sun could beam straight into her little yard.

As it was doing now. Faith removed her bra, arched her back, closed her eyes and enjoyed the warmth of the rays on her skin.

Adam's lusty groan raised the temperature ten delicious degrees.

"So this is your secret tanning bed," he said, dropping his boxers.

God, she loved the way he adjusted and changed gears without much hesitation. She wasn't the most spontaneous person in the world, but throwing caution to the wind was so much easier when the person with her wasn't afraid to follow her into the tempest.

His sex jutted hard and proud, and Faith's mouth watered to taste him, this time completely. She released the knot on the drawstring bag and drew out a tightly rolled, thin grass mat and a bottle of suntan oil. Not the kind of lotion with SPFs so strong they blocked out the rays entirely. She was careful to keep her time in the sun limited, so a small protection factor was sufficient to make sure she didn't burn. Although, with what she had planned for Adam, a little sizzling flesh was more than in order.

She rolled out the mat and invited him to lie down.

"No doing. I won the race upstairs, remember?"

She licked her lips. How could she forget?

"Yes, but I have the suntan oil," she said, waving the bottle at him.

After a moment, he surrendered—momentarily. She had no doubt he'd reclaim his dominant position sometime very soon.

"Face down or face up?" he asked.

What a choice! She relied on the practical side of her mind to formulate an answer. "Face down. For now."

He complied, throwing himself to the ground like a marine about to do push-ups on demand. She bit her lip, impishly considering that in a few minutes, he wouldn't be so far off the mark.

Tossing his sunglasses aside, he cradled his head on his arms and squinted up at her. "Just what do you have in store for me?"

She wiggled the oil bottle at him. "A slow massage," she promised, straddling his back. "Then, we'll wing it."

He hummed his consent, but an underlying tone led Faith to believe he had something very specific in mind—something she possibly hadn't thought of herself. She swallowed a derisive snort. She could be very creative when she put her mind to it. Very creative indeed.

CHAPTER ELEVEN

BY THE TIME SHE FINISHED applying the oil to Adam's back, describing Faith as hot would have been an understatement. He'd groaned and moaned and hissed his pleasure at her slick and thorough massage. From the tight muscles of his neck to the rigid curve of his buttocks to the tapered arch of his foot, she'd explored every inch of him. And she liked what she learned.

The next step, however, could push her into uncharted territory. Up until now, Faith had thought she'd maintained a bright and positive social life, full of family and friends, activities like surfing and sunbathing and dancing until dawn.

Yet, like it or not, Adam's presence reflected the full story. Yes, she had a good life—family- and career-wise. But something crucial was missing. Or at least, it had been missing until Adam literally pushed her against a wall and forced her to confront the truth.

She was lonely.

Although, for the last twenty-four hours, she'd been anything but.

"Time to flip over," she said, moving out of the way so he didn't have to roll onto the grass to do as she asked.

He glanced over his shoulder. "Isn't it my turn yet?"

The possibilities his words conjured drew the moisture from her mouth. "Not quite yet."

With catlike grace, he rolled into a sitting position, his elbows braced boldly on his knees. "If you keep touching me like that, the only part of me that will be exposed to the sun is my back. So I'm now…covered."

He slid his gaze down her body, brazenly appreciating every inch of her that wasn't covered.

"Doesn't mean you've had enough, does it?"

She dropped to her knees in front of him, making an erotic show of pouring a stream of oil into her palms, then rubbing the emollient until her hands glistened, slick and glossy. She placed her palms on his shoulders, swirling the coconut lubricant across, then down, taking particular care in coating his nipples.

He surrendered, lowering himself back on the mat while she massaged his neck, chest and arms. Then she skipped down to his feet, covering his legs, loving how her hands had to tickle through the hair on his calves and thighs. He'd thrown one arm across his eyes to block out the sunlight, so when she abandoned the oil in favor of her mouth to glaze his sex, he hardened with both pleasure and surprise.

He tasted musky, rich, earthy. The sensations enthralled her, especially when his groans became breathless, wild and deep. To have such power over a man like Adam thrilled her more than she'd thought possible. She drew him to the brink. Then, just when she thought he'd tumble, he forked his hands into her hair and eased her aside.

"My turn," he said simply.

She didn't plan to argue, but when she slid against his body, the suntan oil transferred from his skin to hers. Now he was no longer greasy, just smooth and slick and hot.

He situated her on the mat, pouring more oil into his hand with wicked intentions dancing in his eyes.

"I'm pretty well covered, thanks to that switcheroo," she said, her tone light, teasing and ever hopeful that he wouldn't take the easy way out.

He didn't disappoint her. "Doesn't count. It's not the oil I want all over you, but my hands. The suntan oil is a lame excuse for some pretty fantastic exploration, don't you agree?"

The minute he slid his palms over her breasts, she had neither the strength nor the inclination to argue or resist. She relaxed, allowed her heavy lids to drop over her eyes, and fully enjoyed the sensations he created with his hands, tongue and lips. The scent of toasted coconut, sweet and brimming with a million memories, lured her into a dreamlike state between reality and pure, unadulterated pleasure.

As she had done to him, he saved the most intimate kisses for last. He parted her thighs slowly, a light touch encouraging her to bare herself fully to him. When his tongue dipped into her sex, the pulses and waves of sensation found their center. She arched her back, and he grabbed her hands, holding her still until climax was one lick away.

She had no time to clear her head when he moved aside, donned the condom, then slid back over her. Lubricated and warm, their bodies glided into a perfect rhythm. She barely had to move for him to thrust into her deeply, but once contact was made, movement was all she wanted.

She grabbed at him, unable to clutch him tightly, thanks to the oil. He solved the problem by ensnaring her hands in his, then balancing them over her head. He kissed her, aroused her, spoke to her in words only lovers understood, until the climax neared, and then, together, they broke the barrier between physical pleasure and spiritual bliss.

When Faith returned to earth, she noticed she was thirsty,

hot and slick. And yet, she'd never felt so alive in her entire life—and never more loath to leave the private little garden that surrounded them.

Adam shifted, resting his head on his elbow. "I like how you sunbathe," he commented, punctuating his compliment with a kiss on her nose.

She licked her dry lips. "Does that mean you'll consider sneaking over here from time to time to join me as I soak up the rays?"

His smile dissipated and his jaw seemed to freeze at her lighthearted suggestion. "I'd rather not sneak."

Heaviness settled in Faith's chest, and it had nothing to do with Adam's body on hers. That was the most comfortable, most bearable weight she'd ever experienced. But slightly twenty-four hours into their affair, they were now facing a moment she'd hoped they could put off, at least a little longer.

"You know we have to," she insisted. "You could lose your job if people knew about us."

"Why? We're both consenting adults. We don't have the same boss."

She tilted her head, wondering if their sensual interlude had somehow loosened the wiring in his brain. This wasn't nuclear physics—this was city politics. Courage Bay might be progressive and advanced in many areas, but basic human nature didn't change with the size of the metropolis. In the eyes of his superiors, and maybe more important, the men he commanded, Faith was the enemy. She didn't have nearly as much to lose as he did, though she wondered how many clients would pay her retainer if they knew she was sleeping with the detective who meant to put them in jail.

"This isn't about workplace romances, Adam. Your department has been under a lot of pressure lately, some of it due to me." She stroked his cheek, wanting to erase the increasingly serious expression on his face. "Don't get me wrong. I don't want to stop seeing you. I just don't think public displays are good for your career right now, do you?"

His lips pulled down into a clear and dangerous frown. "I don't suppose it would help your career, either."

"I don't know," she teased. "Maybe my clients will think I have an advantage." She tried to smile, but realized the expression probably came off more like a painful grimace. "Look, do we have to worry about this now? We're still working on this case together." She slipped her arms down, curling into his body as best she could. "You're still my big bodyguard, aren't you?"

After nuzzling his neck for a few moments, Faith relaxed as the tension in Adam's muscles slackened. She understood that he wasn't the type to sneak around or lie to his friends, so as much as she desired a clandestine affair beyond this case, she realized she might not get her wish. When he kissed her forehead, then her nose, then each cheek, she knew she'd learn to deal. She wanted Adam now. She wanted Adam in the future, too, but if she couldn't have him, that's the way the waves broke on the shore. She'd move on. She'd have to. He wouldn't leave her any other choice.

IF ADAM HAD HAD A VOICE in the matter, he and Faith might have lazed in her private sunbathing haven for much longer than the hour they allowed themselves. He knew he had a job to do—an investigation to conduct, a murderer to catch—but damn it if for the first time in his life, something else had a shot at competing for his attention. Actually, someone else. Faith.

They took turns in the shower. While she washed and blow-dried her hair, Adam received the call he'd been expecting. Tim had found Felix Moody's mother, but she'd been on her way to work as a housekeeper at a fancy hotel on the coast. They'd have to wait until tomorrow to interview her, or stop in at her job. Adam made notations of the address and the name of her supervisor. According to Tim's initial call, however, Delia Moody hadn't seen her son in at least a week—and she wasn't happy about it.

Mia Peters proved easy to track down. She still worked at On Target Gun Range, though she'd been promoted from instructor to manager. She worked until seven o'clock that evening, giving Adam and Faith just enough time to fight the rush-hour traffic, such as it was in Courage Bay, and confront the woman who may or may not have tried to kill Faith.

"You sure you want to come with me?" he asked, for likely the twentieth time. "I could drop you off at the precinct until the interview is over." He had a hard time processing that they'd been together for only a little more than a day. Or that less than twenty-four hours ago, someone had tried to kill one of them, both of them…or—a scenario he found impossible to believe—neither of them.

"I'm going," she answered, sighing with exasperation. "I'm not in any danger, Adam. You'll be standing right there."

"So will Mia Peters," he pointed out, slipping into his loafers. "With deadly weapons in very close proximity."

Faith swiped a wine-colored lipstick over her mouth, then tossed the tube into her purse. "She's not going to try to kill me in front of the chief of detectives."

Faith had chosen to wear black, a tight pinstriped suit with a white, button-down blouse that was tailored to her curves and sported wide lapels and a plunging neckline. Even though he was supposed to have been concentrating on getting dressed himself, he'd found himself fascinated by every step she took to enhance her natural beauty. From the colors she chose to put on her face to the thin silver chain she'd wrapped around her tummy so that a tiny medallion teased from beneath her jacket, Faith grew more and more alluring with each moment.

His voice was hoarse when he replied. "You have a point."

As they drove to the gun range, they chitchatted, with Faith recounting a few wild tales from her road trips to various beaches with her sister. He had no trouble believing Kalani Apalo was a master on a surfboard, but Faith riding the waves proved harder to picture. He probably hadn't been on a board since high school, so he declined her offer to take him out first thing tomorrow morning. They were, after all, potentially on the run from a sniper. Frolicking out in the open, with high cliffs around them and an ocean to drown in, didn't seem prudent to the cop in him. The man in him simply preferred playing indoors with Faith, relegating all outdoor activities to her secret garden.

On Target Gun Range was in a small town not far from Courage Bay, and when they arrived, Adam didn't recognize any of the patrons or the management. The Courage Bay Police Department had its own private range that officers could use anytime. On Target wasn't fancy, but the weapons in the display case looked clean and legal. And Mia Peters, who entered her office in slim black slacks, a simple blue button-down blouse, heeled boots and goggles, looked every inch the part of an efficient shop manager.

"Ms. Lawton, how can I help you?" she greeted Faith, removing the goggles.

The smile seemed genuine, and the soft twang of the woman's southern accent injected her tone with real graciousness. Faith shot Adam a surprised glance, then extended her hand to the woman who, less than three months ago, had threatened her life.

"This is Detective Adam Guthrie of the Courage Bay Police Department. I was wondering if we could ask you a few questions."

Mia nodded, her ponytail swinging as she shook Adam's hand. Her gaze swept over him with barely checked interest, and Adam bit the inside of his mouth to keep from blushing. "Sure. I get cops in here all the time. Have a seat. Can I get you something to drink? I just brewed fresh coffee."

Again, Faith seemed stunned by the woman's courteous attitude. Adam took out his notebook and flipped to a blank page. Perhaps Faith had her clients confused?

"No, thank you," Adam answered. "We just need to know where you were yesterday afternoon around five o'clock."

It was Mia Peters's turn to be shocked. Her green eyes widened to the size of half dollars. "Excuse me?"

"There was a shooting at the Courage Bay courthouse yesterday afternoon," Adam told her, watching her carefully, attempting to gauge her reactions, sniff out any clue to her involvement or guilt.

"I know, I saw it on the news. That crazy doctor was murdered." She turned to Faith. "You were his attorney. You were there."

Faith only nodded.

"I don't understand. Why are you asking me about it? Did the weapon come from our gun shop?"

After clearing her throat, Faith answered the question.

"Someone tried to kill me yesterday." Her voice held a slight tremor. Either she still didn't believe the bullet had been meant for her, or being in the presence of the woman who had threatened her life was unnerving her.

Adam doubted the second explanation. He knew from personal experience that Faith wasn't easy to intimidate. And nothing in Mia Peters's body language reflected any antagonism or rage. None at all. Which was odd, judging from Faith's description of her last skirmish with the woman.

Mia glanced back and forth between Adam and Faith, obviously perplexed. "And you think I had something to do with the shooting?"

Faith leaned forward. "You did threaten my life a few months ago—or have you forgotten?"

"What?" Mia slumped back into her chair and placed her hands at her temples. "Oh God. Oh…my…God. Yes, I remember, but…" Her eyes welled but she didn't cry. She took a deep, calming breath, struggling to keep control.

Adam had seen a lot of women turn on the waterworks to manipulate, but he'd never seen one turn them off for that same reason.

"I was so screwed up then, Ms. Lawton," Mia explained. "I'd been with Roland for two years. Met him at a gun show in Los Angeles. He was so classy. He really snowed me good—all the gifts he bought me, big promises he made. Never having to work again. Mansion in the valley. Summer home in Vail. I didn't grow up with much and I've worked here forever, but I hadn't gotten a raise or promotion in years. The former owner didn't like that I wouldn't sleep with him, and he'd put the word out to other range owners that I was unreliable. I think he didn't fire me just to avoid a lawsuit.

Anyway, when Roland was arrested, I was in a real bad place. I was desperate to get Roland off so he could take care of me again, make things better."

"But now?" Adam asked, abandoning his pencil. His gut screamed that Mia Peters had nothing to do with the shooting, but he had to hear the whole story before he decided for sure.

"The range changed ownership about a month ago, and believe it or not," she said sheepishly, "the new owner is a great guy. A real entrepreneur. He's scheduled a major renovation that's starting next week. We hit it off instantly and he promoted me to manager. We're running the place like partners. I don't even see Roland anymore. The only time I think about him is when I want to remind myself about how far I've come in such a short time."

She stood and crossed around to Faith. "Ms. Lawton, my behavior in your office was horrible. I didn't mean any of the threats, I swear. I've had no contact with Roland and I wouldn't do anything to jeopardize all I have right now, especially by trying to kill someone."

Faith pressed her lips together, nodded, then locked stares with Adam. She obviously believed the woman. Good, because so did he.

"Just to be sure, do you have an alibi for yesterday afternoon at five o'clock?" he asked.

Mia pressed her hand to her chest, exhaling with relief. "I was teaching a concealed permit class. We started at five. The classroom part lasted an hour, and then we spent another hour on the range. I have eight guys and two women enrolled, Detective. I can give you a copy of the roster."

Adam accepted the copy, and after answering a few curious questions Mia had about the sniper, they prepared to leave.

Faith turned to Mia just as they were about to exit her office and held out her hand again.

"I'm sorry, Ms. Peters, that I suspected you of trying to kill me."

Mia grinned, her eyes again glossy with emotion. "No apology, Ms. Lawton. I can be a real raving bitch when I'm desperate. It's not pretty. You had no way of knowing I wasn't some crazy lunatic."

Mia took Faith's hand. They shook professionally, but then Faith placed her other hand over Mia's, giving her a gentle, friendly squeeze. "We're all crazy lunatics from time to time. I hope you stay away from Roland McGee. Even if you lost this job tomorrow, you don't need a guy like him to hold you up. You can do that yourself, I'll bet."

The smile that spread over Mia's face seemed to light the room. "Damn straight."

As they left the building, sunset had descended. Adam wished they were near the water, but instead, the mountains blocked the view of the sun drifting down into the Pacific. Still, the brilliant violet and orange hues added a romantic air even to the dusty, dry atmosphere of the parking lot.

If he was honest with himself for a minute, he'd admit that Faith's presence made him wax poetic. Who would have guessed? Not him.

"Well, that's that. Mia Peters was the only person who had a motive to hurt me. I'm assuming you're crossing her off the list."

"You assume correctly," he said, resisting the urge to cup her elbow as they walked.

He scanned the parking lot, suddenly uneasy. Only about six cars, all locked tight and empty, remained, probably belonging to employees, since the range had closed while they spoke to Mia Peters. Not a single car or truck rolled down the highway just outside the entrance, an access road.

"So now it's time to focus on Felix or the possibility that the person who shot George Yube wasn't aiming for either of us," she said.

Adam opened his mouth to agree that she might have a point. The bullet that skimmed by his ear changed his mind.

CHAPTER TWELVE

NOT AGAIN!

Faith dove toward the car, but not before another volley of bullets rent the air. Adam slammed into her on the way down and he rolled to block her body with his, contorting his arms to reach his weapon. He drew, but with nowhere specific to aim, they could only wait and pray they got out of this alive.

"Damn," Adam said. "We've got no cover. I should have—"

"Can we get back to the building?"

Adam glanced around for his dropped keys. He fished them out of the parking lot gravel, right beside the tire. He disengaged the locks, but the flash of his lights must have alerted the sniper. The jerk used four good bullets to shoot out the windshield.

"Looks like he doesn't want us to go anywhere," Adam quipped.

Faith gulped for air, but her voice came out steady and strong. "I have no trouble complying with his request. We're not moving. Why is he still shooting?"

Adam shook his head, then combed his hand through his hair, right at the place where he imagined the bullet had nearly sliced off his ear. Who knew why this maniac did anything? God, another few inches and Adam would have been shot through the brain. He had to thank God this guy wasn't a crack shot—but at the same time, the sixty-four thousand dollar question had finally been answered.

Adam could no longer doubt who the sniper's bullets were intended for. The shooter was after him.

Part of him sagged in relief, knowing that as long as he got her away from here, Faith would be safe. She'd been walking slightly ahead of him and to his left. If the sniper had wanted Faith dead, she would have provided the easier target.

Unfortunately, the other part of him—the part that resented that this lunatic had tried to snuff him out—got pissed off real quick. Whoever the hell this asshole was, Adam wasn't going down without a fight.

"I don't know what his plan is," he said through clenched teeth, "but I'm not waiting around here like a bull's-eye."

He scooted around toward the driver's door. With the glass shattered into a tight cobweb across the front of the vehicle, the shooter likely couldn't see if Adam attempted to enter the car. If he could put Faith into the back seat on the floorboard and then drive around to the back of the building, they'd have a shot at getting out of here alive.

"What are you doing?" she asked frantically, when he reached up and flipped the handle. The door opened an inch. The interior light did not go on—probably damaged by the gunfire.

"What does it look like I'm doing? I'm getting you the hell out of here."

"Adam, the gun range is closed. Someone inside probably heard the shots. They've called 911 by now. We should just sit tight and wait for the police."

"I am the police," he growled.

"Let me be more specific, then. You're one man with a .38

against some crazed loon with a scope and a rifle. You're out-gunned, Adam. Deal with it."

He smirked, though the expression did nothing to soften her steely glare. She sure got tough and bossy when she was in danger. Probably better than weepy and hysterical, but at least he knew from experience that she could be reasoned with even in the most tense situations. Although, once he really thought about it, he'd rather not have any knowledge at all about how Faith reacted to life-threatening situations. Above all else, he wanted her safe. Never in his life had someone else been injured because he'd screwed up. He'd do whatever it took to get her out of the line of fire.

"Do you hear sirens?" he asked.

She cocked her head to listen, then answered, "No."

"Where's your cell phone?"

"In the car," she said. "Yours?"

Adam dug into his pocket and cursed. No service. The mountains must have blocked the signal.

"We're on our own here, Lawton. The longer we wait, the longer he has to change positions and get a better shot. Look around. The mountains surround us on three sides. You want to wait around and let this guy pin us down like ducks frozen in a pond?"

"It doesn't freeze in Southern California," she snapped, but with a frown that told him he'd made a point she simply didn't want to concede.

Adam grinned. "Well, it's going to have to be freezing somewhere farther south before I give in to some kook, even if he does have a bigger gun and a better view. Get in the car, Faith. A moving target is always harder to hit."

She hesitated, but her eyes bored into his. Yes, he could see her fear, but he could also see the mechanisms of her brain working on the formula for action he'd just given her. Get in the car and we'll get to safety. Sit here and die.

She crawled to him on her hands and knees. He opened the door only a few inches and she squeezed through, keeping her head low. Once she was in, he closed the door tight and opened the driver's side. The trick would be starting and flooring the car without hitting anything on his way to the back of the building. He scanned the parking lot one last time, memorizing everything he saw and trying like hell to judge distances.

His best bet was to move in reverse. A straight shot back about fifty feet, then a quick left spin and straight on would expose the side and back windows to the sniper for only a few seconds. They hadn't parked that far away from the building. He could do this. He could save Faith. And himself. He gulped air, psyching himself up with the same positive mantras and chants he used when competing on the ball field or when preparing to confront an armed and dangerous criminal.

When his confidence hit a peak, he dashed into the car, folded himself low in the seat, turned the key, yanked the car into Reverse and punched the gas.

Gravel and dirt spun and cracked. He heard dings against the car, but Adam couldn't tell if bullets or small rocks protesting against his speeding tires were to blame for the sounds that made Faith yelp. Didn't matter. He jerked the steering wheel, throwing the car into as close to a controlled spin as he could manage. Faith screamed again when a back wheel jumped, likely over a parking barrier. After a fast gear-shift, he punched the gas again and propelled the car behind the building. Except for scraping the doors against something—probably the mailbox he'd noticed earlier—they were mere inches from safety.

He jammed his foot down on the brake. "You okay, Faith?"

"Just dandy."

"Stay down."

"Why do you keep telling me that? Does the word *duh* mean anything to you?"

He exited the car and crept to open hers, grinning at her sarcastic humor despite the danger. The minute he poked his head around the door, he was treated to a clear and unhampered view of her shapely legs and thighs. An ill-timed come-on lingered on his tongue, but before he could proposition her about back seats, the exit door of the gun range burst open.

Mia Peters leaned halfway out, gesturing with her arm in a circle, as if the motion would propel them to safety at the speed of her hand. "Come on! We called the cops! Get in here."

They didn't have to be asked twice. After he'd helped Faith out of the car, they made a quick dash to the door. No one fired. Had their escape spooked the shooter, or did his location keep him from pursuit? And for how long?

Adam hustled Faith and Mia away from the back door and toward the cavernous shooting range. Once he saw Faith throw herself into a chair, he jogged back to the door, and locked and bolted it. When he returned, the women were sitting in a close huddle.

"Anyone hurt?" he asked, glancing around at the terrified expressions of Mia and two other female employees who both looked as if guns scared them beyond reason, even if they did work around the things all day long.

"We're all fine," Mia said. "Unless one of you is hurt? Janie here had one foot out the front door when the first shots were fired. She ran back in and alerted us."

Adam narrowed his gaze. If he wanted to be with anyone

in the middle of a sniper attack, people familiar with guns were a good choice.

"From which direction was the sniper shooting?" he asked Janie, a butch brunette in a ponytail and high-tops.

"Northeast," she answered, pointing toward the front of the building, where the hill was heavily wooded. "About halfway up. I told that to 911 when Mia called."

"That's a private road up there," Mia added. "It snakes around to a subdivision on the other side of the hill. But it's no short jaunt. Must be one powerful gun he's got."

Powerful? Sure. This wasn't an everyday weapon—likely not the same one he'd used at the courthouse, either. Still, no wonder the guy had little accuracy. He wasn't exactly close by, and wind and a hundred other natural conditions would play on a bullet shot from so far away.

"Did you see anything else?" he asked Janie. "A car? The shooter?"

Janie shook her head, looking both despondent and resigned. Then, she pursed her lips and seemed to think hard.

"I only looked up for an instant," Janie said. "Other than a quick flash to let me know where he was, I didn't see anything else."

"A flash? A gun barrel, maybe?" he asked, desperate for information that could point them to the sniper.

"No, probably the sun's reflection off the sight. But if he was a real professional, he'd know how to angle his gun so as not to give away his position, especially at sunset."

As Adam mulled over that logical conclusion, Faith reestablished her steely calm and asked, "Where's everyone else?"

Mia had directed her into a chair, and the one-time suspect had her hand pressed on Faith's back as if she meant to push her head between her legs if the attorney showed any signs of passing out.

Mia shook her head. "They're in the gun room, loading up. If you're going to have a gun battle, this is the place to hole up. The front door is locked and all the glass is bulletproof. We're safe here."

Adam strode forward, pulling out the .38 he'd reholstered just before jumping into the driver's seat. "This isn't a gun battle. This is a sniper situation. I need to contact the police chief."

"Is this Zirinsky's jurisdiction?" Faith asked.

Adam cursed. It wasn't. But since this was an ongoing investigation, he could pull some strings with the locals. The community where the gun range paid their taxes abutted Courage Bay. More than likely, Max Zirinsky knew the cops in charge.

"The locals will be here soon. We'll deal with jurisdiction issues then. But Max needs to know what is happening."

Faith nodded, combing her hand through her hair and cursing at the bits of dirt and gravel she found there. She couldn't believe that only minutes after eliminating Mia Peters as a suspect in the threats, they'd run smack-dab into the real killer—still shooting, yet still hiding, using distance as an effective cover. For a blissful few moments, she'd imagined she and Adam could steal a bit more time. Not so. The danger had just ratcheted up to code red.

Adam struggled with his cell phone. "Still no signal."

"The phone is this way," Mia volunteered.

Silence pressed down on them until sirens wailed. Faith dashed to the front window in time to see the blue lights atop three patrol cars wind up the private road on the hill across from them. Adam had Max on the line, and when he returned to her side, he informed her that the chief and a detail from Courage Bay were on the way.

"Any information on Felix Moody?" she asked, knowing the investigation had turned, whether Adam liked it or not, to his most vocal enemy. They hadn't had a moment to discuss the shooting, but she knew he'd almost been hit. He probably didn't realize that he'd suddenly developed a habit of combing his hand through his hair—on the left side. Right where she guessed the bullet had ripped between them as they crossed the parking lot.

"We've got a mole in Moody's neighborhood who has a lead. I'm going to meet with him tonight."

She stared at him. "You're meeting with *Felix?*"

"No, the mole."

"Still," she said, turning and grasping his arm just above the elbow, "Adam, it's obvious now that you are the target. Either that, or this guy couldn't hit the side of a barn with an elephant gun. I was in front out there, but the bullet whizzed closer to you."

He jabbed his fingers through the hair at his temple. Again. "I know. That's why I've got to go after Moody. If he's not the shooter, the investigation is back to square one."

Faith swallowed, knowing Adam wasn't the type to live in fear. She couldn't imagine him holing up anywhere beyond a few days, any more than she could imagine him letting someone else take over the investigation now that he knew he was the target. He'd delegated enough of the detective work up until now, obviously operating on the premise that his time was better spent protecting Faith. They had, after all, found marvelous ways to pass the time. But now things had changed. The case had just turned *very* personal.

"You're going after him," Faith guessed.

"Wouldn't you?" he countered.

She inhaled but didn't respond, knowing the answer wouldn't help her keep him safe.

"Stay with me," she begged. "We were going to figure this out together, remember? Felix likes me. I can help."

Adam shook his head. "I won't put you in danger, Faith. Moody may like you right this minute," he said, then lowered his voice, "but that won't mean squat if he finds out you've been sleeping with me."

"You mean, now I'm a liability?"

"Not exactly. But you've been shot at enough, don't you think? If I'm the real target, you'll be safer away from me."

She released his arm. Suddenly, touching him brought no comfort, no passion. Just cold loneliness.

"We don't know for sure that you're the only target. The evidence is circumstantial at best."

He nodded, his gaze fixed outside the window as two more police cars pulled into the parking lot, one more from the local department and one from Courage Bay.

"Sometimes circumstantial evidence is all we have to go on. Max has agreed to continue your protective detail for a few more days. Until we're sure where this case is going…"

"But I'm no longer a choice assignment, huh?"

The comment was meant as a joke, but the crack in her voice ruined the punch line. She crossed her arms and tried not to look defensive, struggled to keep her emotions in check. She couldn't protect Adam. He was the one with the training and experience to make sure he didn't get hurt. And yet, she wanted to be with him, provide a second set of eyes. She had a few talents she could offer him beyond the bedroom, mainly her connections with the current suspect and her analytical mind.

"Faith," he said, his hand reaching out for hers. "I can't put you in more danger. If anything happened to you because of me, I don't know what I'd do. Please don't ask me to keep you in danger just because you're still lusting after my bod."

His joke worked. They both dissolved into laughter, just as the police entered the building. From that moment on, Faith hardly had two seconds to speak to Adam. They were all interviewed separately, though once Adam flashed his badge he was able to leave the building and join his colleagues outside. She could only watch from the window.

He came back in shortly after a second car from Courage Bay tore into the parking lot. Max Zirinsky, his boss, remained outside, but Adam returned with a tough-looking uniformed officer named Chandler.

"Tad Chandler, this is Faith Lawton."

He nodded. "Ma'am."

Faith eyed the man, not the least bit skeptical that he could scare off even the most determined killer with just a scowl. He was as mean-looking as a heavyweight boxer, with dark hair, dark eyes and a perpetual scowl. She shivered, then awarded Adam silent points for choosing his replacement with care.

"Nice to meet you, Officer. Just where is Detective Guthrie banishing me to?"

Chandler didn't so much as glance in Adam's direction. "Back to your family, Ms. Lawton. I'll take you there myself, then pull the first shift making sure you're safe. My partner is on her way. She'll take a second position."

Faith glanced at Adam. "Two bodyguards?"

His grin didn't quite reach his eyes. "Better safe than sorry. Chandler here and his partner, Pam Cortlandt, will switch off in shifts. Zirinsky's orders. Hopefully, we'll clear this case quickly, if no one screws up."

"Including you," she pointed out. From what she'd witnessed, Adam wasn't a reckless cop. He was logical, methodical. Calm. But she'd also watched his eyes turn cold and determined when he spoke about how the sniper had nearly killed him.

"I'll be careful if you will," he answered.

That gave her an opening. "Sounds like a deal, if…"

"If what?" Adam asked, hands on hips.

Chandler crossed his arms over his massive chest and widened his stance, apparently very interested in the deal Faith was about to strike.

She squared her shoulders. "If you let me interview Delia Moody myself."

Adam sniffed, his gaze steady, his chin set in stone. "Why?"

Always willing to listen to logic. She loved that about him—that and so much more. "She trusts me. Delia, for the most part, is an honest, hardworking, down-on-her-luck woman. A lot like my own mother. Felix has let her down, lied to her, manipulated her, used her love for him against her for years. If I ask my questions the right way, I might find out more about Felix than just where he's been hiding."

He nodded slightly, following her reasoning. "If Moody is our shooter, he might be on his way to his mother's right now, looking for an alibi or someplace to crash."

"I'll see her at work. If he is on the run, he won't go to the hotel. Too many people around."

"More people means better cover," Adam countered.

"Yeah, but I'll have this fine officer with me. If you want, I can even bring my father. I have a strong suspicion that once Chandler here delivers me to the doorstep of my family, I won't be leaving without an escort who bears a Hawaiian surname."

She smirked, but secretly cherished how protective her family could be. Now wasn't the time to spout off about independence and self-reliance. They'd instilled those qualities in her long ago. In the face of a killer, she needed her family, her friends and her colleagues. And so did Adam.

He nodded to Chandler, who read the quiet communication and stepped away. Adam cupped his hand under her elbow and guided her toward Mia's office, though they didn't go inside. And even after he leaned forward to speak softly into her ear, he didn't let go of her. She didn't want him to. The contact, tenuous and tentative though it was, might be all they would share for a few days—maybe longer.

"Faith, I trust you to be smart about this. Don't put yourself in any danger. There's no need."

"And I have no desire to put myself in danger, Adam. If you haven't noticed, my instincts for self-preservation are fairly well honed. Besides, I have something to live for, remember?" She snaked a single fingertip up his arm, relying on the commotion around them to mask her intimate touch. "The anticipation of our next secret rendezvous might drive me crazy, but I won't lose my ability to think. Not until you take that away yourself, understand?"

From the way his irises darkened, he fully comprehended her meaning. If she had to entice him to take care of himself by promising another night of great sex, then so be it. She wouldn't exactly be sacrificing her morals or her heart. She cared about Adam more than she could say—to him or to herself. Everything had happened so fast between them, and under stressful circumstances. She needed time to sort out all the particulars, but the bottom line was clear.

She didn't want Adam to die. Not today, not tonight—not

ever. Even if she couldn't have him once the case was a bitter memory on a yellowing police report, she still wanted him alive, happy and, hopefully, cherishing the memories of their wild affair.

CHAPTER THIRTEEN

WHEN ADAM WALKED into the parking lot to clear his stuff out of his car so the windshield could be repaired, he hadn't expected to see his brother, Casey, inspecting the damage. His motorcycle, gleaming in black and silver chrome, leaned on its kickstand, looking every inch the powerful hog it was. This wasn't his department-issued bike, but his special edition, 100th Anniversary Harley-Davidson Fatboy. Adam licked his lips, the center of his gut fluttering with the possibility of commandeering his brother's iron and chrome ride and taking to the open road with no destination, no timetable, no speed limit. But seeing as that action wasn't exactly the smartest thing for the target of a sniper to do, he'd have to put the adventure off. As usual.

Casey, obviously off duty in his torn, faded jeans and Dodgers T-shirt, turned when he heard Adam's steps crunch the gravel. He hooked his thumb at the shattered windshield, a wry grin on his unshaven face. "I knew you always hated your official police sedan, but this is a little extreme, don't you think?"

Adam grinned, slapped his brother on the back. He wasn't too surprised when Casey held on for a moment longer than usual, executing the kind of half hug that men were infamous for. He had, after all, almost been killed. Again.

"Maybe they'll upgrade me to a convertible," he joked.

Casey rolled his eyes. "Right now, I'm hoping they'll find you one of the cast-off Popemobiles with the bulletproof glass. You're a pain in the ass, but I still kind of like having a brother. Who is this guy?"

Adam shook his head. "Not sure." He gazed up at the hill, and through the trees could see a few patrol cars parked at the side of the private road. Had they found something? "Give me a lift up there, would you?"

Casey nodded and yanked out an extra helmet. Adam put it on, but when he turned toward the building, he saw Faith and Officer Chandler on their way out. His stomach dropped, but he pasted on a smile and gave her a wave, which she returned. Damn, he hated leaving her. He hated turning her safety over to someone else, even if the likelihood of her still being in danger was slim. Even if he might be the cause for the danger she'd faced so far.

Oh, who was he kidding? He didn't hate leaving her because he thought she might get hurt. He hated leaving her because she was the single most exciting, beautiful, smart, alluring woman he'd ever met.

"Who's that?" Casey asked.

"Faith Lawton," Adam answered, his tone even.

"The attorney? I went to school with her, didn't I?"

Adam grunted his acknowledgment. In response, his brother eyed him skeptically, taking his sweet time buckling his helmet strap beneath his chin.

"Hear you've had her in protective custody since yesterday."

Adam scowled. "So?"

Casey nodded and mounted the bike. Adam climbed on behind him. The roar of the engine effectively blocked any further discussion, and Adam was glad. Like Adam, Casey was a certified bachelor. Unlike him, Casey skirted the edge between playboy and player. His devil-may-care attitude extended to all aspects of his life, even his career in law enforcement. Casey was a great cop, but he rode a bike, volunteered for dangerous assignments and generally walked on the wildest side he could walk without landing in serious trouble.

And his mind hardly ever strayed from the topic of women, meaning that if Adam showed the least clue that his interest in Faith went beyond this case, Casey would pick up on it. Adam didn't much care about that, but Casey would also have questions and he'd want answers—answers Adam couldn't give.

They made it up to the secondary crime scene quickly, where Adam found Max Zirinsky squatting near the side of the road, supervising as a technician poured plaster into a wood frame that likely surrounded a tire print.

"Anything?" Adam asked, marching over to his boss.

"Quite a bit, actually, for this case," Max said. "We've got a track here and one shell casing so far from over there." He pointed toward the trees nearby. "Doesn't look like the same gun as yesterday, but that doesn't mean it wasn't the same shooter. He could have a whole collection. And," he said, waving over one of the techs, "we have this."

He held up an evidence bag. Inside was a half-crushed beer can stuffed with tissue.

"It's trash," Adam said, eyeing the can skeptically.

Max shook his head. "It's fresh trash. Take a whiff—the beer isn't stale yet. Our shooter might have indulged to fortify his nerves before he shot."

Adam slipped on the latex gloves he'd stashed in his pocket, then took the bag. "Maybe that's why the bastard missed. You going for prints and DNA?"

The tech took the bag from Adam and headed back to the department's van.

"DNA is too slow. I'll be happy with a print."

Adam would throw a party for a print. "What about witnesses?"

"None but the woman from the gun range. I'm talking to the media in an hour. We'll put out a call and see if anyone else saw anything."

A quick glance around and Adam shook his head. This road and the one below it, even now, were practically deserted.

Max straightened and Adam wondered if he was going to be pulled off the investigation now that the evidence pointed toward him being the target. If Max ordered him into protective custody, he was pretty sure he'd go nuts.

"Anything on the note?"

"Other than bad grammar, no. No prints, nothing remarkable about the ink."

"Tim went out to the accountant's office and verified that the stationery was from a batch that was thrown away," Adam added, knowing they'd met yet another dead end. "The accountant had the printer dispose of the bad letterhead, which went to recycling."

Max blew out a breath in frustration. "They put it out on the curb?"

Adam nodded.

"So anyone could have had access to the stationery."

"Yup." Adam looked around, knowing his time would be limited on this investigation unless he came up with something useful. "There's a neighborhood on the other side of the curve," he volunteered.

"I already sent some patrol cars up there, but whoever it

was has had plenty of time to drive to the top, turn around and take off without anyone noticing. Still, we'll check it out."

"Mind if I take a look?"

Max pressed his lips together, and Adam knew the moment of decision had come.

"I don't have any desire to attend the funeral of my chief of detectives."

"I understand," Adam assured him.

"I don't think you do, but I know you're a good cop. Not reckless." Max glanced at Casey, who was leaning on his bike, arms crossed, puffing up a bit as a female officer strode by.

Adam coughed, hiding a grin. Everyone had his brother pegged as a daredevil, but if he ever wanted someone to watch his back, he'd pick Casey over just about anyone, any day of the week. But he also welcomed the chance to change the subject.

"My brother is the best motorcycle cop you've got."

Max grinned and shoved his hands into his pockets. "Not denying that. I just don't want you going off half-cocked. I know you suspect Felix Moody."

"He's the only suspect we have. According to his attorney, Moody spent a good amount of her billable hours complaining about me."

"Threatening you?"

"In a braggart's way, yeah. He knows I've kept the heat on him these months since his release. He hasn't been able to pull off one scam. That can't sit well with a career criminal like him. And he had sniper experience before a dishonorable discharge got him booted from the service."

Max's eyebrows shot up. "That's interesting."

Adam nodded. Another piece of useful information

provided by the lovely Faith Lawton. Man, they did make a good team. There was no denying that.

"And," Adam added, "no one has been able to find Moody since the shooting. It all adds up to justifiable suspicion, if nothing else. I think we need to bring him in."

The police chief walked toward his car. "Sounds like a plan. But I want you to check with Slade before you follow that line of investigation."

"Slade's the mole on Moody?"

Adam had known Simon Slade for years. He was an old-timer, a crook who'd run the gamut of illegal operations since before Adam was born. After an eye-opening stint in federal prison, Slade had returned to Courage Bay in an unusual capacity—professional snitch. Adam and everyone else on the force went to great lengths to protect the old man's position. Information he provided had led to many successful arrests and prosecutions. And he gave up the goods for free.

"I thought Slade liked Moody," Adam said. He'd pursued this avenue before, years ago. "He wouldn't help us at all with the murder investigation."

Max leaned into his car and removed his cell phone. "Just go listen to what the man has to say," he insisted, waving an acknowledgment to a technician who'd shouted his name. "If anyone knows anything significant about Moody, it'll be him."

Adam agreed, and after reviewing the evidence himself—three spent bullet casings and the tire print from a new-model four-wheel-drive truck—he bummed a ride back into town with Casey. The whip of the wind on his face, arms and back and the rush of the speed combined to offset the creepiness of almost being shot earlier by a gunman he couldn't see and couldn't defend himself against—short of hiding out in some hole.

By the time they reached the intersection in depressed Victoria Park, two blocks away from Slade's bar, Adam was even more determined to bring Moody into custody. A few hours of questioning might reveal if his old nemesis had had anything to do with the killing of George Yube and the threats on his life and Faith's.

Casey stopped the bike but didn't kill the engine. "So, do I look too much like a cop for this neighborhood?"

Adam grinned, then yanked the tail of his polo shirt out of his pants. He should have stopped by his place to change, but then again, Slade liked it when cops came in, so long as they didn't stop and drink. Made him look like the go-to guy for criminal activity, which was how he got all his great information. Adam figured that Slade fed information to the perps the same way he helped law enforcement. *Quid pro quo* for betraying his element.

"You never look like a cop," Adam said.

Casey grinned. "Thanks, bro."

Two central streets ran through Victoria Park. At the crossroads stood an area the police nicknamed The Lair due to frequent criminal activity. Casey parked the bike on the sidewalk. Two guys with long beards and tattoos stopped to admire the machine, so Casey hung around. Adam pushed through the doors to Slade's establishment and was immediately greeted by the stench of stale cigarette smoke and spilled beer. The *crack* and *pop* of billiards broke through the dueling sounds of loud, slurred conversation and blues on the jukebox. He found Slade, as always, behind the bar, puffing on a Monte Cristo cigar.

Adam caught his eye. The old man nodded toward the back of the room and Adam followed him there.

"Detective Guthrie," Slade greeted, his voice permanently gravelly thanks to years of smoking and a bout with throat cancer. "Who you looking for this time?"

Adam tried to fight the instinct to look over his shoulder. He'd come into Slade's bar armed, but he couldn't quite keep his back to the wall as he preferred. "Felix Moody."

"Moody?" Slade said, then extracted his cigar and spit on the floor. "That punk?"

At that moment, Adam knew this trip was worth the trouble and the stench. "I thought you and Moody were compadres."

The old man skewed his leathery face in disgust. "Bad enough he deals drugs. Now he's using 'em, too."

Adam cleared his throat, attempting to hide his surprise. Few of the dealers around here, especially upper-level crooks like Felix Moody, actually used their own wares. The competition for territory and customers was too stiff. A crook had to be sharp to stay alive. What had changed for Moody?

"When did this start?"

"Few months ago. After he got out, but couldn't take a piss without some cop calling it in. Moody didn't like the pen. Likes his privacy. He was free, but couldn't pick his nose without the world knowing about it. Made him crazy."

Adam bit the inside of his mouth. He'd been entirely responsible for the twenty-four/seven tail on Moody. At the time, he'd hoped either that he'd catch the guy breaking the law and put him away for good, or that the pressure would push him out of town. Moody was always on the edge of sanity, so Adam couldn't imagine how whacked-out drugs would make him. If he'd been crazy enough to kill before, Adam could only imagine how bloodthirsty he was now.

"Why doesn't he just leave? Start fresh somewhere else?"

"He was thinking about it. Said he had business to finish first."

Adam's entire body tensed. Revenge business, perhaps? "You know where he hangs out?"

Slade shook his head. "He don't come in here no more. I gave him shit for shooting up, so he lit out. You checked with his mama?"

"Not yet. I have someone on it right now. How does mama feel about his drug use?"

Slade chomped on his cigar, turning the stogie so that the ash flitted to the floor. "She's a God-fearing woman. That boy'll be the death of her."

Adam nodded, thanked Slade and met Casey outside. Felix Moody had to be brought in. Now. Adam couldn't allow Moody to be the death of anyone—himself included.

WITH A WEARY SIGH, Faith slid into her father's car and allowed Maleko to close the door behind her. She didn't know which had been worse—having her father escort her to the interview with her former client's mother or feeling like an idiot for helping free Felix Moody in the first place.

Warrant irregularities or not, one thing became clear after speaking with Delia Moody. Both she and Delia had been manipulated and duped. Felix had been guilty as sin.

Maleko got into the driver's seat and started the engine. "Seat belt," he said to Faith, who with a patient grin complied with his request.

Her safety and happiness always ranked first with him. Had she known whom to contact, she would have nominated him for Father of the Year.

On the drive back to the restaurant, where she was camping

out until Adam gave the all-clear, Maleko made no attempt at small talk. She glanced in the vanity mirror, catching sight of the faithful Officer Chandler following in his patrol car. But after a few minutes and a turn onto the highway, Faith realized they weren't going back to the restaurant. She sat up and read the exit sign. They were headed toward the beach.

"Where are we going?" she asked.

Maleko took a deep breath, his weathered, sun-kissed hands strong at ten and two on the steering wheel, his eyes never leaving the road. "I thought you could use a little peace, the kind only the ocean can give you."

She turned as far around in her seat as the seat belt would allow her. "And my heavily armed shadow doesn't mind?"

Maleko laughed. "I'm your father. What choice did he have?"

Faith relaxed in the seat, smiling. To the world, Maleko Apalo was an easygoing showman, the consummate entertainer who embraced the free-spirited Hawaiian culture he'd left behind years ago. But Faith knew that beneath the fun and the frolic was a spine of steel and a sharp mind. How else could he deal with a powerhouse wife like Lu? Not to mention two headstrong daughters.

But mostly, the man had a heart the size of the Big Island itself. The minute they rolled into the parking lot and the cool ocean breeze slapped against the car, Faith's body lightened. If she couldn't have Adam, this diversion would work wonders.

They parked in the moonlight, alongside a half dozen other cars, all but one empty. The minute Chandler pulled in beside them, the activities of the couple inside stopped abruptly. Faith laughed and thought of Adam, entertaining a brief fantasy of them making out in the back seat of his big, department-issue sedan. Maybe being caught by one of the men he supervised. What a scene that would make! Still, for all the scandal and angst such a scenario might inspire, she couldn't help speculating about how much fun it would be.

She couldn't believe how connected she felt to Adam after only a couple of days, and she thanked God she hadn't quite realized at the time how close he'd come to dying just a few hours ago. How did police officers' wives deal with that fear all the time? Did they do as she did and simply try not to think about it? Live for the moment?

They got out of the car and descended the wooden steps to the boardwalk and then to the shore. Though it was September, summer still spiced the nippy night air with the scents of suntan oil and baked sand. Faith kicked off her shoes. Maleko did the same. Officer Chandler, who trailed about ten feet behind them, didn't bother. He alternated between watching them and watching the parking lot above them, his flashlight poking into the shadowy areas near the rocks. He caught another kissing couple. Faith shook her head, amused. And jealous.

The roar of the Pacific beating the shore lulled her into a cocoon of sound and sensation. The wind and rustle of the palms, the strong scent of salt, the grit and bite of sand, shell and rock beneath her feet—all transported her to a different world. Unfortunately, her worry followed her to this new place and almost blocked the sound of Maleko's sympathetic voice as he spoke close to her ear.

"You couldn't have known he was guilty, Faith. Even the mother didn't know until after he was released."

She nodded, still sick to her stomach that she'd helped a killer walk free. According to Delia, who'd initially convinced Faith to take Felix's case on behalf of his children, she herself was now being punished soundly for her web of lies by a son who'd betrayed her. The children Delia had produced in Faith's office on the day of her initial visit hadn't been Felix's kids at all. They were his nieces and nephews, the offspring of his sister. True, the family relied on Felix to help feed and clothe the children, but since his release, he'd done nothing but spend what little money he had on hustling for drugs. Delia had taken on two additional jobs to fill the shortfall and constantly had to fend off threats from Felix's associates in the drug trade. She was terrified for her daughter and grandchildren.

The older woman had become nearly hysterical with humiliation and rage when recounting how her son had finally reduced himself to a common junkie. She'd chased him off for good after she caught him mixing meth in her kitchen.

Tears had streamed down her face as she confessed that in one of Felix's drug-induced rages, he admitted that he had indeed killed the man he'd been convicted of murdering. He'd stashed the gun in Jasmine's apartment in an attempt to set her up for the crime. Felix had screamed and cursed and roared. How could the cops not have blamed her? She'd been the guy's ex-lover. She had a record, including charges on battery and assault. He'd never killed anyone before. He'd never done anything worse than selling smack to kids. Why hadn't they arrested the bitch instead of him?

Why? To Felix, there had been one answer—Detective Adam Guthrie.

"I think Felix killed George Yube, Maleko. I think he was aiming for Adam and hit Yube by mistake. If that's the case, then I'm partly responsible for George's death."

Maleko cleared his throat but then was silent. He'd made his opinion regarding George Yube clear months ago, when

Faith had first taken on the case. He wasn't the type to repeat himself, but he also wouldn't mourn a man he thought guilty of crimes as serious as Felix's.

"The only person who deserves blame is the man who pulled the trigger," he said finally. "He made his choices. You've made yours. You need to learn to live with that."

"But what if he hurts someone else before he's caught? Delia said she hasn't seen him in a week, that none of his friends have seen him, either."

"Maybe he left town," Maleko reasoned.

"Maybe, but there's every possibility that he's the man who also tried to kill Adam today. Adam heard the bullet fly right by his ear. Another inch or two…I couldn't live with myself if Adam gets hurt because I helped Felix out of jail."

Maleko hugged her a little tighter. "Faith, was the evidence against Felix properly obtained?"

"No," she said, hating how argumentative and high-pitched her voice sounded.

"Then you did what you were supposed to do. You aren't a judge. Meting out justice is not your role in the system. You're a defense attorney and you look out for the rights of those who are arrested. Maybe if your mother had had an attorney as good as you, she never would have gone to jail."

Faith hugged Maleko closer. Yes, she missed her mother. She mourned for her each and every time she walked into, or even passed by, her home office, filled with the paperwork from the bogus arrest and conviction. If she had the chance to change things, she would want her mother back in her life. But she couldn't change the past any more than she could predict the future.

"I'm worried about Adam," she said simply.

"He seems very capable. I'm sure he's taking every precaution."

Faith frowned. She'd called Adam from the hotel immediately after her interview with Delia. He'd assured her several times that he was safe and had someone watching his back while he looked into Felix's possible involvement. He'd already learned about the ex-con's drug use, but having the verification from Delia seemed to help. Faith had wanted so desperately to do more, but when he'd disconnected the call, she'd had no sense of when she'd talk to him or see him next.

"He's a very intelligent man," she confirmed.

Maleko nodded. "Probably the smartest you've ever brought home to meet us."

She grinned, knowing where this conversation was leading and not entirely surprised that her foster father had swung their chat in this direction. Though Lu, as a woman, had the reputation of being the family matchmaker, Faith knew that Maleko never separated himself from anything his wife took on as a project. Like any successful couple, they were a team in every sense of the word, just as she and Adam had turned out to be in the short time they'd been paired together. As friends. As lovers.

God, she missed him. And they'd been apart, what? Three or four hours?

"But if he's so smart, he wouldn't have gotten mixed up with me, you know," she said.

"That's a ridiculous thing to say. You're a wonderful woman."

"I'm married to my job."

"Only because you haven't had a better offer from a decent man," Maleko countered.

"And why is that?" Faith asked, indignant. "If I'm such a great catch, why am I still out in the ocean, swimming free?"

Maleko wrapped his arm around her shoulders and gazed down at her with total disbelief. "And here I thought you were some sort of genius, whizzing through law school, passing the bar on your first try. I had no idea you could be so dense." He attempted to soften his criticism by giving her a little squeeze. "Thankfully, you only seem to be stupid when it comes to men."

She opened her mouth to protest his insult, then promptly shut it. Yes, she'd had lots of relationships, most of which had ended amicably—but only because in the long run, little passion existed between her and her lover. She always picked nice guys. Smart guys. Safe guys. Men outside her professional circle. Accountants and business owners, even a baseball player. But despite the diversity, none of them ever challenged her, ever involved themselves too deeply in her life—and eventually, they bored her. Every one of them was the exact opposite of Adam Guthrie.

Everything about him thrilled her to the point where she could hardly form a coherent thought. Every inch of her yearned to learn more about him, explore him—and not just in the physical sense. She wanted to know more about his childhood, his family. His plans and hopes and dreams for the future. But mostly, she wanted to know how the hell two people on opposite sides of the justice system could ever remain together once the going got tough.

The pressure was inevitable. She had no intention of giving up her career, nor did Adam. Sooner or later, they'd have to face off in court—or worse, burden their clients and co-workers by having to excuse themselves from a case. She couldn't see how their relationship, if indeed they established one, would survive another cross-examination like the one that had prefaced his saving her life yesterday afternoon. At the time, he'd been just another cop she could dissect on the stand. Now he was a man who knew some of her most intimate secrets. A man who had touched her heart.

"Am I supposed to thank you for calling me stupid?" she asked Maleko, even if she had no evidence or proof with which to counter his claim.

He laughed. "Only if it makes you see how pigheaded you can be. You may not have been born into our family, but you've inherited that trait from your sister and your mother."

"Pigheaded? Don't you mean 'afraid of commitment'? Terrified that I'll put my heart on the line just to get it trampled? I loved my parents, and they didn't exactly put my needs first, did they?"

That stopped him. He halted, then held her at arm's length with wide-eyed amazement.

"Well," she said sheepishly, "it's not like my stupidity extends to my ability to analyze myself. Look, I don't want you to think for one minute that I haven't learned to love from you and Lu and Kay. But that trust was a long time coming. How can I just fall in love with Adam? Without thinking, without working the logic through? I know what's wrong with me…I just don't know how to fix it. How do I change the very things I like about myself so that I'm not afraid to take a chance? Especially when the odds are against us."

Maleko took Faith's hand, and together they walked ankle deep into the surf. The chilly water of the Pacific rolled up the sand, teasing her toes and legs. They stood side by side, looking out into the darkness, the stars twinkling against the inky night sky, the moon a silver sliver casting shadows on the surf. After five minutes, Faith stopped waiting for her foster father to speak again, to impart some wisdom that would make her path clear. She should have known he wouldn't tell her, even if he knew.

The Malekos had taught Faith so many valuable lessons over the years—how to be self-sufficient, how to take risks, how to have fun. The most valuable lesson, however, had been how to love. Her foster family had done all they could to heal the wounds of her tempestuous childhood and give her the confidence to dive into the ocean of life, even when the riptides were treacherous.

Now it was her time to put all that knowledge to good use. As soon as she figured out how.

CHAPTER FOURTEEN

Two DAYS. How Adam had lasted this long without seeing Faith, he had no idea. After a tip from Slade, however, he had made the decision to break the rules. Rumor on the street was that Felix Moody was looking to hook up with his former attorney, and Adam was going to make sure the meeting never happened.

He'd called Sunsets and had Dispatch alert Chandler, but Adam had to see for himself that Faith was safe. For the last forty-eight hours, he'd fought his instincts to check up on her by throwing himself into the task of finding Moody, and though Adam had caught sight of the man as he dashed into a crowd at an outdoor mall, Moody remained in the city, but on the loose.

When the crushed beer can from the crime scene at the gun range had come back with a partial print that matched Felix Moody's, the intensity of the manhunt had heightened to critical. The cops circulated APBs, and with Max's permission, they'd also greased the palms of a few reliable informants, hoping to catch a break. They'd staked out Delia Moody's house and workplace, Slade's bar and Moody's last known girlfriend. They'd turned the heat up so high, it was only a matter of time before Moody burned his own hide and got himself caught.

In the meantime, Adam had kept a low profile—and until

now, he'd kept away from Faith. Max Zirinsky would burst a blood vessel if he knew where Adam was heading now. The scene with Max this morning still played in Adam's head like a bad movie, one in which he'd been cast as the reluctant star.

He'd gone into Max's office with a fresh cup of joe and a hopeful attitude, searching for an update on the physical evidence gathered by several agencies so far. The report from the fire department on the blaze in the stairwell. The bullets found at the courthouse, as well as those in his car and the spent shells on the dirt road above the gun range. The note left in Faith's file. He'd plopped into the chair across from Max's desk, never expecting the first words that shot out of his boss's mouth.

"I hear you're sleeping with the enemy."

Adam had nearly choked on his coffee. He threw himself forward, trying to avoid a stain on his shirt as the drink spewed from his mouth. "Excuse me?"

Max didn't stop scribbling on the report he'd been working on when Adam had entered. "Talk around the water cooler is that you and Faith Lawton are mixing it up."

Adam remained silent. Mixing it up wasn't an accurate term. More like falling hard and deep. At least, on his end. But he wasn't about to share this with his colleague. He respected Max, but Adam's personal life was just that—personal. He'd been discreet, so he couldn't imagine who was dishing about his love life. And he didn't really care.

"You've got to think, Adam," Max had continued. "Think real hard and with the part of your anatomy on top of your head, not below your waist."

Adam balanced his mug on the edge of Max's desk. "Chief, is this discussion really necessary?"

"Damn it, Guthrie, you think I enjoy dissecting your sex life? I don't give a shit who you sleep with, so long as she's over twenty-one." Max threw his pen onto the desk, knocking over an empty foam cup and spilling a dribble of coffee onto his blotter. "But I'm not the be-all and end-all of city government. I am, however, the one whose job it is to deal with the calls from the city council and the mayor, asking when we're going to catch the sniper so they can pencil the press conference into their day planners. They're still smarting over the department's screwups in the Yube case, and searching for Felix Moody is dredging up more bad memories. And instead of reviewing evidence and tossing out theories in the squad room with my detectives, I'm sitting on my ass in this office, putting together a budget proposal that needs the approval of the city council and the mayor—two entities who aren't exactly big fans of Faith Lawton. Are you seeing where I'm going with this?"

Adam could have been a smart-ass and said no, but Max Zirinsky rarely lost his cool, and since he still hadn't ordered Adam off the sniper case and into protective custody, Adam had decided to err on the side of caution. He knew exactly what the top cop meant. Any whispers of a conflict of interest between the chief of detectives and the very defense attorney who'd humiliated his department would not be tolerated.

And yet, where did Adam find himself at midnight on a Sunday night? Rushing to check up on his forbidden lover.

Despite his boss's subtle edict, despite Adam's best sense and judgment, he couldn't stay away after hearing Slade's tip. Faith was one stubborn woman and she had to understand how dangerous Moody was, even to her. He was a wanted man with shrinking prospects. Who knew what he'd pull next?

Though most of the diners had left the restaurant, Adam knew the staff and Apalo family would remain in the main dining area and kitchen for hours after closing. According to Officer Chandler, Faith planned to stay and lend a hand. No one could imagine any impropriety or conflict of interest if they were just discussing the case, right? In public. At 12:08 a.m.

Right.

Adam exited the car. With his parents out of the country, he'd taken the liberty of borrowing his mother's Mercury Grand Marquis, a car no one would associate with him. He'd circled the restaurant three times before selecting a space, and he wasted no time jogging inside. The biggest risk he faced tonight was seeing Faith and not being able to touch her, taste her. He missed her, and as far as he could remember, he'd never missed a lover. Not since high school, anyway.

Kalani saw him first. She quietly stopped wiping down a table and crossed the room. "You supposed to be here?" she asked, typically blunt.

"No," Adam answered.

She grinned. "Good for you. You've got your priorities straight."

"Where's Faith?"

He sensed her before he saw her, slowly walking out of the kitchen with a tray of fresh votive candles and refilled salt-shakers. The minute their eyes locked, Faith halted. Kalani bustled across the room and took the tray, then shooed Faith toward Adam.

Did she really need shooing?

"What are you doing here?" she asked, her eyes devoid of any indication of how she felt about his presence.

A stone immediately formed in the pit of his stomach, and several sharp pebbles lodged in his throat.

"I got word Felix Moody is looking to meet with you," he answered tentatively, wondering how much of a fool he'd made of himself by showing up here tonight. A cautionary phone call would have been enough. Facing her in person had been his choice, his excuse to soothe the ache he'd experienced since leaving her at the gun range. But maybe this connection he'd felt to her had been one-sided? Maybe she hadn't missed him at all. Maybe she was glad to be back in her old world, away from the danger and uncertainty and conflict he'd brought to her life.

The corners of her mouth quivered, as if she was attempting to suppress a smile.

Or maybe, her feelings matched his.

"I'm glad you came," she said, "even if you shouldn't have. Felix can't get anywhere near me here."

"I had to see for myself."

"But you shouldn't be out and about like this."

Adam shoved his hands into his pockets, trying to keep from touching her. "Both times, our sniper has shot in broad daylight. I'm betting Moody's partying right now in some hellhole, not creeping around looking for me."

"Or for me," she reminded him with a gentle smile, touching his sleeve, showing him she didn't really care *why* he'd come, just that he had. "No luck finding him, huh?"

Adam growled in frustration, moving his arm so her fingertip would press against his flesh. "No, but the partial print gave us cause to issue warrants. And we think we've identified the tire track from the dirt road across from the gun range. We've got the style of tire, but we're waiting for a report on make and model of the truck to match with stolen vehicles. If Moody hasn't trashed his ride by now, it could lead us to him. It's not much, but it's something."

"What do you think Felix wants with me? Do you think he knows about us?"

"No way. My guess is he's looking for representation again. He's in a tight spot now, and frankly, only a lawyer of your caliber could work him loose."

She smirked. "He's barking up the wrong tree with me."

"But he doesn't know that. You need to stay sharp until we have him in custody. He's got nothing to lose. He's more dangerous than ever."

Adam suddenly realized that all the waiters and busboys who'd been working so hard in the main dining area just a moment before had mysteriously disappeared. Other than whispers from the kitchen and the occasional movement of the swing door, they'd been left alone. No doubt, the uniform assigned to Faith had been shanghaied out of the way as well.

"Where's Chandler?" he asked.

Faith glanced over her shoulder. "Last I heard, he was doing a sweep of the back alley, which, of course, he can only reach through the kitchen. In the few days he's been my shadow, he's developed quite a taste for Lu's teriyaki chicken. I have a feeling that once I'm safe and sound, he's going to have to go on a diet."

Adam chuckled, but her reference to the end of this crisis brought up a topic he knew he had to address, which cut his laughter short. In fact, he wondered if a need to lay his cards on the table with her about the future of their affair hadn't been the real reason he'd sought her out tonight. The conversation with Max weighed heavy on his mind. By nature, Adam followed rules. He understood and respected proper procedure, and while he preferred dealing only in facts rather than innuendoes and suppositions, he understood fully how the appearance of impropriety could harm his department.

"Faith, we need to talk."

Her eyebrows shot up. "That sounds serious, and since we've already discussed Felix, I'm thinking you mean we need to talk about us."

He nodded.

She blew out a breath, apparently not looking forward to this inevitable conversation any more than he was. "Okay, then. But let's find somewhere private, because…" she said with a whisper and nod toward the kitchen, "the walls seem to have ears here."

She led him into the lobby, and Adam was relieved to see Officer Chandler break Kalani's grip on his arm in order to follow. He was a good cop, and despite the Apalo family's blatant attempt at matchmaking, Chandler had a job to do. Adam, however, wanted privacy, so he ordered Chandler to make a sweep of the parking lot and then take a break.

Faith led Adam through the bar to a private room that defined "outdoorsy" even more than did the main dining hall. Tall windows stretched from floor to ceiling, but a stone fence surrounded the windows on the outside, blocking any access from the alley. Lush tropical greenery and trickling waterfalls filled the space between the windows and the wall, creating the illusion that the room was surrounded by a living rain forest. Emerald outdoor carpeting blanketed the floor, and twinkling white lights canvassed the entire ceiling, which was painted a midnight blue, with silvery sweeps of night clouds for added effect and sparkle. But the tables and chairs were lined up against the wall as if the room hadn't been used in a while.

"What is this?"

"Special party room," Faith volunteered, walking in the semidarkness toward the farthest window. "Mostly for bridal showers and wedding receptions. We have a lot of couples who elope to Hawaii, but come back here to have a reception for their family and friends. Great place, isn't it?"

Her voice sounded enthusiastic, but her body language conveyed an entirely different message. Dressed in a sleeveless blouse in turquoise blue, denim jeans that ended mid-calf and sandals, she hugged her body, as if a chill had somehow slinked into the air. If it had, it was thanks to his surprise visit.

Adam closed the distance she'd placed between them, hovering behind her, aching to warm her skin himself. His palms itched to rub up and down her arms, to swing her around, pull her against him and kiss the expression of doubt on her face into oblivion. But the one time Adam had surrendered to indulgent spontaneity, he'd ended up in bed with Faith. Not a bad outcome so far as cause and effect went, except that he was nearly certain that the pensive tilt of her lips and glossy look in her eyes were telling him to take things a little slower.

"Do you want me to leave?" he asked.

Faith spun around, her gray eyes wide. "What? No! I mean, I—" She turned back toward the window. "I just wasn't expecting you tonight, that's all."

He could feel the muscles in his jaw tighten, and his stomach roll and pitch. This was all so complicated! Or was it? He wanted her. For tonight. Tomorrow. The week after. He wanted a serious shot at investigating every aspect of

Faith Lawton's life—her needs and wants. He was desperate to know if the rapport they'd established so quickly had been a fluke, or a taste of what could evolve with time. Didn't he deserve that? How could he allow his career to stand in the way of loving a woman as strong, remarkable and sexy as Faith?

He yielded to temptation and touched her. Lightly. A single finger running up and down the length of her arm. "I don't know about you, but everything that's happened between us has been unexpected."

When she leaned back into him, Adam's chest tightened. Dare he allow himself to hope that the signals she'd been sending were crossed? That she didn't regret getting involved with him?

"Unexpected and unexplainable," she said. "We're such different people."

"We're not, Faith." He went for broke and wrapped his arms around her waist, pulling her flush against him. She didn't protest, but instead relaxed into him, giving him leave to place a single kiss on the crown of her head. "In the two days we spent together, we discovered so much common ground."

"Other than mutual desire, what would that common ground be, exactly?"

He curved his body around her, trying to spy the hint of humor he heard in her question. He saw no clues.

"We both believe in justice."

"No, we don't." She spun around, but didn't break out of his embrace. Instead, she squeezed her arms through his and mirrored his hold. "You believe in justice for the guilty. In punishment and accountability. I'm working toward justice for the innocent, the unfairly accused."

"It's still justice," he insisted.

She frowned. "Maybe to you and me, but what about to your boss? I'll bet if Max Zirinsky caught wind—"

Adam groaned. He was normally a decent liar…had to be when dealing with criminals. But dealing with Faith was something else entirely. He couldn't tell her anything but the truth.

"He's already heard, then," she concluded.

Adam shook his head. "Only rumors, which I neither verified nor denied. I told him my personal life had never affected my work in the department and it never would. And it won't. Faith, what we have is between us. The rumors in the mill right now are just because we're spending so much time together."

"And we won't once the case is over?"

"Not where others can see us. We can be discreet."

"Do you want to be?"

The question stopped him. He leaned back, exploring her expression. She was dead serious—and there was no mistaking the fact that she found the prospect distasteful.

"I'm always discreet, Faith, no matter who my lovers are. I don't broadcast my personal business to the public. Do you?"

She shook her head. "Of course not, Adam. But at the same time, I'm not into hiding, either. It's been a long time since I've been involved with someone, and while being discreet is one thing, sneaking around is something else altogether. I want to have the luxury to go out, have fun. I want to meet your friends and your family and have you do the same. But we'll both suffer if we take this any farther. If my clients find out I'm involved with you, they may not trust me to be on their side in any case that involves the Courage Bay police department. But then, I have plenty of business from Los Angeles and San

Diego. I'll survive. But you—I can only imagine what the consequences could be for you. Your life is here…your career. Things could get ugly, all because of great sex."

Adam pulled her close, inhaling the sweet scent of her hair. "Can you think of a better reason?"

"Adam, be serious."

"I am! Look, I know things might get tense, but I'm willing to take the chance if you are. If there's one thing I've learned since being shot at twice in four days it's that life is too short to let go of something that might turn out to be amazing, just because others could object."

She nodded, but the doubt in her eyes was as clear as the pink lip gloss on her mouth. "We're not talking about gossips and busybodies, Adam. What about your boss? The men you supervise? How they react is important, whether you like it or not. Can you deal with some of them losing respect for you simply because of what I do for a living?"

Her words struck hard. Adam hadn't really allowed himself to think too much about his fellow detectives. Blowing off the concerns of politicians and higher-ups was one thing—but what about his men?

"I want to give this a go, Faith. I really do. I'll deal with whatever comes."

She reached up, curled her arms around his neck and pulled herself up to kiss him. "No, *we'll* deal."

The minute their lips connected, two days' worth of longing exploded between them. Her lips parted greedily for him and he matched the thrusts of her tongue. Adam felt trapped, unable to touch her and hold her as his body and heart insisted. If not for the threat of someone walking in on them at any second, he would have folded her onto the floor.

But as he feared, a knock sounded. They pulled apart, and while Faith righted her clothes and hair, he stalked to the door.

Kalani was on the other side. "You don't know how much I hate interrupting," she claimed, bouncing from foot to foot as if the discomfort made her unable to stand still.

"Not half as much as I hate you interrupting," he joked, until he spied the dark look in Faith's sister's eyes. His chest tightened. Something was wrong.

"What's up, Kay?"

She looked reluctantly at the front door. "It's Officer Chandler. He went out to search the parking lot and he's not back yet."

"I told him to take a break," Adam explained, grinning. Leave it to Kalani to keep tabs on the good-looking police officer. Should he be the one to tell her Chandler was married?

"I know, but he told my father he'd come back inside for his break, and Dad was going to show him how to mix up the marinade for the chicken. But he didn't come back. I went out looking for him and he's not around."

"You went out?" Adam asked, dashing toward the entrance. He doused the lights in the lobby, then stood flat against the wall, peering cautiously through the tinted, double-glass door. The lot looked nearly empty. Adam's car was right up front, and a few others—probably employees'—filled the farthest spots.

Kalani followed behind him, with Faith just behind her, though they both remained cautiously in the main dining room.

"Adam, what's wrong?" Faith asked.

He scanned the lot as carefully as he could, then, after switching off the lights in the main room, jogged to the window behind the bandstand, which would give him a clearer view.

"Chandler's not out there."

He whipped out his cell phone and dialed Dispatch. He ordered them to contact Chandler. They waited in tense silence until the dispatcher returned to the line—with troubling news.

Adam disconnected the call. "No response from Chandler. They're sending backup."

But backup might not arrive in time. If Chandler was hurt, seconds could make the difference between life and death. Adam stalked to the door, knowing full well this could be a ruse meant to lure him into the open. But if he had to choose between his safety and Chandler's life, he knew which he would pick.

"Adam, where are you going?" Faith asked, her eyes frantic as she latched onto his arm.

"He could be hurt."

"His radio could be broken," she reasoned.

He nearly growled. "Then why isn't he back?"

"Maybe he's smoking a cigarette."

Adam grabbed her hand and pried her fingers free. "Chandler runs marathons. He doesn't smoke. Faith, I know this could be a trap, but I can't let a good man pay in a vendetta that is meant for me."

"Aren't the police sending other units?"

He growled in frustration, torn between good sense and the immediate need to help an officer in trouble. Only, he had no real proof Chandler was at risk. He couldn't go rushing out into the night without hard evidence, especially if doing so meant leaving Faith alone.

A slim chance remained that Chandler's disappearance had to do with Faith, not him. What if someone diverted her protection to get to her? Would Felix Moody go that far?

Under the circumstances, Adam couldn't take a chance by leaving Faith's side, even if her whole family and their waitstaff were here to protect her.

"Fine, we'll wait," he told Faith, glancing aside in order to ignore the smug smile on her face.

He shuffled them to the back of the bar area, far from doors and windows. He ordered the chef to secure the back exit, and Maleko volunteered to double-check the front entrance and the emergency exit in the hall beside the bathrooms.

Adam kept his gaze off Faith, who was still grinning as if she'd won a national debate rather than a simple argument. What did he care? Better she be cocky than dead.

DESPITE THE CROWD around them, Faith didn't take her eyes off Adam for a moment. Not even after two police units rolled into the parking lot, sirens blaring and lights flashing. Like a responsible cop, Adam remained in the restaurant. He waited while two uniforms swept the entire building, the parking lot and surrounding areas.

There was no sign of Officer Chandler. He'd been assigned to protect Faith, and while she'd completely cooperated with him, not for one minute had she actually thought she'd been in any danger. The leaded weight of dread sat in the pit of her stomach, making it hard for her to watch Adam, who stalked to and fro like a caged animal.

Finally, after the second set of cops reported in, Adam had had enough. She could see his resolve in the glare in his eye, and despite the heaviness in her body and soul, she stood.

"Two of you stay here and coordinate getting these people safely to their cars," Adam said, sweeping his hand toward the terrified wait staff. Faith tried to swallow, but for the last tense twenty minutes she hadn't been able to speak more than a few words. In two days, her family and all their staff had become friendly with Officer Tad Chandler, and his partner, Pam Cortlandt, who'd pulled the day duty. If anything happened to the policeman because of her, Faith wasn't certain what she would do. She dealt with crime on a daily basis, but not since childhood had she been a victim. How Adam faced such uncertainty every day was beyond her.

He continued barking orders, and suddenly, Faith realized he was working his way toward the door.

"I want someone with Ms. Lawton and the Apalo family at all times until we figure out what the hell is going on."

Faith jumped to her feet the minute Adam turned toward the door. "Where are you going?"

He hesitated but did not face her. "I have a job to do, Faith. You're safe here."

"But you're not safe out there!"

At this, he spun. "What am I supposed to do? Hide? Spend the rest of my life behind locked doors so some maniac won't shoot me?"

She thrust her hands on her hips. "Works for me!"

He stepped closer and lowered his voice, not that it mattered. Every eye in the place was on them as they argued like lovers.

"It doesn't work for me, Faith. It never will."

One of the uniforms dashed to Adam's side, radio in hand. "Detective Guthrie, we've got a report of a man with a gun three blocks from here. Matches Moody's description."

With an expression she was almost fool enough to think was apologetic, he turned away from her.

"Where?"

"Violet and Wilder."

"Who's responding?"

"Four patrol cars. Zirinsky, too."

Adam marched toward the door, ordering the officers to remain behind. With a hard slam, he forced the door open. Faith stepped forward to stop him, but she was detained by a tug on her hand.

"Please, Ms. Lawton," the new policewoman begged.

Faith had spun around to demand that the officer free her, when two sounds cracked across her consciousness. First, a gunshot and shattering glass. Second, a howl of pain.

Adam!

CHAPTER FIFTEEN

WITH THE OFFICER practically wrapping herself around Faith's body in a stationary tackle, Faith watched, helpless, as the other three officers spilled out of the restaurant, one shouting into his radio for immediate backup. With guns drawn, they moved into position, blocked by the awning and several large planters. Faith had no idea what they meant to do. Could they save Adam? Could they see the shooter? Damn, they'd blocked her view. She couldn't see anything!

"Let me go!" she screamed.

Cortlandt used all her strength to keep Faith still, but Faith struggled with equal determination. She just wanted to know if Adam was alive! She had to see. A split second later, the cop yelped and loosened her hold, and Faith made her break toward the door. A quick glance over her shoulder told her she would very soon defend her sister Kalani on charges of battery on a police officer, but she'd win. This was justifiable.

Faith managed to make it to the door before the woman caught up with her. She hardly felt her biting grip on her shoulders when she caught sight of Adam sprawled on the ground next to his car, his legs and torso visible against the gray gravel.

"Adam!"

"Please, Ms. Lawton."

"Adam." The second time his name came out choked. She couldn't breathe and dropped to the ground. Air whooshed out of her lungs and her vision began to swim in a dark, dizzying vortex. His head was partly beneath the car. Was he shot there? Was the dark spot still imprinted on her eyelids blood?

One of the cops dashed toward his patrol car, his partner close at his heels. Radios crackled with voices and screeches while the oxygen was sucked out of the air around her.

Sirens. Tires. Shouting voices. Gravel biting into her skin. Tears flowing down her face. The patrolmen had moved their car, not to pursue the shooter but to block Adam's body from another sniper attack. Suddenly, Faith saw movement. His leg? She wasn't sure! Had he moved, or had one of the cops shifted Adam's body?

She attempted to scramble to her feet, but the policewoman held her down.

"Please, Ms. Lawton. Tucker and Smith have medical training. The ambulance is on the way. If you get yourself shot and he lives, he'll see to it that I'm the next one in the hospital, understand?"

Faith struggled for a few more moments, until the cop's words sank in. Yes, she understood. She couldn't do anything for Adam—except stay safe. She stopped fighting and dropped back to the ground.

The fourth policeman, after shouting a string of orders, jumped into his own car and raced off. The echoes of "officer down" emitting from the patrol cops' radios resounded in her ears. At the entrance to Sunsets, the cruiser nearly collided with an ambulance, but they swung to avoid each other, sirens wailing. Faith could hardly process what happened next.

A stream of howling patrol cars sped down the street like

race cars in pursuit of the checkered flag. Every fourth or fifth car tore into the parking lot, creating a wide perimeter of red and blue lights. Conversations raged over the radios, but none made any sense in her muddled brain. She tried with all her might to do nothing but pray as the paramedics worked on the man she loved.

Yes, the man she loved. How could she not love him? From the beginning, he'd possessed all the qualities her dream man should. She'd had her eyes opened to the fierce devotion, innate sexiness and caring nature of the man with whom she'd been thrust into this life-or-death battle. She'd known from the first kiss that he was a man she could never resist.

And now, facing his injury, she knew she loved him. But if he lived, she knew she couldn't spend another moment in his life. Not if facing the possibility of his death was a daily occurrence. Her heart couldn't take the pain. She wasn't strong enough, she thought, sobs catching in her throat. She wasn't brave enough.

The place swarmed with cops in blue and black. She recognized the SWAT members from her rescue just a few days before, and even one of the paramedics. One of Courage Bay's finest was down. They'd move heaven and earth to care for one of their own, Faith knew. And still she prayed, reciting over and over every litany she'd ever learned. Finally, the crowd surrounding Adam parted. He was on a stretcher, but his hand moved. He was alive!

Faith glanced over her shoulder. The policewoman had blended in with her brethren, so Faith dashed off, determined to see Adam before the ambulance took him away. She pushed through a wall of cops, nearly fainting with relief when she realized his eyes were open and he was struggling to remove the oxygen mask.

"Faith," he said weakly as she grabbed his hand.

She gulped down a big breath and swiped away the tears she suddenly realized were streaming down her face. "I thought I told you not to get shot. Can't anyone in this department follow procedure? I'm pretty sure nearly dying isn't in your standard operating manual."

He chuckled, but the laughter cost him. Pain glazed his eyes. The paramedics had cut away his shirt, and a bright red stain erupted on the gauze taped just below his collarbone but well above his heart.

"Sorry," he said, his voice wheezy with pain.

"Shut up," she ordered.

He nodded his compliance. She scooted alongside as the paramedics lifted the stretcher into the ambulance, and knowing she couldn't stop herself, she grabbed his hand. His eyes locked with hers, and though no words were spoken, she knew at that moment that his feelings for her ran as deep as hers for him. As much as the words pushed at her lips, fighting to break free, she swallowed them back. What good was love if one of them was dead?

A gentle hand locked around Faith's arm and she turned to find Officer Cortlandt drawing her away.

"I'm going to the hospital," Faith insisted.

Cortlandt shook her head, her eyes shiny. Oh God. Faith realized then that Chandler, Cortlandt's partner, was still missing. "We need to secure this area first. Keep you safe."

Faith pressed her lips together, determined. She admired the cop for her loyalty and duty, but Faith had just about endured enough of having the police tell her what to do. With a screech, she doubled over, as if horrible pain racked her stomach. In seconds, paramedics had her in their clutches.

Only a few moments after the first ambulance had pulled away with Adam in the back, Faith followed in the second.

Once she arrived at the ER, Faith experienced a miraculous recovery, and after trading blustery threats with a rather large nurse, she was released. Fortunately, although Officer Cortlandt hadn't let Faith out of her sight, she was occupied with a new arrival—Tad Chandler, beaten and bloodied.

"What happened?" Faith asked, touching Cortlandt lightly on the arm. The blond policewoman looked pale, and Faith knew exactly how she felt.

"They found him dumped on the side of the road by the railroad tracks. A cruiser speeding toward the restaurant nearly ran him over."

"Is he shot?" Faith asked, certain the policeman's injuries were somehow related to the attack on Adam.

Cortlandt huffed out a sigh, hooking her hands on her gun belt as if she needed somewhere to put them. "No. Four guys jumped him in the parking lot and kicked the shit out of him."

"Why?" Faith asked, knowing the most likely explanation was that whoever shot Adam had wanted to make sure no police were around to catch him.

The cop rubbed her palms vigorously over her cheeks, as if needing the friction to keep awake. "He doesn't know. Have you found Detective Guthrie yet?"

Faith gestured to a room a few doors down. "They'll be sending him up to surgery soon. He's stable. He'll be okay. Chief Zirinsky said he'd call me over as soon as Adam could talk."

Another ambulance arrived at the emergency room bay, throwing the already chaotic scene into total bedlam. Faith and Cortlandt found two chairs out of the way and sat without speaking until they received word that Chandler had four broken ribs and a torn ligament near his eye, but would recover fully. Adam, on the other hand, had suffered blood loss that would make him weak for a few days, but otherwise he would have no permanent damage from the gunshot once the bullet was removed. Faith insisted she had to see him, and when Cortlandt walked her to the door, she found Max Zirinsky leaning over his bedside.

"I thought I told you not to get shot," Max growled.

"I told him, too, Chief," Faith stated, walking into the room as slowly and calmly as she could force her feet. "He doesn't listen very well."

"No," Max said, glancing accusingly at her. "He doesn't."

Faith stood her ground. "Do you have a problem with me, Chief Zirinsky? Other than the usual, that is?"

Max scowled. He obviously didn't like being called on the carpet by some woman he considered public enemy number one. "Depends on how you define 'the usual.'"

Faith crossed her arms, narrowing her gaze, trying to decide the best avenue to take in this showdown. Adam attempted to clear his throat to divert her attention, but she ignored him. She loved the man, but she wasn't going to back down on his boss while there was still blood pumping through her veins.

"If you want to dislike me because I uphold a citizen's constitutional right to effective representation, that's your prerogative as chief of police. Animosity between defense attorneys and police officers is as old as the justice system itself. But you can't stand in the way of Adam and me closing that chasm in our personal lives. If we choose to be friends, it's none of your business."

The chief glanced back at Adam before he spoke. "Frankly, Ms. Lawton, I don't give a damn about your personal life or

Guthrie's. My main concern is that he stay alive long enough to *have* a personal life. And I'd prefer if he didn't have to pull disability to do it."

"That's my main concern, as well. See?" Her smile was only half-genuine. "We've found common ground already."

Zirinsky snorted, then turned back to Adam. "She's a pistol. Sure you have an ample supply of Kevlar to protect you?"

Adam's grin was slight, but real. His eyes held a glazed look, so she knew he'd been medicated. She also knew he might not remember this conversation so fondly when his head was clear. She'd just told his boss to butt out of their business.

The bullet might have missed all vital organs, but Adam had to be in pain. And what was she doing to ease his discomfort? Arguing with his boss.

Nice, Faith. Real nice.

Quietly, she slipped around Max and stood on the other side of Adam's bed. As much as she didn't give a damn about the chief's opinion, she resisted reaching out for Adam's hand, and instead, laid her palm on his pillow, right beside his head. She turned to Max, who watched them with narrowed eyes.

"Did they catch the shooter?" Faith asked.

The chief's frustration was evident in the furrow of his brow. "No, but we found a truck parked behind the building across from your parents' restaurant. The tires match the vehicle associated with the shooting at the gun range. We ran the VIN. It was stolen two days ago."

"From?" she asked.

Max frowned. "Market Street. Two blocks south of Felix Moody's last known residence."

Adam cleared his throat again, but the sound was rough and raspy. Faith found a cup of ice chips nearby and spooned a few into his mouth, which may have satisfied his thirst, but definitely deflated his ego. He scowled at her attentiveness, and Faith resisted the urge to slap him on the arm for being such a…guy.

"If you didn't go and get yourself shot, you wouldn't need help," she snapped.

He peered at her with those fathomless caramel-colored eyes. "I've suffered worse indignities tonight than having you serve me," he countered, then winked.

Max just shook his head.

Adam winced as he turned back toward his boss. "Any prints on the truck?"

"Wiped clean, but we found powder residue on the seat and a single shell on the floorboard. As soon as the doc yanks that bullet out, Masters will run it down to the lab for comparison. In an hour, we'll know if they match. We also found a ball cap in the truck bed, caught under some tarp."

Adam perked up. "Hair samples?"

Max grinned. "We're pretty sure. In just a few, we're going to know if Felix Moody is really our man."

Officer Cortlandt came in, her eyes weary but her smile bright, with a report about Chandler. Max left immediately to check on his other injured officer, leaving Faith and Adam alone. After ten tense seconds, a nurse bustled in, assessed Adam's antibiotic IV, recorded his temperature, adjusted his pillows and announced they'd move him to surgery in ten minutes. Adam remained as still and silent as possible, except for the tic in his cheek. He was obviously enduring the medical attention with the last of his patience.

Faith had to hide a grin. She hadn't had that much experience, but the cliché that men made the worst patients was apparently based in truth. He didn't complain aloud, but his body language and silence shouted, *Leave me alone.*

The minute the nurse disappeared, however, he turned contrite eyes on her. "Sorry I got shot," he said.

She opened her mouth to speak—but what was the appropriate response? And how did he do that, anyway? How did he know exactly the right thing to say?

God, she hated him. Well, she hated how much she loved him. That counted for something, right? Wouldn't that be enough to keep her heart from splitting in two?

"I'm sorry, too." A painful truth constricted her chest, and despite her resolve not to turn this bedside chat into a regret-fest, she couldn't help saying what had weighed so heavily on her mind since her retreat to the beach with her father. "If I hadn't helped Felix Moody beat that murder rap, he wouldn't have been out on the streets tonight gunning for you."

Adam leaned back into the pillow, his eyes half-closed. "You were just doing your job. Just like I was when I arrested him and when I pressured Zirinsky to keep him under close surveillance. The scrutiny from law enforcement obviously tipped him over the edge."

"That and the drugs," Faith said, her stomach aching again with guilt. She'd taken the case to help Delia Moody and her grandchildren. Instead, she'd played a part in a scenario that pushed a bad man into becoming downright evil. Killing a fellow drug dealer was bad enough—shooting a police officer and abandoning his mother, nieces and nephews was insane. And Felix obviously felt no compunction about taking innocent lives in the process. She'd almost been shot. Twice. By a man who claimed to be indebted to her.

Made no sense. But then, people sustaining themselves on

drugs and anger rarely did. She knew this firsthand from the few memories she had left of her birth father.

Now her doubts forced her to question her initial instincts about George Yube. The evidence, before it was tainted, had been nearly indisputable in regard to his guilt. And yet, she wouldn't have undone her actions in his case. The chain of evidence was a sacred link between truth and justice. But was helping to free guilty men and inadvertently punishing the police department for acting with human foible really why she'd taken up the law?

"Do you think Yube's shooting was an accident?" she asked.

Adam yawned, a definite side effect of the painkillers and the fact that it was nearly four o'clock in the morning. Once the anesthesiologist got a hold of him, he'd be out cold.

"Who knows? Doesn't matter. Moot point. Moody has to be stopped. If he really is only after me, he doesn't give a damn who he hurts in the process."

"But how did he attack Chandler and sit in wait for you at the same time? Who were his accomplices?"

"Probably recruited some homeboys to take Chandler out in order to get to me. He could do the same to anyone else I'm close to. Including you."

Adam reached for her, but the IV line caught his hand. Faith slid onto the bed, careful not to shake the mattress, and twined her fingers gently with his. "You don't have to worry. I don't think Felix would hurt me. I got him out of prison."

"But you wouldn't represent him again. And if he knows we're involved—"

"He doesn't know," she argued, her voice sharper than she'd intended.

Adam's eyes drifted to half-mast, and if he noticed her

flash of anger, he didn't acknowledge it. "He doesn't know now, but—"

Two things occurred to Faith at that moment. One, she didn't like where this conversation was going. As much as she'd claimed earlier that she didn't want to remain involved with Adam because she couldn't stand the stress of his dangerous job, she also wasn't ready to walk away just yet. She cared about him deeply, enough to know that the seeds of love had already been planted in her heart and that eradicating the growth wouldn't be easy. Fear of what *might* happen could be powerful, but she was more frightened of what might *not* happen if she didn't give their relationship a fighting chance.

The second fact dangling in front of her was emphasized when a fresh-faced uniformed policeman entered Adam's room. He took a position beside the door when Tim Masters walked in and waved Faith over.

She looked at Adam. He was asleep. Biting her lip, she glanced at the officer, then threw caution to the wind and placed a kiss on Adam's lips. She had a strong suspicion that once she left tonight, she wouldn't see him again until Felix Moody was in custody.

"Ms. Lawton?"

Faith crossed the room, her muscles aching with exhaustion. Now that she knew Adam would live, every ounce of energy seemed to have fled her body. She rubbed her eyes, transferring dark lines of melted mascara and eyeliner onto her hands.

"Yes, Detective?"

"Your sister is outside, waiting to take you home."

She nodded, glancing back at Adam for a moment. "Has his brother been notified?"

Masters stretched his shoulders beneath his wrinkled jacket. He'd probably been called to the hospital out of a deep sleep.

"Took us a while to track him down, but Casey is on his way now. Should be here in ten. Detective Guthrie will be well looked after, ma'am. But Chief Zirinsky thinks you'd be much safer if you went home. Now that Felix Moody is our prime suspect, he's reduced your protection to occasional drive-bys at your home and office."

"I thought Felix Moody was looking for me."

"The tip didn't pan out, ma'am," Masters answered. "And we don't believe Moody will go anywhere public. His face is on every station in this part of the state. We do suggest you remain at your parents' restaurant, because of the crowd."

She nodded again, frowning. She agreed that Felix wouldn't try to contact her now. He'd shot a cop. His freedom wouldn't last much longer.

Masters's voice dropped to a barely audible volume. "The chief also suggests you stay away from Detective Guthrie, and out of the line of fire, until after Felix is in custody." He whipped out a business card and handed it to Faith. "He said you can call him anytime for updates about Detective Guthrie's condition and on the progress of the case. He doesn't want you to get the wrong impression, ma'am. He really just wants you to be safe. Says he owes it to his top detective."

Faith took the card. She didn't argue despite the urgent need burning up her throat to scream and yell and protest her polite but definite dismissal from Adam's life. Just like a man to pawn his dirty work off on an underling. Who did Zirinsky think he was, anyway? Sure, his orders were logical, based on facts made painfully clear by the events of the past few days, but she didn't have to like them.

Still, tonight, Felix Moody had unleashed his murderous evil in the parking lot of her parents' restaurant. Any one of the members of her family, or their staff, could have been hurt in the cross fire. Even Officer Chandler, a man trained to protect himself, hadn't been spared. She couldn't ignore the fact that as long as Felix remained free and she continued her association with Adam, his target, none of the people she loved would be safe. She turned and watched Adam sleep for a few moments, her chest tight.

She'd walk away and stay away. For now.

"When he wakes up, can you tell Detective Guthrie that I expect a phone call from him immediately?"

Masters frowned, but nodded. "He'll be under twenty-four-hour police protection, Ms. Lawton. The whole department is out looking for Moody. I don't think it'll be long before we drag him in."

Faith swallowed and closed her eyes. Only two days ago, she would have protested the cop's wording, made some comment about making sure Felix's rights were followed to the letter of the law. Tonight—this morning, more accurately—she didn't give a damn. She just wanted the killer off the streets.

CHAPTER SIXTEEN

WITH A GRUNT, Adam slid his arm off his desk, allowing the sling to catch the weight with a tug. God, he hated this. He hated not having complete mobility in his arm. He hated the orders from Zirinsky that chained him to his desk. He hated the two vigilant officers standing outside his door, shadowing his every move, limiting his freedom of movement to the police department and his new home in an undisclosed safe house. But most of all, he hated not seeing Faith.

He'd called her once a day for the four days since his surgery. They'd spoken for only moments each time, but the sound of her voice had done more for his recovery than the meds or the excruciating physical therapy. Funny how one little bullet could rip through muscle and knick bone and cause all sorts of trouble.

And yet, that same bullet had solidified their case against Felix Moody. Adam drummed his fingers on the ballistics report that provided an irrefutable match between the bullets used to kill George Yube and the one that had torn the hole in Adam's shoulder. The DNA from the hair found in the cap discovered in the stolen truck matched Moody's DNA, which had been registered in a national database with his prior conviction. Adam had long since resigned himself to the fact that the two-bit hood he'd once considered nothing more than a nuisance to the system had morphed into a desperate killer. In Moody's twisted mind, Adam had ruined his already miserable life. Revenge was a powerful motivator, especially to someone who'd lost his business prospects, his family and his freedom.

And yet, they still didn't have him in custody. His friends and family insisted that Moody had abandoned Courage Bay for good, but Adam's gut told him otherwise. He'd known Moody for years, and never once had Moody left home, except for his stints in prison. Adam believed Moody would run this time, but he'd be back. And when he surfaced, they'd have him. The entire force had vowed to leave no stone unturned in this investigation. And Adam had put a plan in motion to nudge things along.

But how long could Adam wait? Until they had a lead on Moody's location, Adam was in personal lockdown. He couldn't do his job, couldn't live his life, couldn't see Faith—until this whole mess was wrapped up. His patience was wearing thin. Lying in that hospital bed a few days ago, he had realized that life without Faith wasn't any life at all. He loved his job, but he wouldn't let political nonsense block his happiness. Good cops did not kowtow to small-minded politicians. He'd already laid down the law with Zirinsky, informing the chief that if his association with Faith was jeopardizing his job, Max might as well fire him now.

True to type, his boss hadn't called his bluff. They agreed to take the flack as it flew, and reevaluate what was best for the department if and when the time came.

Worked for Adam. Now he only had to see Faith again without putting her in danger. Unfortunately, there was only one way—catch Felix Moody.

A knock sounded, and through the glass Adam could see

Casey, dressed in his uniform and holding his helmet against his hip. He grinned, feeling only partially guilty for what he'd done to jump-start the case—especially since he'd dragged his brother into a situation no one in their right mind would designate as procedurally sound.

"How's the warden treating you?" Casey asked, throwing a quick glance toward Adam's watchdogs before he shut the door behind him.

"Could be worse," Adam answered. "I could be in solitary."

Casey plopped into the chair across from Adam's desk, the very same chair he'd sat in when Faith had commandeered his office. He couldn't help inhaling deeply, in the vain effort to pick up a whiff of her subtle perfume. Instead, all he could smell was the faux-pine residue of cleaning products. He nearly sneezed.

"You practically are in solitary," Casey said, his voice loud and clear, all the better in case someone was listening. With a nod and a wink, he verified that he'd accomplished his unconventional mission. Now they just had to work the conversation in the right direction.

"Have you managed to sneak Faith into your room at night?" Casey asked.

Adam frowned, but knew this talk was necessary. Two brothers shooting the shit would not garner any unwanted attention.

"This isn't high school, Casey. Moody is dangerous. I won't jeopardize her again."

That part was entirely true. The only thing dishonest about this exchange was the unspoken subtext regarding Casey's mission today. Never before had Adam asked him to act in a way that some might consider dangerous and maybe even unethical. Usually, Casey worked that angle on his own. But Adam knew if anyone would come through for him, it would be his fearless kid brother.

Casey balanced his helmet on his bouncing knee, glancing again at the door. His brother didn't sit still well, making him a perfect candidate for the constantly moving motorcycle squad, even if the same behavior had caused loads of conflict at the dining room table when they were growing up.

"Seems to me the risk might be worth it. You don't think a hot babe like that is going to wait around for you forever, do you?"

Adam used his unhurt arm to shuffle the files on his desk, needing to do something to keep from using that same arm to wring his brother's neck. Casey wasn't supposed to have come here to discuss his love life. Far from it. But he forced himself to remain calm, knowing that the last thing he needed was his brother pushing him into doing something stupid— like seeing Faith before she was safe—with juvenile-based gibes. Actually, that was the second-to-last thing. What he really didn't need was to be discussing his love life with his brother at all.

"Drop it, Casey. I'm doing the right thing. I'm concentrating on getting Moody off the streets and verifying that he's the shooter beyond a reasonable doubt, so that when he goes to prison this time, he stays there, no matter who his attorney is."

Casey drummed his thumbs on the helmet's visor. "You sound like an attorney yourself."

"Maybe I need to so a conviction will stick."

"Maybe you can just make sure his previous hotshot mouthpiece doesn't represent him again."

"That's not a problem," Adam said, knowing Faith would

never take Moody on as a client again, though he wasn't so sure she wouldn't end up representing one of the creep's brethren in the criminal lowlife league.

"That's good to know, I guess. But *sooner* or later, you're going to catch Moody," Casey said, emphasizing the very word Adam wanted to hear. "And after him, you'll catch some other murderer, drug dealer, bank robber…you can fill in the blank. Eventually, one of those perps you collared will hire Faith Lawton as his defense attorney, and you're going to be facing your lover in court. Are you ready for that?"

With a growl, Adam realized what his brother was doing. Casey had information for him, but wasn't about to give it up until he'd said his piece about Faith. Fortunately, Adam had considered that question so deeply over the last couple of days that the answer popped out of his mouth quickly and without forethought.

"Yes."

The quickness and decisiveness of Adam's answer caught his brother off guard. His eyebrows popped up high. "Really? It's going to suck—you know that, right?"

"Yes, Casey, I know that, too. But if Faith and I really care about each other, really respect each other—and I think we do—then we'll deal with the hard times. We aren't the first couple to have to face down major differences of opinion, particularly in our professional lives. We'll make it through or we won't. But I want to at least have a damn chance to try."

Casey grinned, always the first to enjoy the slightest show of temper on his brother's part. Adam knew Casey resented the way his big brother could stay so even keeled all the time, but Adam attributed the talent to nothing more than a personality trait. On the other hand, he might have developed the skill in response to his brother's more volatile nature.

But volatile or not, Casey cared. Enough to spend his break making sure his brother wasn't passing up a chance at a great woman. Enough to put his career on the line with a not-so-routine traffic stop.

"Why are you here, anyway?" he asked, for the complete benefit of the officer standing outside the door. While his bodyguards hadn't been ordered to eavesdrop, Adam wasn't willing to take a chance, not when Casey had taken a risk for him. "Dissecting my love life isn't your usual pastime."

"You don't usually have a love life worthy of dissection, bro." Casey scooted forward on his chair. "But I've got an interesting tip for you."

Adam sat up straighter. This was what he'd hoped for when he'd privately met with his brother this morning and handed him nothing more than a report on the recent traffic violations of one Jasmine Becker, the former girlfriend Felix Moody had tried to set up for murder.

Casey leaned back, grinning. "Oddly enough, I had the rare opportunity to pull Jasmine Becker over today for a faulty taillight."

Adam pursed his lips, determined not to smile too soon in the face of victory. The plan to pull her driving record had only occurred to Adam late last night, when he'd put together a short list of people most likely to turn Moody in for the reward.

"Jasmine Becker? Man, with all the citations she's amassed lately, you'd think she'd get the taillight fixed. Did she happen to mention how she felt about her ex being on the run again? I mean, the man did try to frame her for murder."

Casey shook his head, chuckling. "The bubblehead was too

dense to even realize that's what he'd meant to do. But we were chatting on the side of the road as I wrote up her *warning*," Casey said, emphasizing the word so that Adam knew his brother had opted out of giving the woman a ticket, more than likely in exchange for information. "She mentioned that Moody might be heading out of town. Permanently."

"That's old news."

Casey arched a cocky eyebrow. "Really? Did you know he planned to leave tonight around two a.m.? Seems old Moody has been watching the rotation of shifts in his neighborhood. He plans to blow town right under our noses."

Adam stood abruptly. His chair skittered behind him on the metallic wheels. "Could she be lying?"

Casey slid his helmet onto Adam's desk. "Of course, but I don't think she is. According to her, Moody's been hiding out in every basement, attic and crawl space in The Lair and the rest of Victoria Park. He's called in every favor owed him from childhood to keep someone from turning him in for the reward. A reward, I so smoothly reminded Jasmine, that would not only pay all her outstanding tickets but buy her a new car."

Adam tried to tamp down the surge of satisfaction rushing through his veins. Any regret he harbored over recruiting his brother to explore this avenue vanished. "So Jasmine wants the cash?"

"Funny how the right incentive can remind a girl how wrong it is when her man tries to set her up for murder, even if he did screw it up. I hope we find Moody before she does. She can be a real firecracker when she's pissed off."

"And leave it to you to fuel her fire," Adam suggested, grinning.

Casey polished his fingernails on his shirt, then blew off the nonexistent dust. "If there's one thing I can do well, it's tick off a woman."

"Did you tell Zirinsky?"

"Of course," Casey said, standing. "Duty first, right?"

Adam reached for his jacket, ignoring the shot of pain that nearly made him stagger. He'd stopped taking the pain pills because they made him sleepy. With normal and controlled movement, he could endure the ache, but one wrong move… ye-ouch. He extended his uninjured arm toward his brother, who took his hand and gave it a shake.

"She doesn't know where he is now?" Adam asked, hoping for platinum even if they'd already struck gold. This was the closest they'd come to finding Moody.

"Nope. But she promised to lead us to him tonight if we expedite the reward. She doesn't want to wait for his conviction. Doesn't trust the system. I told her I'd see what we could do."

Adam didn't much care how they dealt with Jasmine Becker, as long as she came through with the information they needed. The bust could go down quick and painlessly, if he planned it right.

Unfortunately, he wouldn't be planning anything if his boss had any say-so. Which he did.

"Zirinsky won't want me there," Adam concluded.

Casey feigned a serious expression. "No, he won't."

Adam chuckled confidently. He respected his boss, but even Max couldn't deny him a ringside seat on this arrest. Not if Adam applied the right amount of persuasion.

"Then come on," he said to his brother, his veins pumping with determination. "Let's go unleash a little Guthrie charm on the chief of police."

FAITH TAPPED HER INTERCOM and called Roma's name. When her assistant didn't answer, she stamped her foot beneath her desk, cursing herself for not installing an intercom system in the small law library she'd amassed and created in the conference room, farthest away from Roma's post and just inside the reception area. Her vigilant assistant spent most of her time away from her desk, doing what she did best—digging for case law. Faith looked at the stack of files about to topple off her desk and couldn't believe she'd waited this long to bring her mother's case to the office.

But if she'd learned anything in the past week, she'd learned that trying to separate her personal and professional lives wasn't worth the effort. They were too intrinsically entwined. Her past and her mother's bogus conviction had made Faith who she was, shaping her career aspirations long before she'd realized she wanted to pursue the law. And while Faith might have someday finally squeezed in the time to prepare the final documents to have her mother's charges posthumously vacated, she had no real reason to wait for closure. She'd been wise with her financial dealings and could afford taking fewer cases for a while.

She'd even gone so far as to dig underneath the bed in her guest room to find her surfboard. She'd spent last night with Kalani, drinking rum and prepping her board for a weekend excursion to the beach. But today, she needed to finish going through the last of these files to fill in some missing names and dates, which she'd never accomplish if the information crashed haphazardly to the floor.

The door between her office and the reception area creeped open.

"Oh, great, Roma—I need your extra set of hands," she said, trying to keep the papers from falling.

But when she looked up, it wasn't Roma in her doorway. She gasped. Felix Moody.

"Hey, Ms. Lawton."

She couldn't speak. He looked horrible. His dark hair was plastered to his head, grimy against his blotched skin. Circles ringed his eyes, and his lips were pale and cracked. His clothes, torn jeans and a filthy T-shirt, reeked, even from a distance. And in his hand, he held a relatively small but lethal handgun.

"Felix, you need to get out of here." She kept her voice as steady as the files, terrified that if they fell to the ground, the sound might startle him into firing.

"I can't, Ms. Lawton. Look, I know you said you weren't my lawyer no more, but I know you went to see my mama last week. You stood up for me when Guthrie threw me in jail and I hadn't done nothing. I'm a wanted man and, Ms. Lawton, I didn't shoot no one."

Faith swallowed. The gun in his hand didn't lend much credibility to his story.

"Felix, I can't represent you now, even if I wanted to. I'm too personally involved in this case. The man you killed was my client."

Felix slipped completely into her office, closing the door behind him with shaky hands. He tiptoed across her carpet and kept his voice low. Obviously, he knew Roma was somewhere in the office.

"I didn't shoot no George Yube. What do I care about some rich doctor who tried to off some bitches? I'm in big trouble here. You're going to help me."

Understatement, Faith thought, though she refrained from

speaking. Something about the gleam in Felix's red-rimmed eyes told her that despite his eerily calm voice, he was a desperate man who might not be thinking clearly. She could understand why. He'd already extended his rampage to include shooting Adam, a police officer. If the men and women of the Courage Bay Police Force hadn't been after him in earnest before, they were likely champing at the bit now. And not necessarily to arrest him, but to make sure he paid in blood.

She took a deep breath and steeled herself for any and all reactions on his part. Running or hiding were not options. He blocked the only door out, and while her office was on ground level, the window likely wouldn't open without a struggle.

"Felix, maybe I can help you," she said, her palm up and outstretched, "but not until you lose the gun."

With an odd slowness, Felix looked down at his hand. He turned the black steel this way and that, as if seeing the pistol for the first time. "I need this."

Faith pressed her hand against her chest, desperate to calm the pounding that threatened to knock her off her feet. Her other hand cramped as she still tried to balance the files on her desk.

"No, Felix, you don't need the gun. Remember? You need me. I can try to help you, but not if you have a gun. It scares me, Felix. I can't think while you're threatening me."

He spun back toward the door, gun aimed outward. Faith said a silent prayer that Roma wouldn't walk in. She might startle Felix. He would shoot. Oh God! What should she do?

As quickly as possible, she gathered a pile of paperwork and laid it quickly into her chair so it wouldn't fall. She kept her eyes trained on him as he alternated between jabbing his gun toward the reception area and turning to her with a lost, vacant look. She gulped in a large breath, then walked around to Felix slowly, her arms out in friendly welcome. If nothing else, she had to keep Felix from hurting Roma, either accidentally or with malice.

"Please, Felix. No one will hurt you here. I don't have clients coming in today. We'll be alone for the rest of the afternoon, until we can figure something out. Please."

She glanced down and noticed he wore no shoes. Closing the distance between them, she could smell the putrid odor of stale alcohol, smoke and scorched-rock cocaine. The pungency transported her back to her childhood, and she had to fight to keep from allowing the bad memories to overwhelm her. With all her willpower, she kept her expression open, honest and amiable. She reminded herself that she'd gotten him out of prison. He considered her someone who could help. He wasn't here to hurt her, but had come out of sheer desperation.

Desperation that could turn deadly if she said or did the wrong thing.

WITH HIS GOOD ARM, Adam clapped his brother on the shoulder as they turned the corner outside Max's office. He should have known his boss wouldn't deny him a chance to witness justice firsthand. While Max did order Adam to stay well out of the way, Adam would be there tonight when Felix Moody was finally brought down.

He passed Flint Mauro in the hallway and nodded respectfully at the SWAT commander, who was, because of the nature of Moody's crimes, arranging the operation. Adam trusted Flint, the man who'd actually faced Moody's sniper rifle when he'd gone out into the plaza to rescue Faith. As Adam and Casey crossed back into his office, he took one last look around the bustling squad room. Mistakes or not, Courage Bay had the best police force in the state, if he did say so himself.

"That went well," he commented, rolling his good shoulder to work out the kinks.

Casey reached for his helmet. "Old Max didn't stand a chance. Wish I could be there, too. Fill me in on the details tomorrow, okay?"

Adam had opened his mouth to agree when his cell phone trilled from where he'd clipped it to his belt. He didn't recognize the number.

"Detective Guthrie," he answered.

"Thank God!"

Adam's muscles went rigid. "Who is this?"

"Roma. Roma Perez, Ms. Lawton's assistant. I should have called 911, but your card was still by my phone, where you left it the other night."

Her voice shook, and Adam heard the hysteria of someone who was desperate to hold onto her nerve while in grave danger. He'd heard it before, more times than he could count.

"Roma, what's wrong? Where are you?"

"At the office— Felix Moody. He's here. He's got a gun."

Adam charged by his brother, back into the squad room. Desperately, he marched toward Max's office as he talked. "Where's Faith?"

"In her office with him. I was working in the back. I didn't hear him come in. Faith moved him away from her door and shut it, but I heard them talking. I grabbed your card and my cell and took off."

He walked into Flint and Max's meeting, gesturing wildly toward the phone. "Where are you now? Can you get out?"

"No," she said, her voice quivering. "I couldn't leave

Faith alone. I ran back into the law library and called you. I locked the door."

Max and Flint stood. He quickly recounted the situation before turning his attention back to Roma. Flint shot out of the door. Max pressed close so they could both hear her reply.

"Is there a back door or window? Some way you can get out without crossing near Faith's office?"

"No. I'm trapped, aren't I. I'm so stupid!"

A normally clear-thinking young woman, Roma had let her fear send her in the wrong direction. Now he and his colleagues had to make sure they got both Roma and Faith out alive. At this moment, though, he simply had to keep Roma calm. Quiet. She'd at least done the right thing by calling him directly. A 911 dispatcher might not have realized the man holed up in Faith's office with a gun was Courage Bay's current most-wanted man.

"Shh," he said, forcing a soothing tone. "You're going to be fine, Roma. Tell me what you can, but whisper." He pressed the button on the side of his cell phone to jerk up the volume. Max shut his office door. "Is he holding her hostage?"

"I don't know. He wasn't yelling or screaming or angry. God, I'm so scared. What if he shoots her? What if he shoots her like he shot George Yube?"

Her quiet sobs rattled Adam to the core. He didn't want to think about the answer to those questions. "Roma, I know you're terrified, but you need to stay calm. Find a closet in the library and get inside. Or hide behind shelves. Under a desk. Whatever you have to do. Be very quiet. I'm giving my phone to an officer who is going to talk to you, keep you together, okay?"

Max opened his door and shouted for Tim Masters, who

was filling up his mug with water from the cooler. Adam swallowed deeply, glad Tim was around. He was a seasoned detective and a real charmer. He'd keep Roma calm until they could work out the next move.

In the meantime, Roma was his only link to Faith. Before he handed the phone over, he briefly considered encouraging Roma to escape through the front door. But what if she stepped out into the open at the same moment that Felix Moody decided to grab a soda from the small refrigerator in Faith's reception area? If Moody didn't know she was there, or didn't care, he wouldn't go looking for her. No, she'd lost her chance to get away clean. Now he simply needed her to stay alive.

Tim took the phone, introduced himself, then listened as Adam ran down the situation so Tim knew what to do. By the time he turned away, leaving Tim to wander near a window for better reception, Max had apprised the squad room of the situation.

"Flint will have SWAT ready to move by the time we go out," he announced, then rattled off the names of the officers he wanted on this detail. At the end, he turned to Adam. "You should be there, Guthrie."

Damn straight. "He might exchange the women for me."

"Let's not jump ahead of ourselves. Let's get to the scene, set up a command, and then we'll contact him and assess the situation. We'll need to immediately evacuate the offices around Ms. Lawton's, but I want it done quietly, understand? No sirens. And no press."

Adam rushed into his office and retrieved his smallest handgun from the safe behind his desk. He'd been shot in his left shoulder, but his right hand was strong enough to pull a trigger. However, he doubted Moody would let him in wearing his service revolver. His backup gun, however—a Smith and Wesson, short-barreled .38 Special—could easily fit inside his sling.

He grabbed the bullets, but couldn't work them into the chambers with one hand. Luckily, Casey entered, and without saying a word, he did the job, then gave the gun back.

"I won't let him hurt her," Adam said, not knowing why he had to indulge the overwhelming urge to make that claim aloud.

Casey braced his hand tightly on Adam's good shoulder, then silently, they joined the rest of the detail on their way out the door.

This would be over today, not tonight. And if Adam managed to bring Faith out alive, he wasn't wasting one more minute worrying about anything else except making her the happiest woman on earth.

CHAPTER SEVENTEEN

FAITH REMAINED STONE STILL, watching Felix pace around her office, barely moving her eyes as he stalked from one wall to the next, pivoting with such force at times that he nearly lost his balance. Every so often, he stopped to rant and rave, to rummage through her purse for candy, gum or cigarettes—none of which she had. She'd offered to call in takeout if he'd put the gun away, but the pistol seemed glued to his palm.

He'd left her alone only once to use the small half bath in the corner of her office, but he'd also left the door cracked open, so that if she'd tried to escape, he'd shoot her. She remained his captive and she still didn't know why.

"I'm not going back to prison," he declared for the hundredth time. "They won't let me out again. Last time was luck—was you and your luck."

He pointed the gun at her for emphasis, and she couldn't help but flinch. "Please, Felix. I don't want to get shot, okay?"

With eyes even redder than before he'd gone to the bathroom, he turned the weapon in his hand. "I'm not going to shoot you. Not unless you make me." The crescents beneath his eyes seemed to cut painfully into his pale skin. "Don't make me."

A faint sound caught Faith's attention. A soft chirping. She looked over her shoulder at the window, but Felix had closed the blinds and she couldn't see anything but the last dying rays of sunlight gleaming through the slats. As she turned back, she realized the noise was coming from somewhere on her desk. Her cell phone?

She didn't move, eyeing the mess Felix had made when scrounging through her purse.

Then, he heard the sound, too.

"What's that?" he asked, his voice pitching upward with fear.

"My cell phone." She glanced at the clock, improvising. "I was supposed to meet my sister at four o'clock. She's probably calling to see where I am."

The lie rolled off her tongue with cool precision, but Felix didn't seem to understand. God, was he that drugged out? Maybe he'd taken another hit when he'd gone to the john. How could she reason with a man strung out on drugs?

She knew the answer. She couldn't. She'd have to try to manipulate his skewed sense of reality. But how?

The cell phone stopped, then a few seconds later, started ringing again. Whoever was calling wasn't appeased by voice-mail.

"Make it stop," Felix spat.

"I'll have to find it, answer it," she said.

"I don't care. Tell them to go to hell."

His response made little sense, but she wasn't arguing. Digging through the piles of paper on her desk, she found the phone and grabbed it.

Before she could answer, Felix launched himself over her desk and snatched the phone out of her hands. The barrel of the gun grazed her cheek and the cold steel injected her entire body with icy fear. He thrust the LCD screen in her face, shouting, "Who is it?" over and over, until she gathered the clarity to look.

She read the caller ID. Unfortunately, it said "Unknown."

"See for yourself," she said, turning the device back toward him, wanting only for him and his awful smell and lethal gun to back away. "It's an unlisted number."

The trilling stopped. Again, only seconds elapsed before it started again. He threw the phone at her, a sick grin spreading across his blotched and mottled face. "Answer it."

Faith did so immediately. "Faith Lawton."

"Faith, it's Adam."

Relief washed through her like a cool summer rain in a parched desert valley. She closed her eyes and took one split second to concentrate only on Adam's voice, so deep, and yet…tense. Did he know where she was? Who was with her? Or was he only calling to check up on her, as he'd done every day since they'd been separated. They'd already spoken once this morning, so she'd have to figure out a way to alert him to the situation.

"This is Faith," she repeated, not wanting to reveal to Felix that the person on the other end of the line was no stranger— to either of them. She also hoped her professional tone clued Adam in to her predicament. "How can I help you?"

"I know Moody is there with you," Adam said, speaking quickly.

She contained a sigh of relief by focusing on Felix's gun.

"Is Moody still armed?" Adam asked.

"Yes," she answered calmly, glancing over at her diploma from law school, trying with all her body and soul not to give anything away. The man Felix considered entirely responsible for his current trouble was on the other end of the line. He might shoot her just for conversing with the enemy.

"Is he drugged out?"

"Yes," she answered.

"Is he pissed at you?"

"No," she said, though in her head she amended it to *not yet*.

"I want to talk to him," Adam insisted.

Faith's stomach turned and dropped, as if hot tar had been poured down her esophagus. Felix was jumpy, volatile and unpredictable. She couldn't imagine his reaction to her telling him that his archenemy was on the telephone, waiting to chat. As it was, Felix had claimed to have come to her office to solicit her help—and yet, he still hadn't asked her to do anything for him except listen to his ramblings. Her instincts insisted that the criminal had invaded her office simply to lure Adam out into the open.

Of course, that line of reasoning depended on Felix knowing about her personal relationship with Adam. He'd been following them, hadn't he? Adam had been by her side in two of the three shootings. But that didn't mean Felix had the brains to make the necessary deductions.

"Is Max there?" she asked, hoping Adam would realize the implication behind her question.

"Oh, yeah. Max is right beside me. We've hooked the cell to a speakerphone. He and the rest of the detail are listening to our every word. Say hello, Max."

The chief did as his lead detective requested, but he did not sound amused, though he was at least cordial. Still, Faith couldn't contain a small smile. She needed to keep her wits about her and a dose of humor could be the key. Her life was on the line. She couldn't lose her head to panic or fear, not when Adam was so close that she could practically feel his love through the phone line.

"We're in the parking lot, Faith," Adam told her. "We have

a sniper behind your building, but your blinds are drawn. Can you open them?"

"No."

A pause. Adam's silent disappointment crackled over the line, but Faith knew Felix would never let her open the blinds, not when he'd specifically closed them so they would have privacy.

Her skin crawled.

"Okay, we'll take another tack," Adam concluded. "Faith, Roma is inside, hiding in the law library. Keep Moody out of there if you can. Tim Masters has her on my cell phone. We want to get her out. Does Moody realize she's in the office?"

"Don't think so," Faith answered. "Hasn't mentioned it."

She glanced up at Felix, who seemed for the moment to be completely unconcerned with her conversation. He paced back and forth in front of her desk, muttering and mumbling, gesturing with his gun and ranting to no one in particular.

"Do you know what he wants?" Adam asked.

"Not really."

"Faith, I know you don't think my speaking to Moody is a good idea because Moody hates me, but that is exactly the reason why I might be able to goad him into letting you go. Please, you need to trust me. I need to speak to him. Put him on."

Faith bit her bottom lip. If Felix were clearheaded and sober, she might have insisted on negotiating with him herself. But she'd been with him for over an hour and his condition and mood changed like traffic lights at a busy intersection. One minute he was calm and cool and appealing to her sense of justice to help him, the next he was railing about police brutality and conspiracies. He was one step away from paranoia, and the distance between sanity and insanity was short. He hadn't tried to hurt her, but more than once he'd threatened to do so if she didn't give him what he wanted. Trouble was, she still hadn't been able to pin him down on exactly what that was.

She had no choice. She had to trust Adam and the rest of the Courage Bay Police Department to do their jobs and get both her and Roma out of this mess alive. She had to trust Adam, the man she loved, to take care of her, to put her safety above all else. Twice he'd already kept her from dying. Third time was the charm, right?

"Okay," she agreed, and was about to extend the phone to Felix when she heard Adam shout.

"Wait!"

She pulled the phone back to her ear. "Yes?"

"Faith, I love you."

She nearly dropped the cell on her desk. Not only had Adam confessed the very words bursting in her heart, he'd said them in front of the entire department. She swallowed her emotions and compressed her response into a simple, "Thanks."

Suddenly, Felix jumped toward her again. "Who the hell is it?"

She yelped as his fingernails scraped her hand, yanking her fist back after dropping the device. "It's for you!" she yelled back, unable to contain the rage simmering through her. What the hell was she doing wasting her time here? Adam was just outside. He loved her. He'd made the pronouncement to every man and woman who worked with him. He obviously didn't care who knew, or how it affected his career. Well, neither did she, damn it. For the first time in her life, she was willing to give love a chance, no matter the price she might pay. She deserved a great guy like Adam Guthrie, and she wasn't about to let Felix Moody stand in her way.

She sat back and crossed her arms. He stared, wide-eyed, at the phone, as if he wasn't sure exactly how to use one.

"Felix, talk to him," she said in the calmest voice she could muster. "He's the only one who can get you out of this alive."

"HE AGREED TO THE EXCHANGE," Adam announced to Max as he disconnected the call, having disengaged the speakerphone feature once Felix got on the line. The background noise had made him nervous, and from what Adam could interpret from the sound of the guy's voice and strange ramblings, he was already panicky as it was.

"I don't like this," Max said, saying nothing Adam hadn't expected to hear.

But this hostage situation was a police matter, and the first and only priority he had was getting Faith and Roma out of harm's way. He knew Max had the same goal.

"There's no choice, Chief. If we convince Moody that I'll buy him the time to leave town without getting his head blown off, he may drop his guard long enough for us to grab him."

"You might get shot," Max said, eyeing Adam's shoulder as a tech hurriedly attached a listening device to the back of Adam's neck, then ran a wire into his pants. "Again."

"Been there, done that."

Max marched with Adam toward the edge of the inner perimeter they'd set up with patrol cars and barricades. The police chief had kept the media two blocks away, and thanks to an emergency court order signed by Judge Craven, they couldn't broadcast a single word or image that might push Felix Moody over the edge. Yet despite every precaution they'd taken, no one could predict the outcome of this operation. Adam accepted the odds were against him, but he was willing to play the luck card one more time.

"You do realize he may just lure you inside and murder you both on the spot. That is what he's been trying to do for the last week, in case you've forgotten."

"I haven't forgotten," Adam muttered, carefully containing his anger. To keep Faith alive, he had to keep his brain clear of rage and vengeance. He had to go in and do his job. End of story. "But I'm the one he has it out for, Chief, and he won't be satisfied with anyone else. As soon as Faith and Roma are clear, SWAT can take whatever chances they need to. I'll either draw him outside or open those blinds. You take it from there."

"And plan C?"

Adam gently patted his sling. "I'll do whatever it takes, boss."

In his long-sleeved shirt and sling, Adam looked as unarmed as he could. He started up the walkway to Faith's office, twenty armed patrolmen, five detectives, two dozen SWAT and an undisclosed number of expert sharpshooters watching his back. Without some gift for foretelling the future, he couldn't guess how this operation would end. However, he knew he had the cream of the California crime-fighting crop behind him. If any team could make this work, it was Courage Bay's finest.

He opened the door to the office slowly and found the reception area empty. He walked in, arms and hands clear and visible, not that it would matter to Moody if he were armed or not. At this point, everyone knew who and where Felix was. If he killed Adam now, he'd have nowhere to run. Did the guy care? Had his drug-enhanced paranoia spawned a capacity for suicide? So many possibilities existed, not one of which Adam could pin down, not even after Moody swung open the door to Faith's office.

Adam's heart nose-dived and his entire body stiffened with cold, steely fear. Moody had Faith locked in front of him, the barrel of his gun jabbed beneath her chin. If his fingers so much as shook too violently, Faith would die.

"I'm here now, Moody. Let her go. You don't need a shield."

"Right! You think I don't know this place is surrounded. I ain't getting out of here alive without her. I'm not stupid."

Adam took a tentative step forward. Faith's gaze fixed on him, but despite her terrified expression, he saw strength and resolve in her eyes.

"No one has ever called you stupid, Moody. You were smart enough to hire Ms. Lawton here for your appeal. Now you want me to believe you'd kill her? The woman who single-handedly got you out of prison? Come on, man. No one believes you'll hurt her. You're not a murderer. We all know that now. You're just a desperate man. Trade her for *me,* walk with *me* outside, and the cops will take you seriously. They know you'll blow my head off."

Felix yanked the gun away from Faith and pointed it straight at Adam, his eyes wild and his grip unsteady. The barrel shimmied from side to side in Moody's hand. The bullet could fly anywhere.

"You ain't shitting, Guthrie! I'll blow you away right here. Teach you to get in my business."

Adam swallowed a grin as he glanced at Faith, watching how she worked her fingers around Moody's arm, trying to inch herself free.

"You're right, Moody. If I hadn't gotten in your business, if I hadn't kept my men on your ass twenty-four/seven, you'd be back on top of the heap again, wouldn't you. Running the neighborhood, raking in the cash. Instead, you're trying to figure out how the hell to get out of here alive. Shoot me now and you're toast."

Sweat beaded on Moody's forehead, making his hair mat against his face and neck. His hold on the gun was strong, but his arms shook and he swayed from side to side as Faith struggled to remain standing, her fingernails biting into his arm.

Just a few more minutes, babe. I've got him thinking. I've got him working the possibility. Hold on.

Finally, Moody jabbed the gun beneath Faith's chin again, this time with a painful thrust that made her eyes water. Adam's entire body tightened with rage.

"Tell him!" Moody ordered.

Faith opened her mouth to speak, but only a strangled croak emerged.

Adam itched to grab for his gun, but knew he couldn't risk it. Faith would die, and he would likely die with her. If not physically, then in every other way that mattered.

"She can't breathe," Adam said evenly.

Moody looked down, recognized his tight grip kept her from speaking, then released her the millimeter she needed to regain her ability to talk.

"Tell him. Tell him now."

She swallowed, cleared her throat. "Felix says he's innocent. He says he didn't try to kill you. Wanted to, but didn't. Says he's being framed."

Adam pretended to be shocked at this disclosure. Of course Moody would claim someone was trying to set him up—such assertions were his *modus operandi*. Adam remembered clearly each and every interview he'd had with Moody in his murder case where he'd insisted over and over that someone—his girlfriend, in particular—had framed him for the murder of his rival.

It wasn't true then and it wasn't true now. But Adam didn't have to let Moody in on his doubts yet. Not if he could use them against him.

"Who is framing him?" Adam asked Faith. If Moody had come this far to have Faith speak for him, Adam had to go the distance, make the man believe that his claim was at least slightly credible.

"He doesn't know."

He turned to Moody. "Any guesses?"

"That's your job to find out! I ain't going back to prison for something I didn't do. Not again. Not ever again!"

Moody must have loosened his grip on Faith, because a split second later, she was slipping down toward the floor, out of his hold. Moody stepped back and aimed his gun at Faith, leaving Adam no more time to negotiate. He yanked the .38 out of his sling and fired. Moody flew backward. Blood spurted from his shoulder. He swung the gun in Adam's direction, but Adam fired again.

This time, the bullet stopped him. Permanently.

Faith crawled across the floor, clawing out of her office with a desperation in her eyes he'd never seen before and hoped never to see again. He fell to his knees and gathered her against him as close as he could, flinching when the front door burst open and SWAT swarmed inside.

They didn't speak for a long time. The minute Flint Mauro verified that Felix Moody was dead, Adam led Faith outside to the waiting paramedics. Roma was brought out soon after, and though Faith had been the one to face off with

Moody, she spent the next half hour soothing and calming her terrified assistant. Once Roma was calm, Tim Masters took Faith's statement, and Adam could have given him a raise on the spot for the respect and care he used in the questioning.

Adam watched from the sidelines as the forensics team photographed and cataloged the crime scene inside her office, knowing but not caring that there would be an internal investigation of the shooting. In his entire career, Adam had never killed a criminal in a shootout, but he'd known the day would come. At least he felt entirely justified. The man had been crazy on drugs, paranoid and delusional. He'd pointed his gun at the woman Adam loved after terrorizing her for days. Adam knew he'd had no other choice, but hearing those exact words from Faith the moment Masters gave her permission to leave lightened his heart considerably.

He smiled at her selfless greeting, wrapped his good arm around her and ignored the throbbing ache in the other. The best medicine he could imagine was Faith in his embrace.

"Doesn't make it easier. I didn't sign up for this job to kill people."

"I know. You gonna be okay?" she asked, pulling away only enough to look at him directly.

"Me? I'll be fine. I'm not the one who was held hostage by a maniac."

"No, but you're the one who had to shoot him."

He snorted. "Didn't feel as good as it should have."

"You didn't think it would, did you?"

"Of course not. But I'm done thinking about Felix Moody." He filled his lungs with the scent of the outdoors, sweetened with the perfume that belonged only to Faith. "All I want in my head right now are the million possibilities of what you and I will do to erase this afternoon from our minds."

Her grin lit her face like a bright pink sunrise over the blue-black ocean. That's where they'd go, Adam decided. Tonight. As soon as possible. To the beach. They'd make love on a blanket spread on the shore, and in the morning, he'd watch her ride the waves.

"Anything coming to mind?" she asked. Her eyes twinkled with delicious wickedness.

"A few favorites are rising to the top," he said, turning slightly so she pressed full against him. A rush of desire surged through him, dulling the pain as his blood rushed away from his arm and focused on the parts he needed to bind Faith to him. For tonight. For the future.

"Really? I want to hear about these favorites, but first, I have something to tell you. Something that can't wait."

Her mouth turned down in a frown, and her gaze darkened from glittering silver to stormy gray. His chest tightened, then relaxed. They could handle whatever she had to say. They'd survived more than he'd ever imagined he could with any woman, any cherished lover. No obstacle, not a killer nor their contrary careers could stand in their way now.

"Lay it on me," he said, attempting to chase away a smile with a serious tone.

"Okay." She stepped back and hooked her hands behind her, pacing a few steps as if she were about to interrogate a witness. Adam stood up straighter, but a smile tugged at his lips. Try as she might to muster an inscrutable expression, he'd never seen a worse bluff in his life. She'd never shown such weakness in the courtroom, but here, with him, only the real Faith could shine through.

She loved him. And now she was going to say it. Great detective that he was, he had it all figured out.

"You think I'm going to confess my love, don't you," she said, her gaze narrowed.

Caught, he released the arrogant grin he'd been holding in so tightly. "Yes."

"You think I should, don't you, since you announced your feelings for me in front of your entire department."

He bounced slightly on the balls of his feet, buoyant at the emotion coursing through him. Yeah, this love thing was not half-bad. He covered a chuckle with his hand. Not half-bad at all.

"It's only fair and reasonable," he said. "I mean, this is a matter of emotional justice, don't you think?"

She opened her mouth to protest, giving Adam the impetus to snatch her against him and cover her lips with his.

Whatever Faith had wanted to say fled her brain the minute his tongue twined with hers. God, he tasted good—a heady combination of need and lust and home. She slipped her arms around his waist and held on tight. Never in her life had she experienced such a whirlwind of rightness, and she wasn't about to allow the tempest to pass her by.

He released her mouth, allowing her to murmur the words she'd wanted to say to him for what seemed like so very long. "I do love you, Adam. It scares the crap out of me, but I can't fight it. I can, however, fight whatever obstacles stand in our way. I mean, I can fight so long as you fight with me."

He inched his good arm around her, holding her with such clear possessiveness, her bottom lip quivered and her eyes welled with emotion.

"The two of us could take on the world and win, Faith."

She glanced over at the police swarming over the lawn in

front of her office. Every once in a while, one of them shot a perplexed or concerned look in their direction. "We might have to take on the world," she concluded, undaunted as long as Adam held her fast. "I'm ready, are you?"

His next kiss answered her question. And the next. And the next. And the next.

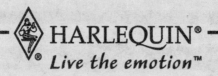

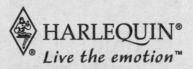

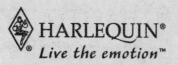

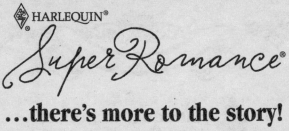

...there's more to the story!

Superromance.
A *big* satisfying read about unforgettable characters. Each month we offer *six* very different stories that range from family drama to adventure and mystery, from highly emotional stories to romantic comedies—and much more! Stories about people you'll believe in and care about. Stories too compelling to put down....

Our authors are among today's *best* romance writers. You'll find familiar names and talented newcomers. Many of them are award winners—and you'll see why!

If you want the biggest and best in romance fiction, you'll get it from Superromance!

Exciting, Emotional, Unexpected...

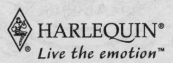

Live the emotion™

Harlequin® Historical
Historical Romantic Adventure!

*Imagine a time of chivalrous
knights and unconventional ladies,
roguish rakes and impetuous
heiresses, rugged cowboys
and spirited frontierswomen——
these rich and vivid tales will
capture your imagination!*

*Harlequin Historical . . .
they're too good to miss!*